A Vintage Murder

**Center Point
Large Print**

**This Large Print Book carries the
Seal of Approval of N.A.V.H.**

sequel to *Silenced by Syrah*

A Vintage Murder

A Wine Lover's Mystery

MICHELE SCOTT

CENTER POINT PUBLISHING
THORNDIKE, MAINE

This Center Point Large Print edition
is published in the year 2009 by arrangement with
The Berkley Publishing Group,
a division of Penguin Group (USA).

The text of this Large Print edition is unabridged.
In other aspects, this book may vary
from the original edition.
Printed in the United States of America.
Set in 16-point Times New Roman type.

ISBN: 978-1-60285-359-1

Library of Congress Cataloging-in-Publication Data

Scott, Michele, 1969-
 A vintage murder : a wine lover's mystery / Michele Scott. -- Center point large print
ed.
     p. cm.
 ISBN 978-1-60285-359-1 (library binding : alk. paper)
 1. Large type books. I. Title.

PS3619.C6824V56 2009
813'.6--dc22

2008037428

To my son, Anthony,
who reminds me
not to take myself so seriously.

Acknowledgments

This book would have never been written without the help of a man I have never had the pleasure to actually meet: Geoff Cardwell, Officer in Charge, Barossa C.I.B., South Australia Police. He was instrumental in helping me learn as much as possible in a short amount of time about the Barossa, and I am indebted to him for that. E-mail is a good thing for a writer. Geoff, I hope we meet one day and share a glass of Shiraz together. I would also like to thank Sandra Harding and Mike Sirota, who continually champion me. Along with Karen MacInerney, who is a dear friend and one of the best writers I know. Thanks for listening to me whine, K. A big thanks to my husband and kids and even our dogs and cats who sometimes had to wait for dinner. I will now take you all to Cold Stone. I promise. This time I mean it. The book is done.

A Vintage
Murder

Chapter 1

Nikki Sands could not believe where she was and
what she was doing. But what she really couldn't
believe was with whom she was doing it. She
looked out the car window. The valley was breathtaking, covered in grape vines, with soil the color
of buttered toffee as the sun cast its morning rays
across the landscape. Although she'd seen plenty
of vines working at the Malveaux Winery in Napa,
this was different. She was far away from home.

She couldn't help but smile. Even inside the car
she could smell the rich soil and the aroma of ripe
fruit that hung in the air. God, it was intoxicating.
She breathed in deeply, closing her eyes. When
she opened them again, she shook her head in
amazement. Was it possible that she actually sat
smack dab in the middle of a Monet painting?
Because if that was at all possible, this was what
it would feel like—kind of blurred but completely
serene. Peaceful. Yes that's where she must be—
in the middle of a painting. The view spread out in
front of her: rolling hills of green set behind a
charming village filled with church spires rising
high from ancient stone buildings, and amidst it
all were rows of manicured vineyards. Napa had
charm in and of itself, but this place felt almost as
if Nikki had been tossed back in time to a yester-
year of simplicity and rustic elegance.

The last forty-eight hours had been a whirlwind, and even though she still had some jet lag, everything in her world felt right. Well, almost everything. She knew that on another continent, in another part of the world, she'd left someone with a broken heart, and that did not feel good. In fact, she knew she'd have to deal with it, with *him* sooner than later, or the guilt would eat her alive. There was a part of her that couldn't help feeling like a monster for making the choice she had, but the logical side—the one not connected to her heart—helped her realize that by making that choice, she'd actually wound up sparing him more pain in the long run. The truth was, the relationship she'd decided not to pursue would've never worked. No matter how hard she would've tried to convince herself that it was right, her heart would've belonged to someone else, and it was that "someone else" she was now with.

And when the man beside her took her hand and gave it a squeeze, a surge of electricity shot up from her toes and warmed her entire body, confirming that yes, she'd made the right choice. He glanced over at her. "I can't believe you're really here with me." Nikki's stomach swirled with a mixture of nerves and something she hadn't felt in years—passion, not lust, but real passion. "I really can't believe it. I didn't know if you would come. I'd hoped." He pulled the car off to the side of the road.

"What are you doing?" she asked.

"This." He took her face in his hands and kissed her. "Thank you for being here with me," Derek said and then kissed her again.

"There's no place else I'd rather be," she replied.

Derek pulled back onto the road. They were on their way to the Hahndorf Winery in the Barossa Valley of Australia, to meet with the owner, Liam Hahndorf, and his wife. Derek's goal was to secure a distribution and licensing agreement with Hahndorf Wines. The popularity of Australian wines was on the rise in the States. Derek felt they made a great product, and when Liam Hahndorf had approached Derek, he saw the potential in the deal. Essentially, the Hahndorfs would send certain vintages to the States with the Malveaux name on them. The Malveaux Winery would then distribute them in the U.S.

"Tell me a little bit about Liam Hahndorf," Nikki said. "You've obviously met him before and you think he makes a good wine."

"Yes, he does. He and his wife Grace started the winery about fifteen years ago and they've done well. Liam is a smart businessman. I've met him a few times, and he's real personable. The last time I saw him was about six months ago. He was in L.A. at the same time I was."

"Oh yeah, when you went there for that big-time celebrity soiree and didn't invite me," she joked.

Derek shook a finger at her. "Let's get one thing straight: I know I should have told you a lot sooner about my feelings. I didn't know how you would react. I didn't know how you felt."

How couldn't he have known? She thought her signals had been loud and clear, like a neon sign.

"Anyway, you know what I've been through in the past, so as stupid as it might sound, I guess I was apprehensive about hanging my heart out there again."

"It doesn't sound stupid." Nikki knew all about Derek's unlucky-in-love history. He'd married a conniving, horrid woman who'd totally manipulated him without ever truly being in love with him. "I just wish you hadn't taken so long to get smart, you big dummy."

"Funny, huh? I like funny women, you know."

"You do?"

"Oh yeah. What I'd really like is to take you back to the hotel and have my way with you."

Oh boy, stomach flip-flop right on over, like a pancake on a griddle. "Hmmm."

He held up a finger. "But business first this morning, and like we agreed on the plane, the first time will be an all-day affair." He winked at her.

Oh yeah, *that* agreement. That had been her idea. How stupid had that been? But last night had been kind of sweet. They'd talked all night aboard the Malveaux jet and cuddled, ate excellent food, and drank champagne. Then, after a bottle of Dom

14

Perignon and some slow kisses, the topic of sex had come up.

"Wow," Derek had said after one long swap of the tongue that made Nikki's toes curl.

"Yeah, wow."

He laughed.

"What so funny?" she asked, feeling confused.

"I'm laughing because this is so crazy. You and me." He leaned back in the cushy seat.

"Well, yeah, it is a little crazy, but . . ."

He took her hand. "No, I don't mean crazy in a bad way." He shook his head. "I know how your mind works. I mean crazy in a great way and I was laughing because if our kiss is any indication of . . . well, you know . . ." He wiggled his eyebrows.

Her face grew hot and all she could do was nod.

"You do want to, don't you? Make love?"

Of course she did, but things did feel sort of weird. After all, Derek was her boss and she'd run away with him on the spur of a moment. Holy cow, this was the craziest thing she'd ever done in her life. "Yes," she said tentatively.

"I don't want to push you, Nikki. I can definitely book us separate rooms at the hotel."

"No, no. I want to. It's just when we do, I want it to be special."

"Me, too."

So when they'd landed in the middle of the night, exhausted from travel and emotions, they'd turned in with Derek taking the sofa in the hotel room and insisting she sleep in the bed. Although she'd been exhausted, she'd fallen asleep thinking she sure would have liked having Derek's warm body by her side. Suddenly their idea of making their "first time" extra special seemed extra stupid, because no matter what, it was going to be special.

Nikki set the fantasies aside as they pulled up to the Hahndorf Winery. A security guard waved them to a stop at a kiosk. "I thought this was a mom-and-pop operation in the middle of nowhere. What gives?" Nikki asked.

"You got me. It does seem like overkill, and I had no idea Hahndorf would have security."

Malveaux was one of the larger and more well-known wineries in Napa, and they didn't have a setup like this. Not even close. Derek gave the security guard his name. The man glanced down at a sheet of paper. "Yep. G'day, sir. Says here you're visiting with the Hahndorfs. Okay then, go straight ahead and over the small hill there and you'll see the winery and house."

Derek thanked the man and drove off.

Unlike Napa Valley, which in May would mean summer was near and so was picking season, in the Barossa, May was the end of autumn. Winter would arrive in the next month, just as the heat in Napa started to rise into the nineties.

"What's that?" Nikki pointed toward the middle

of the vineyard, where several trucks were parked, including a large semi. There was also a row of motor homes. She squinted to see if she could get a better look. "I think that's a film crew."

Derek slowed down. "Yeah, it looks that way. You should know."

"It's been a while." Nikki had once played the starring role in a short-lived cop show when she'd pursued an acting career in L.A. The acting had never taken off, and she'd discovered she was much better at managing a winery than she could ever be at playing a detective on TV.

They pulled past the winery, its architecture very chateaulike, reminiscent of the wineries in France. "Jeez, if that's the winery, what must the house look like?"

"Good question. We're about to find out. I'm curious what they're filming out there," he said. "Maybe a commercial."

"I don't know, it seems like a lot of vehicles for a commercial."

At the end of the drive, in an area secluded behind a row of gum trees, a house appeared. It wasn't as opulent as the chateau. Though still quite large, it looked comfortable, like an English-style stone cottage.

Derek parked in the circular drive next to a row of expensive automobiles ranging from the sporty to the luxurious.

"He must like cars," she said.

"I'd say someone does." Derek climbed out, went around to her side, and opened the door for her, taking her hand.

"Such the gentleman."

"My dad didn't send me to private school for nothing. But, I hated that place, especially the etiquette class."

"I'd say it paid off nicely."

"Don't get used to it. I'm only trying to impress you."

"You're funny, too." They walked up a pathway lined with flowers and plants that Nikki assumed were native, because she didn't recognize them. "Someone keeps a lovely garden."

Derek pressed the doorbell. Chimes rang out from the other side of the door.

Soon a young woman in her early twenties swung the door open. She had long sandy blonde hair, large hazel eyes, pouty lips, and seemed awfully thin. She wore tight jeans and a low-cut orange cotton sweater. Nikki thought her pretty in the grunge, Kate Moss way that had hit heights of popularity back in the late nineties. "Oh, the film crew is down in the vineyard. You passed them," she said in a heavy Aussie accent.

"We're actually here to see Liam Hahndorf," Derek said.

"Oh. Dad!" the girl shrieked. "Some man and woman are here for you." She breezed past them, keys in hand. They watched her get behind the wheel of a navy blue Aston Martin. She took off in an apparent hurry.

"Well, well, g'day, mate!" A tall gray-haired gentleman with warm brown eyes and soft wrinkles forming around them appeared in the doorway. "Oh damn, Hannah. She's gone again! Silly girl. She's surprised us by taking a holiday from school. Says she's not sure it's for her. Oh boy, Grace won't be happy about her running out of here like that."

"I won't be happy about what?" A middle-aged woman joined him. Nikki assumed she was the girl's mother. They had the same eyes, and the woman was as thin as her daughter. She also had the same long blonde hair, but hers was pulled back tightly into a ponytail.

"Goodness, we have forgotten our manners. Grace, this is my friend Derek Malveaux. I told you he'd be dropping in with us today for some business. Good to see you." The men shook hands. "This is my wife Grace, and that was Hannah, our terror of a daughter, who blew past you. I'm not sure how we'll survive her." Liam kissed his wife on the cheek. "Grace here is far more patient with her than I am."

"Hardly. You spoil the girl something terrible. Nice to meet you, Derek."

"And you. This is my girlf—ah, my winery manager and my assistant, Nikki Sands."

He'd almost said girlfriend. *Girlfriend?* Wow. That had her in a spiral—a delicious spiral. She understood why he'd used her business title, but she couldn't wait until things were more cemented between them and the formalities could be pushed aside.

"Where are my manners? Come in, you two," Grace said.

They followed her through the entrance across light hardwood floors inlaid with another type of wood in a diamond pattern. Maybe walnut, but it was more reddish than walnut and quite dark. Possibly cherry. "Your floors are gorgeous, Grace. What type of wood are they?"

"It's jarrah wood. A popular wood here in the bush. Somewhat on the expensive side, but I love it. I redecorated the house a few years back and couldn't resist."

"It's lovely. The entire house is."

No joke. The house looked larger on the inside than it had from outside, and Grace had done a great job of turning the manor into a cozy home with warm golden colors, family photos, colorful throw rugs, and leather sofas. Everything about the place spoke of wealth and sophistication, but also of care. For the family it had to be a nice place to live, because it was definitely a nice place to visit. Grace led them out to the back, where the gardens spread out and a lap pool took up a portion of the yard. Behind the pool, a large patch of grass rolled down to a flowing river. Vast woods stretched out across the river.

"This is gorgeous," Nikki said. "What river is that?"

"That's the North Para River," Liam said. "More of a creek typically, but we had some decent rain this year, so we have a bit more water than usual, which is good because the water can be important to the Barossa Valley for viticulture. You can't imagine how lucky we feel to have it run right through the property like this. Good stuff for the vines. Have a seat. Enjoy the view."

"Nikki and I were wondering what's going on here. When we turned into the vineyard, we saw all the activity."

"Oh yes. Hollywood has come to our village. Our place really," Liam replied.

"Hollywood?" Nikki said.

"It's quite a story. We'll have to tell you all about it, but let me grab the contracts for us to go over first. They're in my office. I would also like to discuss some new matters that have come up, Derek. Would you like your assistant to join us?"

Derek looked at Nikki, who could see Liam wanted to discuss things with Derek in private, so she stepped back slightly, nodding to Derek though she wondered what it was all about. "Uh, no. Nikki why don't you visit with Grace? We should be back soon."

"Of course." It felt really awkward to have been holding his hand less than half an hour ago, and now this stilted kind of weirdness.

"Yes, yes. You two take care of what you need to." Grace waved them away. "We'll head into the kitchen and have some tea."

Nikki found Grace to be hospitable, and the tea was warm and soothing. They made small talk for quite a while. Nikki told her about the Malveaux Winery and Grace began to fill her in on the scene they saw when they'd entered the winery.

"You wouldn't believe it. Shawn Keefer is doing a movie here, with Nathan Cooley directing it."

"*The* Shawn Keefer?" Nikki's jaw dropped. Shawn Keefer was only Hollywood's most sought after leading man, and Nathan Cooley was the kind of director everyone in "the business" wanted to work with. He was a genius.

"No kidding. What's the movie about?"

"I . . . don't think I can discuss it. We had to sign a nondisclosure agreement with the film company." Grace lowered her voice and looked pensive.

"Who else is in it?"

"One of those young starlets. The one who is supposedly so brilliant. But she's quite a trouble-maker, from what the tabloids say. We've even had some paparazzi lurking in our midst. It's the pretty redheaded girl. That Lucy Swanson."

"Oh yes, I've heard of her." Who hadn't? Lucy Swanson was a fine actress who'd starred in some successful films. She was also one of the new breed—if that's what they could be called—of Hollywood: young women who spent too much time partying, getting busted, and then going back for more. This one hadn't done any stints in rehab but rumor was that she needed to. At least she supposedly had a work ethic, and that was her main driving force. It might also be her saving grace. God, Nikki really had read too many rag mags and watched way too much tabloid television.

"Yes, well, I can tell you that she is a wild one. Hannah has been spending some time with her, and also one of the crew people. Some good-looking young man—I'm not crazy about it. I'm afraid they're going to get Hannah into trouble."

Nikki doubted that the girl had any problems getting *herself* into trouble. Instead of saying what she thought, she replied, "Really? Trouble, huh?"

"Out partying at all hours." Grace shook her head. "Anyway, tonight we are having an old-fashioned barbecue and the entire crew is joining us."

"Including Shawn Keefer?"

Grace nodded and smiled. "He's quite a cad, that one. He flirts with all the ladies."

"I'd read in one of the tabloids that he is a huge flirt."

"But he is a dear really, once you get to know him. We've had everyone up for dinner on occasion since they've been on the premises."

Nikki noticed Grace's cheeks flush and she wondered if the woman had a crush on Keefer. Many women around the world did. He was on par with Brad Pitt and George Clooney in both the looks and acting categories; definitely a superstar. People loved him, and considering his stature he did a decent job of lying low and keeping out of the limelight, except for a few years back, when he'd gone through a divorce with his actress wife, Fiona. But from what Nikki recalled when that happened, they had remained decent to each other, and she'd made out like a bandit in the settlement. It would be interesting to meet Shawn Keefer.

They talked a bit more about the actors in the vineyard before Derek and Liam returned. "Ladies, would you like to take a trip down to where they're filming? I filled Derek in, and he said that he'd love to go, especially when he heard that Andy Burrow was on the set."

"Andy Burrow, too?" Nikki shot a glance at Derek. "How great!" Andy worked with all sorts of wildlife. He was eccentric and quite a character. Nikki knew that Derek loved watching the guy's show on the Earth Channel.

"I know. Isn't that awesome?" Derek sounded like a kid, but there was also a catch in his voice that Nikki didn't recognize.

It was strange, because he sounded excited about meeting Andy, and Nikki was sure that he would be, but there was something else there that she couldn't put her finger on, as if he were slightly troubled. She wondered if there was a problem with the business deal.

"Liam says that he's not in the movie, but they've got a bunch of wild animals they're working with on the film, and Andy is on hand to train the animals. He brought all of them from his zoo," Derek added.

There it was again—an edge, almost fake. "Sure, I'm in. Let's go," Nikki replied. "This must be quite a production," she said as they climbed into Liam's golf cart, still curious about what was rattling around in Derek's head.

"It is at that," Liam replied. "Quite a group, too. The producer has put up a lot of money to film it and they're looking for one of those big block-buster movies you watch in America."

"I personally can't wait until they're finished. They've created a bit of havoc for us," Grace said, "as much fun as it's been." She glanced at Liam. Nikki couldn't figure her out.

"Did Grace tell you that I wrote the script?"

No she hadn't. Now that was strange. She acted as if she wasn't even certain what the movie was about. "Uh, well . . ."

Grace rubbed Liam's shoulder. "I didn't mention that. I know you don't like to brag much." She smiled at Nikki.

"Since when? I couldn't be prouder, and having Andy here is wonderful. You'll love him."

Derek looked like a kid in a candy shop, he was so excited. For him, meeting Andy Burrow was one of the coolest things in the world. She was excited, too, but also baffled by Grace. "That's great," Nikki replied. "I know what the business is like. It's not easy to even get a screenplay read, especially not a first one. Then to have it made into a movie, no less. You should be proud."

"Oh, this isn't my first go at it. I have a bunch of them in the closet. Been writing forever, but never really thought it would happen, you know. I'm a farm boy at heart. I grow grapes and we make wine. To have this now makes everything complete."

"How did you get the idea for the story?" Derek asked.

"That's a long story in itself," Liam replied.

"Yes it is. We don't want to bore you with it," Grace said. She looked at her husband. "Do we, Liam?"

"Right. Maybe another time."

Nikki thought she heard Grace's voice tighten as she spoke.

A group of people sat around in chairs as they got closer, all looking pretty bored. The camera crew and extras. Maybe they were taking a lunch break. It seemed a little early for lunch . . .

Liam parked the cart just as a horrible scream came from the direction of the trailers parked on the set.

Chapter 2

Nikki and Derek looked at each other and then the people around them. No one moved.

The door to the trailer swung open and out sauntered Mr. Movie Star himself—Shawn Keefer. "She's a lunatic!" he yelled. "I can't work with her. A nightmare. That's what she is."

"Me, a nightmare?" In his wake came Lucy Swanson, long red hair flowing behind her. "You're a joke, Shawn. One big stupid ass of a joke. You can't even get it up!" she screamed. "Freak!"

Whoa. Okay, that was way more information than Nikki needed to know.

Shawn stopped in his tracks, turned and faced her, his face purple. He wasn't yelling, but they were close enough to hear what he was saying. "Let me tell you something, little girl: I am a professional. I'm here to do a job, not make nice or anything else with you, and frankly I find you repulsive. I wouldn't sleep with you if you were the last woman on earth. Do your job and stay out of my way, you nasty pig."

"What? What! Did you hear that?" She was now yelling at another man who stood nearby. "Me a 'nasty pig'?" She laughed. "Wait until the world finds out what a fake piece of—"

"Lucy! That's enough! Come here if you want to keep your job," the other man said.

"Whatever. You should be talking to *him*." She pointed at Shawn. "And that Crocodile Dundee freakazoid. Weirdo calls his animals gorgeous and shit—what's up with that? I'm not going near that snake! I don't give a shit what you say!"

"Lucy," the man said. "I need to speak with you now."

She sighed, indignant. "Fine." She stomped over to the man, who put an arm around her shoulder and escorted her away from the set.

"That's the producer, Kane Ferriss," Liam said. "He'll get her under control. This isn't her first tantrum. Maybe we should see if we can find Andy Burrow. Let me ask someone if they've seen him."

He walked over to a young man who, with that tan, could only be from Southern California. He wore torn jeans and a Sex Pistols T-shirt. Now that brought back memories of the eighties and Nikki begging her aunt for an earring on the side of her eyebrow. Thank God Aunt Cara had told her no way.

"Johnny boy. How are you, mate? Looks like a bit of trouble today. Seen Andy around?"

"Yeah. He's over there with his snakes. That's why the princess is losing it. She doesn't want to do the scene with the snake. But she knew what she was signing on for. She's holding up every-thing." He shook his head and walked over to a table, where coffee brewed.

Nikki couldn't really blame the actress for not wanting to do a scene with a snake, but all the same, her fit seemed over the top. As Johnny mentioned, the actress knew what she was getting into when she signed her contracts.

"Ridiculous," Liam said. "That girl is a royal pain in the arse. I know Andy has all of his critters under control. There he is. He's a good man. Known him for years. Old friend, actually." Liam pointed toward an area next to a group of picnic tables and chairs likely meant for the crew to eat lunch at.

Andy Burrow waved as they headed over. "Hey, mate!" he yelled, smiling brightly. Andy was of average height and medium build. He wore his dark, wavy hair long and had big hazel eyes. He had an innocent little-boy look about him.

Liam introduced Derek and Nikki to Andy. She noticed how nervous Derek was. "So, do you like snakes, Derek?" Andy asked.

"Sure."

"Come on over here then and have a look at my Charlie. He's a beautiful brown snake. Just gorgeous. But one bite from him and you'll be gone in a matter of hours if you don't have the antivenom, which of course I keep on hand. And, that's why I wear one of these when I'm dealing with him." Andy winked and ran his hands up and down his long-sleeved khaki pantsuit. "Made out of Kevlar, you know, just like those vests the police officers wear. So I've got a better chance if one of my critters tries to lay their fangs into me; it's harder for them to get through this. I've got an extra one inside the animal enclosure. He pointed to a barnlike structure made out of what looked like corrugated aluminum siding. "Can you believe the producer had that thing built for this movie? So, what do you say, Derek? Do you want to put the suit on? I'll let you handle my beauty here." The snake eyed them from inside a portable terrarium set on the table. Nikki did not like the looks of him at all.

"Oh God, I don't know about that," Derek said.

"Andy knows what he's doing, mate. Besides, that snake is only one of the deadliest snakes in the country." Liam winked at Derek.

Derek looked at Nikki, who shrugged. "I'm not doing it," she said.

"Oh what the hell," Derek said. "Sure, I'm in."

"And we do have the antivenom as I said," Andy said.

"I don't care if you have antivenom or not. No way am I even getting near one of those," Nikki replied. "I do not like things that slither. Add the fact that they're poisonous on top of it and you can count me out."

"She sounds a bit like our Lucy," Andy teased.

"Oh no, I don't think anyone could be as high maintenance as Miss Swanson," Liam said.

"I hope not." Andy winked at Nikki. "Woman is

a lunatic. See over there?" Andy pointed to a bushy area about fifty yards away. "That's where they want to film the scene with my Charlie and that crazy actress. We've got the glass pane set up. It won't be a problem at all. I'll be standing right there, monitoring everything. I understand they're paying her a ton, so I told her let's get it over with and she started screaming 'bastard' and such at me. So, I told her we'd get a look-alike. We don't have to use Charlie then, if it's such an issue for her. She still kept on and then went after poor Shawn." Andy shook his head. "I don't need the money, you know. I can walk from this anytime. I'm only doing it as a favor to Nathan . . . and of course you, too, Liam. This movie will be a treat if we can get it finished. Nate has done some great cinematography for me and my creatures in the past. Helped us raise money for the zoo, you know. I don't want to let him down, but that actress is plain loopy."

They all laughed.

"Here, why don't we take a quick tour through the animal enclosure." He picked up Charlie's terrarium. Nikki cringed. "Okay, gang, follow me."

Nikki wasn't too sure about this, but didn't want to be a bad sport. Snakes did make her squeamish. They followed Andy into the enclosure, which was about thirty feet long with a pathway down the middle that was ten feet or so wide. On either side of the pathway were enclosed terrariums that housed a variety of reptiles. Down the line were larger areas with small eucalyptus trees in planters where Andy kept a couple of koalas. Next to the koalas were a couple of dingoes. The wild dogs looked to be a cross between a wolf and some kind of domesticated shepherd, only golden in color.

"Those are my babies. Love them to death," Andy said, pointing to the wild dogs. "Do anything for me, completely trained. Been around for thousands of years. The farmers hate them. Kind of like the coyotes in the States."

"Really?" Nikki asked. She kept glancing at Charlie the snake in the terrarium and hoping that Andy wouldn't drop it. What if it shattered and the snake got out?

"Yep. Raised them myself. They were orphaned pups. Then over here in the next space I have Sophie, my kangaroo. She's an odd one. Got to watch it with her. She can throw you a jab or two if you aren't looking."

"Punch you?" Derek asked.

"You bet." They walked on.

"And here is my croc. Ain't he a beauty? Love that guy. Hey, Albert." Andy pointed to the largest enclosure yet. Inside was a huge crocodile.

"They have really gone all out for this movie. For you to bring the animals here and to build this, it's incredible," Nikki said.

"It is." He finally set the terrarium down on the ground. Nikki let out a sigh of relief, and Andy smiled at her knowingly. "We're having a blast but I know my critters, and they're about as ready to get back to the zoo as I am. At this rate with that Lucy, we won't be getting home for a few years." He laughed. "Anyway, here you go." Andy took a burlap-type suit along with a mesh face mask off of a peg. He handed it to Derek.

"Ah, the snake suit," Derek said.

"Yes, just like mine," Andy replied.

"Ah."

"You can pull it on over your clothes, mate."

"Right."

"And you have to put the face mask on. Important, you know. You don't want Charlie to turn around and bite you in the face."

This did not sound like anything *any* human should ever be doing. Nikki was not liking this at all. In fact, as far as she was concerned this was one stupid idea.

Derek pulled on the suit over his clothing. The men reminded Nikki of the dog trainers on TV who work with police dogs.

"I'm going to take Charlie out then. All right everyone stand back," Andy said. He slid open the top of the terrarium and with experienced hands removed the snake.

"My Charlie. He's a beauty, isn't he? The key with these gorgeous beasts is to stay calm, Derek. You keep focused on him, not on your nerves. He does not want to hurt you. See how I hold him out and away from my face. Now, you have the mesh mask on, so that makes things far less stressful. Take a step over here, and let's have a look at him."

The copper-colored snake, in a solid S shape, looked tense to Nikki, who couldn't help feeling sick to her stomach. Andy had his right hand tight around the middle and his left up closer to the head. Nikki clenched her fists, and it was all she could do not to scream out to Derek to get the hell away from there. But at the same time there was something amazing about the way Andy remained calm. She had to admit it was pretty damn riveting.

"Want to hold him?" Andy said.

Derek nodded, though with a slight hesitation. Andy explained how to hold the snake and handed it over to Derek. Nikki held her breath.

"Good, good. Now relax and pay attention to your breathing. See how he is staying perfectly still. This is good, mate. He is not feeling threatened by you."

Thank God.

"Hey, Andy, we're ready for you," a man yelled, standing at the entrance of the structure. Derek stiffened.

"Imbecile!" Andy said. "Don't let that shake you, Derek. You're doing great. Stick with the breathing. I've told those morons not to yell when I'm working with my animals. Now, I'll take him

34

from you." Andy reached out and Derek slowly handed him the reptile.

Nikki sighed.

"There you go, Charlie." Andy gently placed Charlie back into the terrarium. "Looks like we have to go and play nice with the diva now. Hopefully she's mellowed out. I don't like being insulted, but what's worse is having my creatures insulted."

He stretched out a hand to Derek. "Nice to meet you, mate. So what did you think?"

Derek took the mask off; a huge smile spread across his face. "Cool. Very cool."

"You're a natural at this. Why don't you and your wife come on down to the zoo and be my guest some time?"

"Oh no, she's not my wife." Derek glanced at Nikki. "My assistant, actually. And yes, we'd love to do that. Thanks, Andy. That'd be great."

"Andy!" the crew member bellowed. "Lucy is ready now."

"Will? Is that you?" Andy asked, squinting his eyes.

"Yes, sir."

"Come here."

A young, burly looking man came down the corridor. His blue eyes looked worried.

"I think I've explained to everyone around here the protocol around my animals, haven't I?"

Nikki studied the guy for a minute. He looked

like the same man who had been at the security kiosk when they came in. He wore a uniform consisting of a button-down, big navy blue jacket and polyester pants.

"Yes, sir. I'm sorry. The director was yelling at someone to find you and when no one was doing it, I volunteered. I was on a bit of a break, getting a soda . . ."

Andy held up a hand. "I don't care. Thank you. But from now on please remember the rules."

The fellow nodded and walked out.

"I know, I know," Liam said, looking at Andy. He turned to Nikki and Derek. "He's a local boy. Nice kid. Known him and his mum for years. Will can be a bit dense sometimes. I was trying to help out when I got him hired on as security. I'm sorry 'bout that, Andy."

"No problem, mate. They shouldn't be making him do an assistant's job anyway. The animals will get over it and so will I, and I don't think he'll do it again. Anyway, I've been called, so I must run on, but I'll see everyone at the barbie tonight, yep?"

They all nodded and started toward the golf cart as Andy prepared for the scene.

"That was something," Liam said when they got back to the house.

"Was it ever," Derek replied. "Man, talk about adrenaline. Here I'm trying to stay calm like he said and you know, all I'm thinking is that I've got this snake who could kill me in my hands. It was crazy."

"I don't get men," Grace said. "Snakes, ooh, disgusting."

"I agree," Nikki replied. "It must be a guy thing."

They chatted for a bit longer after going back up to the house, and then said their good-byes. "Now the party will start at six and it's gonna be great, you two," Liam said. "All casual, nothing fancy. We'll cook you up an amazing feast and have some great Aussie wines from my winery."

"Looking forward to it." Derek shook Liam's hand.

Once inside the car, Nikki slugged him on his shoulder.

"Ouch, what was that for?" he snapped.

"Are you crazy? What were you thinking, messing with that poisonous snake!"

He laughed. "I was perfectly safe. Andy Burrow knows what he's doing, and it was really cool."

"Not for me, you silly snake charmer."

"Snake charmer, huh?"

"Yeah." She smiled and looked at him. "I did kind of like you in that suit."

"You did? Maybe I'll have to ask Andy if I can borrow it, then I can try and charm you, too."

"You already have."

They both laughed, knowing how corny they sounded. It was a comfort level Nikki hadn't ever felt before.

They drove through the village and stopped off at a restaurant for lunch, ordering grilled spicy lamb burgers with a bottle of Shiraz. Waiting for their meal, Nikki asked, "How was the business between you and Liam? He obviously wanted to talk to you in private. Is there a problem? You were acting kind of weird when you both got back."

Derek scratched the side of his neck and then tugged at his earlobe. Nikki had been around him enough that she knew this was something he did when he felt uncomfortable. "No. Not really. The contracts all look good. There are a few more items we need to sew up, but everything is fine. I don't think I was acting weird. I was excited about meeting Andy Burrow."

"You are not telling me the truth. Everything is not fine, is it?"

The waiter showed up with the wine and Derek did the taste test and gave approval. Nikki shifted in her seat impatiently. "What gives? I am your manager and assistant; shouldn't I be aware if there's a problem?"

He sighed. "Right now we are not going to talk business." He took her hand. "Right now, you are my woman."

"Oh yeah. I was meaning to ask you about that. Since we do work together and . . . well, you are my boss, how will this all work? Will there be a posted schedule that states when we can be a couple and when we are all business?"

He laughed. "I know you're not serious. Look, we're both professionals. I think we know when it's appropriate to act as a couple and when we have to be all about the business."

"You're right—and speaking of, I know you were just trying to divert me. So what's the deal with Liam Hahndorf? What's the problem?"

He sighed. "Damn, you are like a pit bull. Okay. There is a problem, but one we can work out, and honestly, I promised Liam that I would not discuss what he and I talked about with anyone."

She set her wine down and crossed her arms.

"Don't look at me like that."

"I'm not just anyone," Nikki replied.

"No. You aren't, but I'm not one to break promises. And I gave Liam my word. When I can discuss it with you, I will. Can we leave it at that and enjoy our lunch?"

"Fine."

"Good. What did you think of Lucy Swanson's outburst?" he asked.

She went with the change of subject. Nikki could respect that Derek had made a promise to Liam and intended to keep it, but being the nosy bug she was, she didn't swallow it easily. "She's something else. I was impressed with Shawn Keefer, though. He handled it well. I don't know—if someone was screaming at me like that . . ."

"And saying the things she said," Derek added.

"As a man, I really would have come unglued, especially in front of all those people."

"Understandably." Nikki shook her head. "I don't know, but I have a funny feeling in my stomach about all of it. Hollywood here in the Barossa Valley and then that Lucy giving such hell to everyone."

He laughed. "You and your funny feelings." He glanced at her. "*I* have a funny feeling that there is something more behind that statement than you thinking Hollywood should have stayed in Los Angeles. What's up?"

"Oh I don't know. I was kind of thinking about Grace Hahndorf's reaction to the movie being made there. At first when we were talking about it she seemed kind of excited about the movie and the big-time actors, but her demeanor changed as soon as Liam told us that he was the one who'd written the screenplay."

"I didn't get that from her."

"I did."

"She could be the kind of woman who feels like that's bragging, and inappropriate."

"It's her husband."

"I think you're reading way too much into it," Derek said.

"Maybe," Nikki replied, but she was not convinced.

They talked a bit more about the goings-on at the Hahndorfs' and what the barbecue might be like that evening. They also discussed the snake incident with Andy. For Derek, it had been exhilarating.

As lunch wound down, they both found themselves relaxed from the wine, and since they weren't far from the hotel they left the car parked where it was and walked back hand in hand.

Getting into the elevator, Derek turned to her. "You know, we do have a few hours before we have to be back out there. We could make some *special* use of the time. What do you think?"

Spicy Lamb Burgers with Marquis Philips Sarah's Blend 2006

Things are starting to heat up nicely between Nikki and Derek, but if Nikki's sixth sense is right, trouble is brewing at the Hahndorf Winery. Now, hopefully you have someone to heat things up with, but even if you don't, invite some pals over and try a new take on an old American classic—the hamburger. These lamb burgers are tasty treats and with a good bottle of Shiraz like Sarah's Blend you'll be pleased you changed it up a bit. So, light up the barbie, grab yourself a nice Shiraz, and get cooking, mate!

The Barossa Valley was settled by German immigrants in the nineteenth century. The area is a warm-weather region. The valley is well known for producing excellent red wines; the Shiraz coming out of the region is some of the best in the world. The Shiraz vines are some of the oldest in Australia, which are prized because, with age, vines tend to lose some of their youthful vigor, which leads to smaller yields and more complex flavors.

Marquis Philips Sarah's Blend 2006 is a smooth, full-bodied Shiraz containing fruit forward flavors of black currant blended with cedar and tosty oak. The Shiraz offers up fragrant aromas of cedar, smoke, tar, blueberry, and black-berry liqueur. Full-bodied, opulent, and structured, this intense, well-balanced Shiraz will age nicely for the next eight years and is a great value.

1 lb ground lamb
2 tbsp chopped fresh mint leaves
2 tbsp chopped fresh cilantro
2 tbsp chopped fresh oregano
1 tbsp chopped garlic
1 tsp sherry
1 tsp white wine vinegar
1 tsp molasses
1 tsp ground cumin
¼ tsp ground allspice
½ red pepper flakes
½ tsp salt
½ tsp ground black pepper
oil
4 pita bread rounds
4 oz feta cheese, crumbled

Preheat grill to medium heat.

Place the lamb in a large bowl, and mix with the mint, cilantro, oregano, garlic, sherry, vinegar, and molasses. Season with cumin, allspice, red pepper flakes, salt, and black pepper. Mix well. Shape into 4 patties.

Brush grill grate with oil. Grill burgers 5 minutes on each side, or until well-done. Heat the pita pocket briefly on the grill. Serve burgers wrapped in pitas with feta cheese.

Serves 4.

Chapter 3

Nikki's stomach twisted. "I th-think that would . . . be great," she stammered. Her response did not come out the way she'd wanted it to, but she'd been out of this game for so long that she couldn't help feeling self-conscious. What if she messed up? Okay, so this stuff was supposed to be natural, and it all just happened. It was lust, heat at its best, right? Did she wear the right panties? Oh God, she hoped she'd put a matching set on. Thank God she'd had enough foresight not to throw her grandma panties into the suitcase. Instead, she'd packed a thong that all the Victoria's Secret models tried to make look comfortable. Please! It was a string going up your ass. No comfort in that. But it looked good. And right now, looking good beat out comfort. But there was that bulge— granted it was slight, but it was there. It was this small bulge that caused the panty line to indent slightly around the hip. What if he noticed it? Oh God, and what if . . . well, she was on top and her stomach didn't look flat? *Why the hell was she even thinking these thoughts?*

"Are you sure?" Derek asked. "I don't want you to feel pressured. I was just thinking—hoping— but Nikki, we can definitely wait."

"No. I'm fine. I'm great. I'm good with this. I want to do it." Oh God. She was *so* in trouble. The heat rose through her body all the way up to her cheeks.

They got off the elevator; Derek grabbed her wrist and lightly pushed her against the wall. He held one arm above her and kissed her neck. He stopped at her ear, where he kissed the lobe lightly.

Oh yeah, she was in hordes of trouble. He kissed her hard on the lips, and she found herself kissing him back just as hard. What the hell, screw the indents from the panty lines. She'd just have to cut out eating two of her favorite foods—bread and cheese. Derek unlocked the door and lightly pushed her onto the bed. He wiggled his brows at her and they started cracking up. Thank God the man had a sense of humor. Nikki wasn't sure she could handle all that mushy "I love you so much" crap and "your body is amazing," blah, blah, blah. All the stuff written for soap operas and movies might work on-screen but for her, some good old-fashioned lovemaking—and yes, a sense that she was doing it right—would be just fine.

Derek had her blouse half unbuttoned as she fumbled with his belt. They were near the throes of passion when they heard the bathroom door open.

"Well, lookie here, what is going on, you two are doing the nasty." Simon, Derek's gay brother, stood in the doorway, toothbrush in hand.

"What the—" Derek said, lifting himself up.

"Oh my God!" Nikki squealed and started buttoning her blouse.

"It's okay, kids. It's about time you two got together," Simon said as he pumped the air back and forth with his hips. Nikki shook her head.

"Simon, what in the hell are you doing here?" Derek asked.

"Listen, don't mind me. It looks like I came at a bad time. I'll just take a little jaunt around town and come back and fill you in on all of the agony I've been through since you both took off."

Derek glared at him. "Bullshit. You've pretty much spoiled the mood, so I suggest you start talking now."

"I'll order us up some tea," Nikki said.

"No tea for me, Snow White. Order me up a bottle of one of those Sauvignon Blancs the Aussies are so famous for."

"Make it two bottles," Derek said.

"You know, instead of room service, why don't we take a walk around the village? We've already had some wine this afternoon. Coffee might be good," Nikki added. In such an awkward situation, finding the right thing to say was impossible, so she played the Pollyanna card.

"Oh no, you two. I don't want to be a third wheel."

"It's a little late for that," Derek barked.

Simon winced. He turned around and walked over to his suitcase, which sat on the verandah.

How did they miss seeing it? Lust. That was the answer. They'd been too far gone to notice anything else.

"I'll just go. I didn't know where else to go or who to turn to. You're my family, but I understand. I know you two want to be alone." Simon rolled his suitcase over to the door and looked at them with a pitiful downturn at the corners of his lips.

As he opened the door, Nikki placed her hand on Derek's shoulder. "We can't let him go. Simon, come on, let's all go down, and you can have that glass of wine in the hotel bar."

Simon looked at his brother. Derek threw up his hands. "Okay, Drama Queen, you win."

Simon hugged him. "Thank you. I'm sorry. I will so make this up to both of you."

Over a few glasses of wine, Simon explained his reason for flying halfway across the world to interrupt what was supposed to be an afternoon delight. "I knew I shouldn't have done it. I mean, Marco and I did have this agreement and it was just so totally wrong. I can't blame him for hating me."

"Slow down," Derek said. "Start from the beginning."

"Well, after Nikki left for the airport, Marco and I had a chat about our relationship and how it was time to take it to the next level and have a marriage celebration. I agreed completely, but he wanted one thing from me. One eensy-weensy thing." Simon pinched his thumb and index finger together. "And I couldn't do it."

Marco and Simon had been partners for years. Nikki had met them three years earlier when she'd gone to work for the winery. At first, the two of them had rubbed her the wrong way with their arrogance and brash behavior, but over time they'd grown on her. They'd turned over a new leaf when they'd gone to a New Age, Zen-type camp in Sedona, Arizona, where they'd met a guru named Sansibaba. Nikki was sure the guy was a charlatan, but Simon and Marco had come back with a sense of gratitude and a soft spot for her. Friendship between the three of them had since blossomed, and she now considered them dear friends. She was bothered to hear there was trouble in paradise.

"I'm afraid to ask," Derek said. "But what is it that you *just* could not do?"

Simon sighed. "I couldn't give up Gianni or Kenneth."

"What? You're cheating on Marco!" Derek exclaimed. "And with *two* men? God, what is wrong with you!" A few heads turned.

Nikki shook her head. "No. I don't think so."

Derek looked from Nikki to Simon and back again. "Someone want to explain?"

"Gianni Versace and Kenneth Cole. I'm right, aren't I?" she asked Simon.

49

He nodded. "We had this deal that we would give up all designer labels for a year. You know, Marco adores Guru Sansibaba and he's been doing this life-coaching thing with a woman from the Sansibaba Enlightenment Center, and his life coach suggested that we give up our labels. She felt it would be good for us to detach from what the designers represent."

Derek put his head in his hands. Nikki could see his neck turning from red to a sort of magenta color. This was not good. "And what is it that those designers represent?" he growled.

"Ego, of course. And, I agreed with Marco that I'd do it. But dammit, I'm like a freaking addict. As soon as I said that I wouldn't do it again, I jumped in the car and went up to that really nice boutique in St. Helena, you know the one I mean, with like all the established designers and the up-and-comers. Place is amazing, and only fifteen minutes from the vineyard. Gotta love it."

"Get to the point," Derek said.

"Right, but gawd, I almost went into the city to Neiman's, too. Good thing I didn't. But anyhoo, I tried to hide all the packages. I was actually using your place to hide them, Nikki, and then Marco caught me going up the stairs and he found all of them. He told me that if he couldn't trust me with this, then he couldn't trust me at all. Then, he packed his things and left. I don't know where he went. He won't answer my calls, or my e-mails, and I feel so alone. I didn't know what to do, so I chartered a jet and I came here. To be with family."

"Wait a minute. You blew how much to get here? You chartered a jet? And oh shit, oh no . . ." Derek's head snapped up. "Who is with Ollie?"

Ollie was Derek's Rhodesian Ridgeback, a big, caramel-colored dog that Nikki had fallen in love with since joining the Malveaux team. He'd become almost as much her dog as he was Derek's. For some time it had been a joke between the two of them as to who Ollie's real owner was.

"Please, Derek, as if I'd leave the animal on his own. No, he's with that adorable girl that Nikki hired. The stripper."

"Alyssa is not a stripper. Well, not any longer. I hired her because she's a good woman and smart and she has a child to take care of."

"Oh God, Snow White, I am so the last person you need to defend anyone to."

Nikki knew he was right. Simon accepted pretty much anyone. She cringed at her new nickname. For the first year they'd called her Goldilocks. She'd been highlighting her hair to fit that Southern California mold for years, but after living up north for some time, she'd gone back to her original darker roots and a new nickname had been born.

"I think the girl is a sweetheart and she's great

with Ollie. I told her that she and the toddler could stay at your place. Hope that's okay."

Nikki smiled. "Sure. It's fine." *Her place* wasn't really hers anyway. It was a room at the Malveaux spa and boutique hotel. Her home had been torched by a killer not that long ago and she'd had to move into the hotel.

"You know what, I've about had enough of this nonsense," Derek said. "You and Marco are freaks. My God, and listening to this Guru Sansibaba—what a crock of shit. This is plain ridiculous, Simon. I suggest you get your ass back on Virgin Atlantic—coach, mind you—because I'm sure you charged that charter to Malveaux, and go find Marco and make up. Quit acting like a woman."

Simon turned to Nikki. "Aren't you insulted by that? Okay, so first off, acting like a gal comes au naturel for me. Second, don't you think that if I could have found Marco by now, I would have done everything in my power to make up with him?"

"Why did you come here, Si?" Derek asked. "What did you think Nikki and I could do for you? You spent fifteen hours in a jet. What's the deal?"

"I was looking for moral support, *brother.*" Simon threw down his napkin.

Uh-oh, time to play referee. Nikki touched Simon's shoulder. "Now everyone just chill. Okay, this is no big deal. Simon needs us right now." Simon pouted. "I know how much . . . I mean, *we* know how much you love Marco." Simon nodded. "And we love Marco, too. He needs some cooling off time and then I'll bet everything will work out."

"You think?"

"Yes. Tell you what. I'll send him an e-mail and see if he responds."

"Really? You will?"

"Of course."

Simon glanced at Derek, who said, "Fine, me, too. I'll try and give him a call, see if he'll take your sorry ass back. Gianni and Kenneth. Jeez, you guys are plain ridiculous."

Simon grinned. "Yes, but you two are the best. I knew you'd come through for me. Now, what do we have planned while we're here in outback country?"

"We're going to a party tonight at the Hahndorf Winery—" Nikki said.

"*We* have nothing planned," Derek interrupted. "Nikki and I have plans. You have to make your own plans."

"Right of course. I'm sorry. I've bothered you enough." Simon sipped his wine and leaned back in his chair.

"Oh for God's sake. Fine. You can come with us to the party. I'm sure the Hahndorfs won't mind."

Simon set his wine down and clapped his hands. "Thank you, and I promise I won't be a problem.

I will not interfere with your good time. You kids should really get to know each other better."

"Simon," Derek warned.

"Right. Okay, well, I think I'll see what I can do about getting my own room."

"Good idea. How did you get into our room anyway?" Nikki asked.

"The maid let me in. I told her that I left my key inside."

"Great security," Derek said.

"Look at me, do I look like a thief?" Simon stood. "See you two at what, around six or so?"

"Looking forward to it," Derek answered, his voice laden in sarcasm.

They watched Simon walk out of the bar. Derek took Nikki's hand. "I'm sorry about that."

"Please. Don't be. You know I love him."

"Yeah, I'm not sure that I do, though. His timing certainly sucks."

She laughed. "You love him, too. You must because you didn't kill him."

"He's lucky I didn't."

Nikki felt herself further drawn to Derek. He was a softy deep down, and as annoying as Simon could be, Derek had handled everything quite wonderfully. Bet he'd make a great dad. Suddenly Nikki found herself feeling brave. Her hand grazed Derek's. "Should we go back to the room and finish what we started?"

He didn't answer right away and an uneasy

feeling came over her. "No. You know what, I think in a weird way it was a good thing Simon interrupted us."

Ooh, she didn't think she liked the sound of that. "You do?"

"Yep. Because the first time we're together should be perfect. That's what I want for you, and that is what we agreed on from the get-go." He leaned in and kissed her cheek, then her lips.

"That seemed pretty perfect."

"No. Not in the way it should be."

"Okay, so perfect, huh? Wow, what does that entail?" she asked.

"I guess you'll just have to wait and see."

Chapter 4

Much to Nikki and Derek's dismay their hotel was booked solid, along with every other place in town. There was a festival going on, and Simon had no place to go, except for the pull-out couch in their suite. So much for the perfect seduction. Nikki could tell that Derek was brooding, and she wasn't exactly thrilled, but they couldn't desert Simon in his time of need. Instead, Nikki shot off an e-mail to Marco in an attempt to locate him, letting him know they were all concerned and that Simon was truly miserable without him.

Instead of romance in kangaroo country, the three of them took turns getting ready in the bathroom, with Simon taking the longest. With the weather downright chilly in the evenings, as winter was just around the corner, Nikki put on a steel blue cashmere turtleneck sweater and a long, wraparound, cream-colored sweater-coat. The combo looked pretty good with her eyes. For pants she pulled on what she called her skinny jeans, meaning for some reason they seemed to hold in anything that needed to be held in without looking like that was what she'd tried to do.

"I so hate you," Simon said when she emerged from the bathroom.

"What?"

"Look at you, you little twit. You even look good in a turtleneck. No one makes a turtleneck look sexy, but you pull it off somehow. No wonder my brother is in lust with you. If I wasn't so gay, I'd be in lust, too."

"Funny." She shook a finger at him.

When she walked out into the front room, Derek's eyes brightened. "You look beautiful."

"See what I mean." Simon shook his head.

"Thank you. Both of you . . . I think."

At the Hahndorf Winery, the barbecue looked to be in full swing with several cars parked out front. Nikki prayed to God that the Australian ideal of "casual" was on par with the same term used in the States. She would hate to see everyone else in diamonds and pearls when she'd chosen a turtleneck and jeans, even if Simon was right that she pulled off *sexy* in them, which she didn't buy. At least Derek and Simon were also in jeans, and there was no arguing that jeans were definitely sexy on Derek.

A valet waited to park the car. "Schnazzy," Simon said, stepping out of the vehicle. "Like you didn't tell me that this thing was a major shindig."

"We were told it was a simple 'shrimp on the barbie' kind of deal and to come casual."

"Huh. So who all is going to be here? As if I'd know anyone in Australia." Simon laughed.

"Shawn Keefer," Nikki replied.

"Oh yeah, you are so funny. First you're a twit in a turtleneck and now you're a comedienne."

"No. I'm not. I'm telling you the truth."

"Okay. Funny girl."

"She is telling the truth. They're filming a movie here at the vineyard. That's why they're having the party."

Simon stopped dead in his tracks. "Stop it. No. Uh-uh. Are you two for real?"

They nodded in unison.

"Oh my God, oh my God. Get me a paper bag. I think I'm going to hyperventilate. Shawn Keefer is here? *Here?*" He pointed to the ground. "Shawn as in *People* magazine's sexiest man of 2005? Please, oh God. And you two let me wear *this*? You said it was a barbecue. Oh no, no, no. I think I'm going to pass out."

Derek took his brother by the shoulders. "Get ahold of yourself. First of all, you look fine. And second, Shawn Keefer is not gay. You wouldn't have a chance with him."

"Please. Everyone in Hollywood is gay."

Derek rolled his eyes and wrapped an arm around Nikki. "I'll pretend I don't know him, if you will."

"Deal."

"Whatever. I'm gonna meet a movie star. But I will kill the two of you for not telling me to wear something a little more stylish. Do I look okay?" Simon ran his hands through his spiky, bleach blond hair. He was a good-looking man, just like his brother. They both had a kind of David Beckham look about them. Tonight Posh Spice had nothing on her. Nikki smiled. A reality show on her own life might actually be worth watching. There was enough craziness to spread around.

"You look great. Stunning."

"Stunning?" Simon asked. He smoothed down his white linen shirt, unbuttoned his suede jacket, and tugged his 7 For All Mankind jeans down around his hips even farther.

"Stunning, and you know if you pulled your boxers out now, above the jeans waistband, maybe you could pass for Slim Shady," Derek said with a sly grin.

"Oh shut up. At least I have style. What the hell are those anyway? Levi's? Oh, aren't you cool."

"Boys," Nikki scolded. "Act like grown men, please. You can go back to sibling rivalry later."

Simon smirked and walked on ahead. Live music was coming from the rear of the home.

"Good to see you, mate," Liam Hahndorf said, pumping Derek's hand. "And you, too." He kissed Nikki on the cheek.

It was true when people remarked that the Aussies were gracious hosts. Everyone they'd encountered so far had lived up to that.

Within minutes, flutes of champagne appeared and they were being introduced all around. Simon's eyes about bugged out when Liam introduced them to Shawn Keefer. Liam had to excuse himself to check on the food and left Nikki and Derek to witness Simon fawning all over the actor.

"Oh Shawn, I loved you in *A Woman to Die For*. The chemistry was fabulous between you and Angelina. Just fabulous. You really should've won the Oscar for that movie."

As much of a fool as Simon was making of himself, the movie star didn't seem to mind at all. His ego ate it up. Actors didn't impress Nikki much. She'd spent enough time in Hollywood to learn that many of them were insecure egomaniacs with superiority complexes. Thus, her acting career hadn't been that difficult to walk away from, especially when she'd found that life could have a hell of a lot more substance.

"That was a great flick," Shawn said. "A lot of intense work, you know."

He crossed his arms over his tan sweater, which was only a shade darker than his skin. Looked as if Shawn Keefer could give George Hamilton a run for his money at the tanning salon. He reminded Nikki of a pretty-boy Clint Eastwood in his younger years. He even had down the eyebrow cock that Eastwood was notorious for. Nikki wondered if he'd studied Clint.

"But this movie here," he continued, "will be phenomenal. You know, you can't go wrong working with Nathan Cooley. He's a genius. And Kane . . . man, the guy is awesome. He's poured so much cash into this thing, and he's banking on it being huge. We all are. It will be, of course."

"Of course." Simon touched his arm as if they were old friends.

"Huh." It was the only word Nikki could muster.

"What do you mean you don't have tequila? I want a margarita." The voice was recognizable from her earlier tantrum—Lucy Swanson.

"Oh yeah, she's the only buzz kill in this deal," Shawn said. "Lucy Swanson. Royal pain in the ass. Chick hasn't even had a real hit and she thinks she's Meryl Streep. Little Miss Diva freaked today on the poor animal safari dude, then hunted me down, thinking I'd come to her rescue. God. Come on."

"You're talking about Andy Burrow?" Derek asked.

"Yeah, man, that dude has some balls."

"Right." Derek leaned into Nikki and whispered, "Would you like to get something to eat?" She nodded. They left Simon to stare and pump mental iron with Shawn Keefer.

Nikki started to say something about leaving Simon with Shawn, when Miss Diva herself bumped into Derek. As she looked at him with her doe-like hazel eyes, Nikki wanted to slap her for just looking all nubile, and . . . well, pretty damn close to physically perfect. She suddenly felt matronlike in her turtleneck and jeans compared to Lucy Swanson's down-to-there silky V-neck black dress. The girl had no body fat—zilch—and had to be freezing her ass off. That gave Nikki some comfort. At least she was warm. But the chill didn't seem to affect Lucy, who smiled coyly at Derek.

"Oh, I'm sorry. I didn't see you standing there," Lucy said.

Nikki couldn't help notice the way Derek looked at Lucy. Okay, probably every man looked at her the way he did—like he was going to start drooling any minute—but still, he was with her, and she couldn't help feeling a sting from the green-eyed monster.

"Lucy Swanson, right?" Nikki asked.

The barely legal actress glanced at Nikki. "Yeah."

"I just read about your latest mishap in the

61

Enquirer. What a shame. You poor thing. I can't believe you had to do community service for what was it, like forty hours?" Derek glared at Nikki and she knew exactly how she sounded—like a jealous old hag.

"Like whatever. That was so lame, you know. I didn't do anything wrong. So like I had a few drinks and well, it's such a lie that I hit that stupid girl."

"Bummer," Nikki said.

"Like who are you guys? I don't think I know you two. You're not from around here. I mean, you have to be American, right?"

"We're from Napa Valley," Derek said.

"Oh cool. I so love it there. I went up there last year after I finished filming. I needed a battery recharge."

More like she needed to dry out, which was hard to do in the land of liquid grape aplenty.

"You guys hanging with Liam and Grace then?"

"We have some business with them," Derek said.

"Right on. I didn't catch your names."

"I'm Derek Malveaux and this is Nikki Sands."

"Nah-uh," Lucy said. "Oh my God. I totally thought you looked familiar. *You're* Nikki Sands? You played Detective Martini. Oh my God. I loved that show. It was so campy."

Who knew that Nikki would find a fan in Australia and that it would be Lucy Swanson? She thought she'd only had one fan in the world and that was a policewoman back in Napa Valley who oohed and aahed over the fact that Nikki played Sydney Martini on what was supposed to be a *CSI* sort of show that only lasted a season.

"Oh this is so classic," Lucy said. "My mom and I watched that show all the time. I mean, well, I was like what, fifteen I guess, and that was before my mom went off the deep end, you know. Everyone heard about that. She was kind of cool back then. But then she just lost it when my dad left and bankrupted her. Now I support her and my brother and sisters. It's a nightmare. But that's another story. So like I don't believe this. What happened to you? I thought you were gonna be like all Heather Locklear, you know. You were perfect for all that soap opera stuff."

Nikki wasn't sure how to take that one, so she used the grin-and-bear-it tactic. "Thanks. Yeah, well, I kind of got a life."

"Oh." Lucy nodded. "I get it. You burned out. I can totally see that, and you probably didn't want to do the whole plastic surgery thing."

Nikki impulsively touched her face and then glanced down at her breasts. Did she need plastic surgery? "No, I really wanted to explore other avenues."

"Cool." She looked Derek up and down. "But I have to tell you that you were one hot chick in that show."

"Thanks."

"All right, well, I'll catch you later. I'm going to go see if Hannah was able to find some tequila in her daddy's liquor cabinet. I thought everyone had tequila."

They watched Lucy walk away. "Charming," Nikki said. "What did she mean that I was one hot chick in that show? Am I not hot now?" Okay, so maybe she wasn't twentysomething hot any longer. She was now inching toward forty and she'd noticed recently that, even with her daily run and eating healthy, nature had caught onto her age, and the pull of gravity had done things to her ass and the back of her legs that she was not crazy about. But plastic surgery? Not her style.

Derek kissed her cheek. "Don't tell me that you're feeling insecure. Come on, she's got nothing on you."

"Yeah, it's me who has about fifteen pounds on her." Oh man, why had she said that?

"You're being silly. She's a kid, and from every-thing that you hear about her, she's a problem child. Relax. I think you're beautiful. In fact"—he leaned in and kissed her earlobe—"I think you're very hot, and I can't wait to get you alone."

Mmm, now that was nice. Real nice.

Liam Hahndorf's voice boomed out, intruding on the moment. "Hello, I'm pleased everyone could make it. Now if you want to get some good food, it'll be up in a moment. We've got shrimp on

the barbie here, lamb chops that are delicious—
my Grace's specialty—salad, and all sorts of wonderful dishes. Of course, an Aussie barbie
wouldn't be authentic without a little roo."

"Roo?" Nikki looked at Derek.

"Kangaroo."

Nikki brought her hand up to her mouth. "Oh
my God, the animals with the pouch that hop
around with their babies?"

He grinned. "I know it sounds horrible, but to
the Australians it's like eating beef. It even tastes
kind of like beef but a bit more gamey."

"You've eaten it?"

"I didn't want to be rude to the host. I kind of
liked it."

Liam continued: "And for your entertainment,
we have our own Andy Burrow to put on a little
show for us. We're real fortunate because we
don't get crocs down here in the Barossa, but
Andy brought some from his zoo, so we'll have
our own tales from the wild side," he said, referring to Andy's popular TV show.

Hmm. Nothing like snakes and crocodiles to go
with dinner. Perfect. Nikki's stomach turned over,
but she'd be a good sport.

Everyone queued up and served themselves
buffet style. Nikki hoped for an opportunity to
meet and talk to Nathan Cooley, the director. Not
that she had any interest in acting. That chapter of
her life was definitely closed, but she would enjoy

chatting with a director of his caliber. She spotted him in line talking with Lucy Swanson and the producer.

Interesting: everyone at this party was either connected to Hollywood, or wealthy like the Hahndorfs. Even so, Liam and Grace were super down-to-earth. Grace had prepared much of the food, with the catering company there to simply help serve. Liam had himself a super-sized barbecue grill and he looked to be completely enjoying himself fixing the meats. They had a service pouring drinks and a couple of attendants picking up along the way, but it was oddly intimate. It probably wasn't the type of party the Hollywood crew was used to frequenting.

The buffet line faced the river that bordered the Hahndorfs' backyard. Rays of the setting sun flashed onto the murky water, making it appear as if a handful of gold coins had been dropped into it. The deck at the Hahndorfs' looked to be made out of the same jarrah wood that Grace had put in the house. The dark reddish color reminded Nikki of the floor of an upscale restaurant back in Napa called Grapes, which then reminded her of the man she'd left to go to Spain on his own—Andrés Fernandez. His sister Isabel was Nikki's best friend and owned Grapes. Nikki knew that she was going to have to deal sooner or later with the consequences of hurting Andrés. And, it wasn't as if she didn't feel a little pull in her heart toward him. They'd been great friends, dated for a couple of months, gotten close to becoming intimate—and he'd confessed his love for her. And, when he'd invited her to Spain, she'd come within moments of grabbing her purse and meeting him at the airport. Then, Derek had called, and the message he'd left her had changed her mind. There'd been a few moments where her head had tried to convince her heart that Andrés was the man she should be with. But in the end, as the saying goes, the heart knows what the heart wants, and Derek Malveaux had grabbed hers and was holding tight.

Everyone sat down around a fire pit on cushy sofas and chairs, eating the amazing food, which for Nikki meant sans roo. To her pleasant surprise the director, Nathan Cooley, took a seat across from them, along with Kane Ferriss, the producer. To her dismay Lucy Swanson and Hannah Hahndorf also joined the group.

"Hey, have you guys met Nikki Sands?" Lucy said, almost immediately upon sitting down.

What was it with this girl? Why didn't she just wave a sign over Nikki that said: "over-the-hill actress right here."

Both men turned to Nikki and said, "No," then introduced themselves to her and Derek.

Lucy piped in again, "Did you guys ever see that show where she played Detective Martini? She was awesome."

Nikki couldn't tell if Lucy meant it or if she was just trying to get her goat.

Thankfully, both men said they hadn't. Also, Derek was sensing Nikki's discomfort and cut in. "So, Kane, you're producing the movie, right?"

Kane nodded, his mouth full of roo. He took a sip of his wine, and Nikki took a gulp. This felt surreal. "Yeah. I'm the producer. We're real excited about this flick. We've got such an awesome cast. Can't go wrong with Shawn Keefer, you know."

Nikki caught Lucy roll her eyes at Hannah, who giggled. "Dude is such a jerk," Lucy said. She whispered something to Hannah.

"Lucy," Nathan warned.

She shrugged. "Well, he is. Look at him over there all buddy-buddy with that stupid snake tamer. Can't stand him either." Nikki felt Derek tense. "And who is that other lame ass he's hanging with? Guy looks all gaga over him."

"That's my brother," Derek said.

"Oh, sorry."

Kane turned his attention back to Nikki. "So, you did some acting?"

Oh God, why couldn't anyone just drop it? She waved a hand. "A while back, you know, silly show. It wasn't really my thing."

He nodded. "You definitely have to be passionate about it. It's like anything: you really got to love this business to stay in it. It sure as hell isn't easy."

Kane Ferriss looked to be the opposite of Nathan Cooley. He had clipped short light brown hair, blue eyes, wore an argyle patterned sweater with khakis. He reminded Nikki of the quintessential Ivy League frat boy.

"That's true," Nathan said. "I'm still working my way up to Spielberg status."

"Oh my God, I love your stuff," Nikki said.

Derek eyed her. Wait. Was she gushing? She was gushing, but not because Nathan Cooley was some hot property. He wasn't attractive to her at all and he didn't seem to care much about his appearance. He wore a faded yellow sweatshirt and jeans with holes. Despite his looks, he was brilliant. Back in the day, Nikki would have died to be in one of his movies. She tried to tone down her excitement. "I mean really, you do put out great films. I'm a fan."

"Thank you very much, Nikki. I may have to check out your old show. Who knows, if you change your mind—ever want back into acting— maybe we could work together someday."

Nikki felt her face flush. She shook her head. "Oh no, you don't want to see my old show."

Derek interrupted. "She works with me. I own a winery in Napa Valley."

"Oh great, here goes Andy Burrow and his show," Hannah interrupted.

Andy walked to the edge of the river and turned around. Lucy and Hannah stood. The actress said, "We'll see you later."

Hannah nodded and seemed to scan the group. Maybe she was looking for her folks, but the way the two of them slithered out, Nikki was pretty sure that Hannah Hahndorf was not supposed to be hanging with Lucy Swanson. It really was none of her business. Derek had reminded her time and again that her curious nature could cause her harm, and she knew he was right. A part of her still felt compelled to rat on Hannah to her parents, because she was pretty sure that the girls were up to no good. Her suspicions had to be dead-on, because a minute later she witnessed the young guy with the Sex Pistols T-shirt—what was his name, Johnny?—excuse himself as Andy brought out one of his "pets." She didn't know what made her watch him, but after grabbing three drinks from the bartender, he disappeared around to the front. Again, she reminded herself that it was none of her business. She should've been relieved that the younger set had scampered away. She turned her attention back to Andy Burrow and Company and decided to let kids be kids. They were probably drinking out front and continuing to talk smack about everyone else.

Andy did his thing with the snakes and even had a volunteer come up onstage. To her relief it wasn't Derek this time but Nathan Cooley, who seemed as enthralled as Derek had been with the creepy crawlies. For the finale, Nathan sat down and Andy turned toward the river, where he commanded a massive croc to come out of the water and up onto the bank. He proceeded to hand-feed the animal. This elicited plenty of oohs and aahs, though Nikki couldn't help feeling relieved when it was over. The jaws of that crocodile made her nervous.

The evening ended on a high note with dessert and good port. Nikki noticed Liam take Derek aside, and their discussion looked intense. Whatever the problem was, be it business or something else, Nikki wanted to know what was going on.

When the men were finished talking, good nights were said with an agreement to meet the following morning.

In the car, Simon couldn't stop carrying on about Shawn Keefer. He went on and on about how wonderful the actor was and how he felt certain that the man was gay.

"Please, Simon. You think everyone is gay," Derek said.

"Uh-uh. I so know this. My gaydar was working overtime and that glorious, gorgeous sweetie of a man is simply hiding in the closet."

"Gaydar?" Nikki asked.

"Of course, dear, like radar but gaydar. Look, I am not one to hide from the truth. I am a homosexual's homosexual, so my gaydar is super-duper strong. Yours just wouldn't be. You're a heterosexual woman."

Nikki and Derek sighed simultaneously. Most of the time Simon's banter was entertaining, but at this late hour it was too much to handle. Derek must've felt the same way. There had to be a way for Nikki to get Simon and Marco back together. The boys of summer—Nikki's reference to the two partners—had to work things out. They were each other's yin and yang, and Marco definitely kept Simon grounded. She would come up with a plan, the first part of it being to locate Marco and talk some sense into him. Granted, it was Simon who needed the sense *knocked* into *him*, but it really was like a piece of the puzzle had gone missing, and it couldn't continue this way.

As they entered their hotel, they had to deal with the tense situation of sleeping arrangements.

Simon pulled out the sofa bed. "Don't mind me, kids. I'll wear earplugs. You just go on and do what lovers do." He winked.

"Simon!" Derek snapped.

"What? I would. It'll be dark and I've got a great pair of earphones. I'll just plug in my iPod. Won't hear a thing. What do you think? Twenty, thirty minutes should do."

"Oh my God," Nikki said. Yes, getting in touch with Marco would be the first item on her morning agenda. "I cannot believe we are having this conversation. *I'm* taking the sofa bed."

"Like hell you are," Derek said.

She frowned. "Come on. This won't work. I mean, not tonight anyway. It's just too weird. It really is, don't you think?"

"I realize that, but we don't have to *sleep* together. I slept on the sofa bed last night, so what's another one."

"Whoa, ho, ho. What's this?" Simon asked. "You two haven't—?"

They both yelled, "It's none of your business."

Nikki shook her head. "No. I'm on the couch tonight."

"No. I'm on the couch," Derek said. "You can sleep with Simon."

She sighed, crossed her arms, and looked at Simon, who shrugged. "Okay, normally that would be even weirder, but . . ."

"Oh honey, I know what you're gonna say, with me, it's like sleeping with a girlfriend." He laughed. "Ooh, even that came out *so* wrong. Any way you look at it, it almost feels incestuous. Whatever." He tossed his hand in the air. "Slumber party it is, and I really am sorry about this. Tomorrow I will definitely find a new place to stay. Promise." He crossed his heart, then paused a moment, his lips turning downward. "No word from Marco?"

"Hang on. It's possible. I couldn't have heard my phone go off at the party. Let me check. I have international coverage, so if he called I would get it." She listened to her cell voicemail, but to no avail. The other boy of summer was off sulking somewhere. "No."

"Oh. Well, I guess I should expect that. I thought maybe he'd rethunk it all by now. Okay, um . . ." He clapped his hands together. "I have to brush my teeth and get my jammies on." Simon headed off to the bathroom.

Derek took her hand. "We may not get to be together tonight, but soon we will. I promise."

Nikki went to bed wondering when that might ever happen.

Aussie Prawn and Scallop Skewers with Rosemount Diamond Chardonnay

What is a woman to do when she comes face-to-face with trouble and a little pent-up frustration? First Simon, then snakes. Throw Lucy Swanson and her Victoria's Secret body into the mix, and there is only one answer—smile and grab a bite to eat. Don't get mad or even, just let it go and grab yourself a prawn and scallop skewer with a bottle of Rosemount Chardonnay and all those issues and frustrations will float away.

No roo meat for Nikki, but the shrimp and scallops were something she couldn't get enough of. The Rosemount Chardonnay is a blend of tropical fruits and soft vanilla notes. It does not contain the buttery oak flavor many California Chardonnays do, and priced under ten dollars, it is an excellent value.

½ cup mango chutney
½ cup orange juice
¼ cup sweet and tangy barbecue sauce
8 pineapple chunks, each about 1" square
12 large prawns, peeled and deveined
12 large sea scallops
8 cherry tomatoes
8 pearl onions blanched, peeled

75

In a food processor or blender purée chutney, orange juice, and barbecue sauce until smooth.

Thread four 12-inch skewers in the following order: pineapple, prawn, scallop, tomato, onion, prawn, scallop, tomato, onion, prawn, scallop, pineapple.

Brush skewers liberally with sauce and place in center of cooking grate. Grill 6 to 8 minutes or until prawns are pink and scallops are opaque, turning and brushing liberally with sauce again halfway through grilling time. Serve with remaining sauce for dipping.

The tangy mango sauce makes an irresistible addition to this Australian seafood celebration. You can find mango chutney in gourmet markets and specialty stores.

Serves 4.

Chapter 5

"Do you come from a land down under? Where women glow and men plunder? Can't you hear, can't you hear the thunder? You better run, you better take cover." Simon belted the famous Men at Work song and tore back the curtains, letting in the hazy sunlight.

Nikki buried her head under her pillow and muttered, "What time is it?"

"Ten thirty, darling girl."

"What?" She lifted her head and peeled back the covers. "As in ten thirty in the morning?"

"Yup. God, wipe that look of horror off your sweet face, it doesn't suit you. I know I'm not exactly a rock star, well . . . but anyhow, I mean, what better place in the world to wake up than in a land where women glow and men plunder? Ah, plundering men . . ."

"Oh my God, and I'm still sleeping. Where's Derek?"

"At the Hahndorfs'. We both got up a few hours ago, cleaned up, had coffee, and you, my love, were still snoring."

Her jaw dropped and she shook her head. "I don't snore."

He smiled. "Yes, you do."

"No, I do not."

"Oh, but you were adorable and neither Derek

nor I had the heart to wake you. You must've been tired."

She got out of bed. "I guess I was."

"Now it's time to de-tousle that mop of yours and get all gussied up, gal."

She touched the top of her head. Her hair did seem to be traveling in many directions. "Gussied up? What are you today? A bad Western? No wait, a bad Australian Western."

He laughed. "Uh-huh, you already got up your get up and go on. Speaking of movies, we are headed back out to the Hahndorfs. That nice Liam and his wife have invited us for lunch. Derek just called and said to get a move on. He sounded tense."

"Tense?"

"Yes, something about shenanigans from Lucy Swanson again and how even though he wanted to negate the offer for lunch, he was feeling sorry for Liam and brood, so off we go. I for one am hardly upset. I can't wait to get another eyeful of the luscious Shawn Keefer."

Nikki slammed the door shut on the bathroom, turning on the shower.

"My, aren't we a tad grumpy in the a.m.," Simon shouted from the other side. Nikki continued to ignore him. "Alrighty then, I'll take that as a sign that Snow White needs herself a little espresso. Be back in a jiff."

She heard the hotel door close. Thank God. Now

she could shower in peace. She had to get ahold of Marco and play cupid.

She had enough time to shower and get dressed before Simon returned, balancing a tray of coffee and a bag of what Nikki figured must be pastries. "My, my, aren't we rather outback motifish today. Here's your coffee and a bite to eat. We better get rolling."

She grabbed the bag and coffee and they headed out, pulling up a while later in front of the Hahndorfs' gate, where they were checked in by security. As they drove inside, they noticed the film crew and their vehicles still out on the back forty. "Why don't we take a little detour?" Simon asked. "Check out the set."

"That's probably not a good idea. Movie sets are busy and we would be an annoyance."

Simon didn't listen as he turned off the main drive and down a side road.

"Simon! Your brother and the Hahndorfs are waiting."

He gave her a wave of the hand. "We're ten minutes early. I just want to see if I can get a peek. Come on, don't crash on my party."

Marco was right: maybe Simon did need a little bit of introspection. He was far too celebrity obsessed. So much for all the money spent on Guru Whatchamacallit. At least Marco had floated back down to earth, but could the relationship between them be repaired if they'd grown so far apart? And, what had happened to make Simon fall off the New Age bandwagon? She sighed. "Fine, but only a few minutes." She glanced at her watch. "I'm timing you."

"Party pooper."

"Can I ask you something?"

He groaned and turned onto another side road. "I'm not sure I like the sound of that."

"You were so into following your guru. I mean, not that I'm big on some of that new-agey stuff, but you know I couldn't stand you when I first came to Malveaux. Both you and Marco were, um, well, there's no other way to say it: basically a couple of assholes."

His jaw dropped. "Tsk-tsk. So not nice." He smiled. "You are right, though. We were a little irritating, I suppose. Here's the dealio. I think the guru thing is cool, and I'm all about improving myself and my relationships. But you know, I'm kind of over being told that I have no depth if I want nice things or designer labels or to spend my money on good champagne. I honestly don't see the big deal in all of it, and Marco, well, he's really getting into the Buddha kind of thing. You know, where you give up all your stuff, and you get your pleasure from within. Pleasure from within? Ooh." He shivered. "How does that even work?"

"There has to be a middle ground somewhere in there for the two of you."

Simon shrugged and pulled up next to a cream-colored Rolls-Royce. "Nice car. See, that's what I'm talking about. I want one of those."

"I guess that's fine. Sure they're nice cars, but when I say middle ground, why not have a car for the purpose of driving? Why do you need a status symbol?"

"Why not? Ooh, this conversation is over, Snow White. There goes Shawn Keefer." Simon got out of the car and started toward the movie star.

Nikki shook her head. How to get him to see the light? She jogged up next to him just as he reached Shawn. What a pain in the butt.

Shawn scowled as he saw them. "Morning," he muttered.

"A good one, too," Simon said.

Shawn shoved his hands inside his jeans pockets and glared at him. "It is, huh? I beg to differ." Simon looked completely wounded, his eyes growing saucerlike. "I've got a movie to shoot, and all I want to do is get it done and in the can." He looked at his watch. "All morning we've been waiting around for Little Miss Lucy to appear. But the diva obviously thinks this movie—and the world—revolves around her, and frankly I don't want to work with her any longer. I've had it."

"That bitch," Simon said. "What hotel is she at? I'll go rouse her for you."

"Oh no. See all these motor homes? We each have one. Well, I do and she does. Nathan and Kane as well. The rest of the crew have to buddy up."

"Sweet," Simon said.

"Isn't she in her motor home then?" Nikki asked.

"Good question. Kane has been banging on her door forever. We shot a few scenes that don't include her this morning because we all figured she needed to sleep off the booze from last night. Rumor is she and Hannah had quite a party out with Johnny, the makeup artist. Kid likes to party with the women and as you can guess, Lucy was along for that ride. I even heard that they crashed Grace Hahndorf's car."

"Seriously?" Nikki said.

"That's what I hear, anyway. Dunno. But this is getting lame. When the wardrobe people tried to get in there, she didn't answer. Kane is trying to locate an extra key right now. The thing is probably trashed. I've got to get some coffee. See ya."

"Poor guy," Simon said.

Nikki rolled her eyes. "Come on, let's go up to the house. You've had your few minutes with Keefer, and I'm sure Derek is waiting."

Simon started to protest when they spotted Derek and Liam coming down the road in the golf cart. "Hmm, looks like they just came to us."

They parked the cart near Lucy's motor home and Simon and Nikki took off that way. When they arrived, Liam was pounding on the door. Derek saw Nikki and gave her a kiss on the cheek. "Drama this morning."

"So I hear."

Kane Ferriss returned, yelling out Lucy's name. No answer. "Here, mate, a man from the RV place brought over an extra key to the house," Liam said, handing it to Kane.

"Thank you. If I can get her up and going, maybe this entire day won't be shot to hell." He unlocked the door and it swung open wide. Something slithered down the stairs. Nikki jumped back along with everyone else as they realized what it was.

"Oh my God!" Kane yelled. "Where's Andy? Andy! Someone get Andy the fuck over here! That's his fucking snake! It's a brown snake!" As the reptile rapidly slithered along the dirt, Kane charged into the trailer.

Andy came running up. "What's wrong?" he asked.

Kane reappeared, his eyes darkening. He brought his hands up to his face. "What's wrong?" he cried, removing his hands and glaring at Andy. "What's wrong? Your fucking snake just killed my actress. That's what's wrong. Lucy is dead."

Chapter 6

Everyone remained caught up in the horror of what had happened to Lucy Swanson as a police car pulled onto the property. Derek placed a protective arm around Nikki, and Simon hung closely beside Shawn Keefer, who appeared to be as freaked out as everyone else. A strange thought occurred to Nikki, who couldn't help wondering if the award-winning actor wasn't acting in the moment. He'd basically claimed he hated Lucy. Was he as upset as he looked over her sudden death?

The one most upset by the tragic events appeared to be Andy Burrow, who kept repeating there was no way the snake had been his. "All of my creatures are locked up securely. I don't take risks like that. There is no way. It had to be a snake from the bush."

Nikki told Derek, "What I want to know is how a snake got inside the trailer in the first place."

He gave her a look she recognized—the one that said for her not to get involved in this. It was true she'd been known to snoop around in the past when she'd had no business doing so. She'd already been responsible for solving a few mysteries back in the Northern California wine country. It was a knack she had, something she figured she'd gotten from her aunt Cara, who'd been a homicide detective for the L.A. Police Department for years, and who'd discussed many cases with her when she was growing up.

"I'm sure that the snake somehow got inside the RV when a door was left open. It's obvious, Nikki, that this has to be an accident."

A uniformed policeman got out of his car and

spoke first with Liam. Simon sidled up next to them. "Oh my God, can you believe this craziness? Poor Shawn. Poor everyone. How will they finish their movie? Shawn is super broken up about it."

Nikki glanced over at the star, now busy pacing in front of his own RV, talking rapidly into his cell phone. Broken up, huh? A minute ago he'd seemed upset by what had happened, but now he was on the phone. What was that all about?

"What do they do in a situation like this, Snow White?"

"I don't know; why would I know?"

"Duh, you used to be in showbiz. They won't cancel the movie, will they?"

"I honestly don't know what they'll do, but I also don't think that's the main concern right now. A woman just died. And, I imagine it wasn't pleasant. My God, sure she was a little obnoxious, but she was a young woman, and talented. It won't be long before the paparazzi gets wind of it and this place will be swarmed. I'm sure Billy Bush has already been put on a plane," she said, referring to the host of *Access Hollywood.*

"Paparazzi are probably already lurking, don't you think?" Simon said. "Like, Shawn Keefer is here. That's probably why I can't get a hotel room and why they have the security guy up front."

"Come on, let's see if there's anything we can do for Liam and Grace," Derek said. "I'll let him know that if this isn't a good time, we can fly back next month when things die down. I'm about ready to get out of here."

Liam was now speaking with Kane as the police officer entered the RV. This was not a good situation at all. Both men looked pale. Derek and Nikki approached them. Simon wisely chose to hang back.

The group turned as they heard a clearly upset Shawn Keefer screaming obscenities into the phone. Kane excused himself and went over to the actor.

The police officer emerged from the trailer. "Yes, looks to be a snakebite that did her in. Those brown snakes are awfully deadly. Bit her right on the leg. Sucker must've gotten down under the covers. Kind of surprising to me, though."

"Why?" Nikki asked. Derek eyed her.

The officer wasn't fazed by her question. "Not from around here, huh?"

"California."

"Oh, California. Well, g'day. Always wanted to visit there myself. Hear it's beautiful."

Liam cleared his throat. "I think the reason Officer Warre thinks it odd that the snake would get under the covers is that they usually like cool places."

"True," Warre replied. "But dark places are good, too. The woman probably shifted, woke him from his slumber and there you have it." His fingers clamped down on one another. Nikki winced. "You say she's an actress?" He turned to Liam.

"Yes."

"Don't watch much TV and never get to the movies. I like to read."

"She was quite a star," Liam said.

"Yep, bad deal. I think it might be best for me to call in a detective. Be right back."

Officer Warre went over to his car and placed the call. Liam turned to Nikki and Derek. "Typical."

"What do you mean?" Nikki asked.

"The police. As soon as Warre found out that Lucy Swanson was a big star he goes and calls in a detective—his superior."

"Why does that bother you?"

"See, the thing is that the police in these parts don't want to be responsible for missing something. He's going to call in someone else to take the heat if this snakebite is more than that . . . which it isn't."

"That's right," Derek said. He looked at Nikki. "Just a snakebite."

"Right, but because Lucy was this American actress and the cop knows there will be media involved, he has to make sure his arse is covered. It's politics here in the Barossa."

Nikki found it interesting that if the cop was calling in a detective, did he actually think there could be something more to Lucy's death?

It didn't take long before another car rolled onto the property. Out stepped a tall, tan, blond, roguish-looking kind of guy. He had the khaki thing going for him with pants and a hat. His long hair dangled past his ears. Many years spent in the sun had weathered his face enough where he could have been in his midforties but looked more like sixty.

Liam waved to him. "Jack."

The man joined them. "G'day, mate, some trouble here in the vineyard, hey?"

"A bit. It's not good. Jack, this is my friend and business associate Derek Malveaux from the States and his lovely assistant Nikki Sands," Liam said. "Nikki, Derek, this is Detective Jack Von Doussa. He is also a good friend."

The detective nodded at them. "Not so good a time to be here, eh, mates? I s'pose I better take a look. Got the call from Warre and of course, he doesn't want to be boss on this deal, not with a big star like this. So, who is she?"

"Lucy Swanson," Liam replied.

He nodded. "Ah yes, this could be a problem if not handled carefully. I'm going to call in a CSE. Warre," he yelled at the officer, who was leaning against his car.

"Yes, sir?"

"Do you have a video camera in your car?"

"Yes, sir."

"Good. Grab it and follow me."

"Video camera?" Nikki asked. "What for, and what is a CSE?"

Von Doussa smiled, his eyes lined with heavy wrinkles. "You're rather inquisitive." He didn't say it in a mean or condescending way.

"Yes, she is," Derek said.

"I'm only curious because my aunt was a detective in Los Angeles for years and she talked about procedures a lot."

"Yes, well, the CSE is like your CSI people in the U.S."

"So you're treating this as a crime?"

"No. I have to cover my arse. See here, this is one of those situations where I need to make sure we go by the book. I don't need my boss giving me a hard time because I didn't follow protocol. I'm going to do it so that there will be no problems down the road." He turned to Warre, who'd just arrived with camera in hand. "Call me in a crime scene examiner."

"It's a crime? I thought it was a snakebite," Warre said, eyebrows raised.

"No, no. I don't think we have a crime here. I need a CSE because this is a well-known person and also a woman." He lowered his voice. "I want you to videotape my examination and I want a CSE here to take stills, because I don't want any allegations that I had a prurient interest when I disrobe a famous actress. Now do it."

"Oh." Warre nodded and hurried off.

"Not the brightest guy around. He got his position through MERIT."

"MERIT?" Nikki asked.

"Yes. Kind of a joke around the department—mates elevated regardless of intelligence or talent. We have quite a bit of cronyism, nepotism, that type of thing. Warre's father is a retired superior who got him the job through a buddy who is now in Adelaide working as an investigator. It's somewhat corrupt. The reason I'm having the video camera go in with me is to prove I've done everything I need to do. I'll swab for DNA at the snakebite, see if we can't locate how the beastie got in there. Oh damn, why didn't I ask? Do we know if the snake is still in there?"

"No," Liam said. "Sucker slithered away and no one around here was going after him, except for Andy Burrow. The producer is saying that it's his snake."

Detective Von Doussa brought his hands to his jaw. "Andy Burrow is here?"

"Yes. He's handling the animals on the set. One happens to be a brown snake, and the producer, Kane Ferriss, insists that it was Andy's snake. Andy says there's no way, and he's gone to make sure that the snake is still secure."

Von Doussa took out a small notepad and scribbled something. He looked up to see another car pulling in. "There's my CSE guy. Must've been nearby. Let's get this done. Can't leave the body for long. I need to get ahold of the pathologist at the state coroner's office, but I'll have to investigate first."

The third man joined them—redheaded with a redhead's complexion of freckles and pale skin. He nodded a curt hello to everyone and a moment later followed Von Doussa and Warre into the RV. Nikki still had no idea what to make of all this.

Liam sighed. "My friends, I have to apologize. Nothing ever happens here. Really. It doesn't. Jack is one of two detectives here in the Barossa and we simply don't get much crime."

"But everyone is saying it's not a crime. That it was a snakebite. You do get those, don't you?" Nikki asked.

"Yes, of course. Brown snakes are common here. Enough so that a short jaunt down the road you'll find the antivenom store. I only said 'crime' because, well . . ." He paused. "You know, I'm not sure why I said that. I suppose it's because Jack called in all of his people to make sure he handles it appropriately. You know he's right, it is all about covering your arse these days. The thing is, he doesn't want anyone around town calling him an oaf or anything. For instance, say the pathologist were to call him next week and tell him she actually died from a drug overdose. He'd be the fool then."

"Is that possible?" Nikki asked. "Everyone insists it was the snakebite."

91

"Anything is possible. It could be she died from something else, I suppose, although doubtful. But say the snake bit her only an hour ago. Then she could feasibly still be alive and therefore he has to be sure that the bite is indeed the cause of death."

"What would it be like, dying from a snakebite?"

"Not like what you think, unless she realized she'd been bitten, and if that was the case, we would've all known about it. I'm sure she would've come unglued and screamed like a banshee. But if you're not aware, a brown snake can bite you and it may only feel as if you brushed up against something. What happens is that a person looks down to see what they've brushed against and, lo and behold, it's a snake. They panic, the poison courses through them and if they don't get the antivenom, they get very sick over the course of a few hours and die. The victim will ache, go into shock, become dizzy and confused, and nauseous. However, what likely happened here is she slept through it. We had a bit of a rough night after the party. Hannah, Lucy, and one of the crew crashed Grace's car. They'd all been drinking. Everyone was okay, but we had a time of it. Grace hashed it out with the three of them. I had to calm her down. And now this. With . . . everything else that's going on." He looked at Derek, and something in his eyes made Nikki think that he'd said something he hadn't meant to. Derek appeared to understand what he was talking about.

Derek patted his shoulder. "If you need anything at all from us, please let me know."

Derek took Nikki's hand. She stood there surveying the scene, with a nagging feeling that, although everyone kept insisting this was an accident, it was anything but. It may be true that the Barossa rarely had murders occur in its quaint valley, but Hollywood definitely had its share, and she had a feeling that Hollywood had come to the Barossa in more ways than one.

Chapter 7

Detective Von Doussa and his crew had exited the RV. Nikki now saw him nodding and talking into a cell phone. He flipped it shut and approached them. "My job is finished here for now. I called the pathologist, who said he's fine with my findings. Warre is calling the funeral director. We've bagged her, so once they show up she can be moved."

"You say that you're okay with your findings. What are they?" Nikki asked.

"She died from the bite of a brown snake. Of course, we took DNA swabs. I mean, DNA is so useful these days, we might as well use the technology. I would like to take DNA from Andy Burrow's snake just to rule out that it was not his snake."

Nikki didn't say her next thought out loud, but if

he planned to talk with Andy to be certain that it wasn't his snake, then he was not ruling out the possibility that Andy or someone could have planted it there. This was going to be interesting. And where was Andy anyway? He'd sure been gone a long time.

"What if his snake isn't in the terrarium, as he insists?" Nikki asked.

"Yes, well, I suppose I'll attend to that if that's the case. I will have to ask how the snake did get out." He nodded.

Nikki faced Von Doussa. "Can I ask you something?"

"Surely."

"Even if death by a snakebite isn't super uncommon, how would the snake get into the RV?"

"Oh, they are wily creatures. And we will be looking into that further."

Derek shot Nikki another one of his looks. "I told you. There's a reasonable explanation."

"But was Lucy in bed? I mean, do you think the snake bit her while she was asleep?"

The detective pondered her question. "Well, I would say that would be likely, as her head was resting on the pillow and the covers were pulled up. Yes, she was in bed."

Nikki nodded. "Isn't it peculiar? I mean, Lucy was asleep in her bed, the snake somehow got into a locked RV, made its way into her bed, bit her, and there you have it."

No one said anything for a moment. The detective finally chuckled. "Yes, that is what I would say. If I had to guess, I think the snake somehow got inside the RV when the door was open. Once inside, he probably fell asleep. The girl came in, went to bed. Maybe he'd gone to sleep in her bed. He sensed some warm blood and took a bite out of her and . . . there *you* have it. I understand your aunt being a detective might make the way we conduct our investigations of interest to you, but are you sure there's nothing more to it, Miss Sands?"

Derek started to say something, but she cut him off. "I think it's kind of strange is all. I have to wonder if someone didn't plant that snake in Lucy's bed with the intent of the snake biting her, killing her, and having it look the way you theorized, that it was all an accident."

Von Doussa appeared to be amused. He then clapped his hand on Derek's shoulder and pointed at her. "You've got yourself a sheila with some spunk now, don't you?" He laughed and shook his head. "Miss, do you know something that I don't? Because this is good stuff."

"She's a regular sleuth," Derek grumbled, squeezing her hand with the obvious intention to get her to shut up.

Fat chance. Nikki had gut instincts and no matter what the detective thought, this whole thing stank big-time.

Before she had a chance to continue her inquisition, Andy Burrow finally appeared. He looked distraught, his eyes bulging, his face ashen. "It was my snake. He's gone. I've been searching the property, looking all over for him and he's gone. And, I tell you, I would bet my life and soul on it that I locked all the terrariums and cages last night. I'm conscientious about that. In fact, you can ask Hannah."

Liam looked at Andy. "My daughter?"

Andy nodded. "Yes, your daughter. It's nothing sinister. She was upset after last night and she'd mentioned to me that she wanted to study zoology at the university. I asked if she'd like to come down and help me make sure the animals were safe for the night. She'll tell you that they were all there, locked up."

Detective Von Doussa eyed Andy. A wave of discomfort overtook the group. It did seem kind of strange that Hannah would go out to check on Andy's creatures before going to bed, especially considering the circumstances of the evening, but Andy came across as a decent guy. He was well known and respected in his field. Derek idolized him.

"What time was that?" Von Doussa asked.

"Late, about midnight. I always make a late-night check and ran into Hannah out on a walk."

Von Doussa jotted all of this information down on a notepad.

"Not only that," Andy continued, "but there's a problem with my suit. The one I wear when I handle the snakes and crocs is on a different peg than usual. You know the suits I'm talking about." He nodded his head at Derek. "They were switched. I'm very specific on where things go, and that suit I let you wear yesterday is the one I let others wear. They were switched. I know it."

"Did you have anything to drink last night?" Von Doussa asked.

"Sure. I had some wine."

"Maybe after a glass of wine or two you thought you put the suit in one place and then set it somewhere else," Liam said.

"No. I have routines that I follow. And I am sure it was moved."

The detective raised his eyebrows and glanced at Nikki, then back at Andy. "If this is true, we need to bag that suit," he said to the cop standing near Andy.

"Yes, sir."

"Well, I'd say that it is possible your spunky little lady here just might not be so crazy after all." He winked at Derek. "Come on, let's have a look at where this snake is supposed to be. The rest of you need to wait around here, in case we need to ask any more questions." He tromped off with the other policeman.

Derek looked at Nikki and shook his head. She

smiled back at him and gave him a shrug of the shoulders. "Sorry."

"Not this time. You will not get involved this time. Right?"

"Right," she agreed, but she also had her fingers crossed behind her back. Come on, she was Nikki Sands, and she wasn't about to pass up the opportunity to get involved in what looked to be one helluva mystery.

Chapter 8

There was nothing left for them to do after the police went to work trying to figure out if what had happened to Lucy Swanson was a crime or not. Nikki felt in her gut that it was, and as much as she wanted answers to quench her own curiosity, she knew that Derek was right. This time, *if* it was murder, she really should mind her own business. Keep practicing that new mantra— *It's none of my business.* Sure. Everyone who knew her had to know that Nikki would never simply mind her own business, no matter how many times she tried to affirm this.

Liam suggested that they all go up to the house, where Grace was preparing lunch. In the golf cart, Liam chattered on about what had happened. "This won't be good for Grace. She's still so upset about last night with Hannah and all."

"Are you sure she wants us for lunch? We can

always go into town and then come back if the police need us," Derek said. "I can't imagine that they would. None of us were even here when Lucy died. In fact, I've been thinking that maybe we should postpone some of our business for a while until things settle down, like I said before. Until *everything* settles down."

Liam frowned. "No. The timing works now. You understand. I know you do. I can't hold off."

There it was again—Liam and Derek speaking in code. Nikki was going to get to the bottom of their secret.

"As far as my Grace, lunch was her idea. She's been making Hannah help her all morning. She wanted to keep her away from Lucy because she feels that Lucy has been a bad influence on our daughter. All three of them—Hannah, Lucy, and the makeup kid—keep insisting they were run off the road last night, but I don't believe it and neither does Grace. They were liquored up and that's what it was. I keep trying to get Hannah to take responsibility for her actions. Oh goodness, listen to me, I sound insensitive." He sighed and shook his head. "Neither of them are aware of what's happened to Lucy. Her death makes me think I shouldn't be concerned about the kids having a good time last night or the car. Of course, I don't want anything to ever happen to Hannah, but all the same, I did some dumb things in my youth."

"We all did," Derek said.

"As far as our business is concerned, what has happened is terrible. I'm sure there'll be some kind of fallout because it occurred on my property. If you want to pull back on negotiations because you're afraid of some kind of negative publicity, Derek, I understand. But really, I don't think this tragedy should affect our business dealings, which are completely separate from the movie, and now Lucy's death," Liam said.

"I'm not concerned over possible fallout. I'm only concerned for you and your family and the timing of it all. I don't want to add any further stress."

"I appreciate your concern," Liam replied. "But it would be best if we try to run life as close to normal as possible. You can put this bad business behind you and go and see some sites later today. I think we should be able to come up with a licensing and distribution deal that satisfies the two of us today and then I'll have the papers drawn up. And, by tomorrow if you want to head back to the States or travel the country here, you'll be free to do so."

Derek nodded. "Sounds good then."

Nikki shrugged. Well, one thing was for sure: even though that itch in her brain was nagging at her to see what answers she could discover about Lucy's death, she wouldn't get the chance. It sounded as if the business between Liam and Derek would be dealt with by the end of the day and they would likely be back on the jet tomorrow. But she did wonder if they would be heading home, or if Derek had any other plans. He had mentioned during their flight over that the trip would be part vacation, and they'd be gone for about a week. It had only been a few days. In light of things though, would he rush them home?

They pulled up in front of the house. "I know this probably goes without saying," Liam said and looked at his three guests, "but I would be grateful if no one mentioned what happened to Lucy. I'd like to tell Hannah and Grace myself."

They all agreed and piled out of the cart.

As they entered the foyer, Hannah hurried toward them. "Daddy?" Her face was tearstained, mascara smeared across her face.

"What is it, love? What's the matter?"

She started crying. "I'm sorry. I'm so sorry. I've done something horrible. Please forgive me!"

Liam pulled her into him and stroked the top of her fair head. He glanced at his guests, all of whom had the sense to retreat toward the front door. "What is it? What did you do, Hannah?"

Grace appeared, a grave look on her face. "Oh yes, she's done something terrible and we are going to have to do something about it. She lied about the car accident last night." Then she spotted Derek, Nikki, and Simon, and she stopped. "But it's nothing we can't take care of as a family later."

"But, Mum—"

"Go wash up, Hannah. Lunch is ready. We will deal with this later. Now, come in. Nice to see you all again. Lovely day, isn't it?"

"What is going on, Grace?" Liam asked.

"Later, dear. We have guests."

"Yes, well, the day is not so lovely. I was going to hold off a bit before I said anything, but Lucy Swanson has died from a snakebite."

Grace's face lost all color. "Oh my God."

Nikki heard a gasp from the stairs and looked up. She saw Hannah turn and continue down the hall, but not before Nikki *thought* she saw a smile on the girl's face.

Chapter 9

Nikki was having a hard time not thinking about the scene that had taken place at the Hahndorfs'. It had been uncomfortable there, and as soon as Liam broke the news to Grace, they decided it would be a good time to leave. Nikki could not get the picture out of her mind of seeing Hannah smile when she heard about Lucy. But *had* she really seen that? Was her mind playing tricks on her? And, what was the deal with Hannah supposedly lying about the car accident she'd been in with Lucy and Johnny?

Nikki kind of agreed with Simon, who'd blathered on in the backseat of the car while driving back to town. He had been saying that the whole lot of them seemed totally dysfunctional, and that Derek should just cancel any business dealings he'd already begun with Liam. He finally shut up when Derek reminded him of their own family's dysfunctional propensities, which included Simon's mother and Derek's stepmom, Patrice, who'd taken the title of stepmonster to the nth degree. Once Derek started in on their family history, Simon didn't say another word, and when they got back to the hotel he said that he was determined to find another room so that they could have their privacy. Nikki felt bad for Simon and she started after him, but Derek caught her by the hand and insisted she allow his brother to sulk.

"We—*you*—can't keep rescuing him. Marco is right. It's time Simon does some growing up, and he needs to go through his own growing pains to do so. We'll invite him for dinner with us tonight, but for now, let him be. Maybe he can work some things out in his head, and who knows, he might actually pull himself out of it for once. But you can't do it for him. Besides, I want to spend some time alone with you. Let's do some window-shopping. Maybe take a drive out to Eden Valley. I've heard it's beautiful, and after what we've been through the last couple of days, I'd like to see some sights and just be with you."

Okay, how could anyone walk away from that? Simon would have to sulk, and even though it left a hole in her stomach to know he was feeling isolated and lonely, she also knew that Derek was right. Simon had to figure some of this out on his own.

They took a driving tour of the three towns that made up the Barossa Valley: Angaston, Tanunda, and Nuriootpa. The towns were only about five miles apart from one another and were serviced by bitumen roads. The scenery was beautiful in between each town with vineyards, wineries, and Australian native trees. They spotted plenty of active wildlife along the way.

They decided to stop at one of the more interesting-looking wineries and see what they had to offer. "I've heard of this place," Derek said. "They do small, boutique wines. Limited editions."

The sign on the front read "Fritz Winery." "What is it with all the German names?" Nikki asked.

"From what history I know, the inhabitants of the Barossa descended from free migrant German and Austrian stock. Supposedly, the Eastern States of Australia like Victoria and New South Wales were colonized by convicts from Scotland, Ireland, and England."

"Interesting. Should we go in? I love these boutique wineries." In Napa and Sonoma there were hundreds of boutique wineries. They couldn't compete with Malveaux as far as sales went, because Malveaux had wide distribution and funds to advertise. However, the smaller wineries seemed to maintain an artisan's viewpoint on the effort that went into making wine. Nikki felt many of them produced better-tasting wines than some of the more commercialized wineries. But she wouldn't tell Derek that.

Walking into the small winery gave Nikki a feeling of going back in time. Maybe it was because they were in a different country, or because the winery itself was an actual barn.

There were a couple of tables. A group of five people sat around one and appeared as if they'd been enjoying a tasting all afternoon. They chatted, laughed, and continued to pour the wine. A woman with long bright, almost orange hair who looked to be in her fifties walked around a long wooden bar, where she took out three bottles of wine and placed them on top. "G'day," she said. "I'm Sarah Fritz. I own the place. I expect you're here for a tasting."

Nikki noticed the woman had a long scar across her right cheek. Whatever had happened to her looked like it had been painful.

"Yes, ma'am," Derek said, pulling out his wallet.

She waved a hand at him. "No charge for the tasting. But you have to buy a bottle of wine." She winked at Nikki. "For your girl." Derek agreed to her terms and she started pouring.

"This is my Sauvignon Blanc. Good stuff. Not

too much grapefruit flavor like so many of them. I think it has a crisp pear flavor myself."

Nikki swirled, sniffed, and did the whole wine-expert thing, which was funny, because although she sold it for Derek and helped manage his winery, she never really considered herself an expert. There was always more to learn and discover about growing grapes and making wine, and about what people enjoyed about wine. "It is good. I can taste the pear."

"You're from the States," Sarah said.

They nodded. "Napa."

"Ah. So are you here for pleasure, or is this a business trip?"

"Both," Derek said and left it at that.

"We've had some meetings with the Hahndorfs," Nikki added. Derek nudged her. Oops, she hadn't realized she wasn't supposed to say anything.

Sarah didn't respond for a second, her face shadowed by what looked to be anger. "I see. Yes, well, I can warn you that you don't want to be involved with that family."

Nikki glanced at Derek, who looked down. He sighed, knowing she would take Sarah's bait. And she did. "Why do you say that?"

Sarah poured herself a full glass of the Sauvignon Blanc and then poured them each a taste of a Viognier. Before expanding on her opinion of the Hahndorfs she gave a brief description of the wine. Nikki sipped it and thought it okay, but wanted this Sarah lady to continue her story.

After another sip of wine, Sarah said, "Liam is a decent man. Quite the entrepreneur in these parts. Rumor has it that he's planning to make a deal with Derek Malveaux. I'm guessing that's you." She raised an eyebrow and Derek nodded, not looking exactly pleased.

Maybe Nikki should've kept her mouth shut. She knew he didn't care to gossip, and she was probably going to catch an earful.

"But I'm telling you the one behind that empire is Grace. She is a control freak and neurotic as hell. Liam doesn't jump unless she tells him to."

"I didn't get that feeling. We've been at their place. Grace Hahndorf seems like a nice woman, and I got the impression that she was hands-off with the business," Nikki said. True, but she did think Grace had some oddities about her.

"Oh no. She puts on a good show. Liam goes right along with it. She's quite the scam artist, I tell you. For Grace it's all about appearances." She leaned in. "Don't you think for a minute that this idea of you labeling his Australian wine in California was his idea. Not at all. Liam is simple folk, like most of us. Grace is a snob. She runs the show. Watch out for her. Such a shame things didn't work out the way Liam wanted twenty years ago."

"What do you mean?" Nikki asked.

"Liam should have wound up with Elizabeth Wells. She was his first and only true love, but she died." Sarah shook her head.

Derek was frowning.

"How did she die?" Nikki asked.

"Fluke. Elizabeth was a zoologist and conservationist. She was trying to save a sick baby koala out in the bush. Guess the mother had died. Anyway, nasty story, but a crocodile got her."

"Oh my God!"

"Yep. Here the poor girl was trying to save one animal only to slip and fall near the river, where the croc got her."

"That's awful."

"Yeah, I know, and then poor Liam winds up with Grace, which is even worse."

"I don't know what you mean about Grace. She really does seem lovely."

"Looks are deceiving."

Derek cleared his throat and set his glass down. He took out a twenty-dollar bill and handed it to Sarah. "That should cover our bottle. Nikki. We gotta go."

Uh-oh. He was not happy.

Sarah called out to them as they left. Derek didn't look back. Nikki turned and shrugged, giving her a smile. She was pretty sure that Sarah Fritz would have some opinions about the two of them to share with the locals.

Nikki followed him back to the car. He didn't say anything for a few minutes as they pulled out of the winery. Finally he spoke: "Why do you always do that?"

"Do what?"

"Ask questions. Buy into what people are saying."

"I didn't necessarily buy into what she was saying."

He laughed. "Sure. What you do is open yourself up to all sorts of B.S. That woman makes shit wine. You tasted it. And she's jealous of Liam and Grace and their winery. That would be my guess. If that story she told were remotely true—and I doubt it—well, it's nobody's business but the Hahndorfs. And you just kept egging her on."

"I didn't do that." Nikki shrank back in her seat. Okay, so maybe she had. But it wasn't like she went looking for gossip.

"Yes, you did, and you do it all the time. It's why you always wind up in trouble, looking and asking where it isn't your business."

She started to say something. He held up a finger. "No. Listen this time. I can see the wheels churning in that brain of yours." She frowned. "Which means you're already willing to listen to the town gossip, see what you can find out about the Hahndorfs. And, whether or not you have consciously realized it or not, I think—no, I know—you're doing it because you want to learn as much as you can, because you have this horrible habit of playing Nancy Drew. And sure as shit, you've already convinced yourself that Lucy Swanson was murdered and you want to get to the bottom of it, which honestly, I don't know why. Even if she *was* murdered, why do you want to go looking for the answers?"

She sat back, trying to be pissed off at him. She didn't like his tone or his accusations, but dammit, her mind was racing with the knowledge that Derek spoke the truth. She had no real answer to his question. The only thing she could say was the first thing that came to her mind, and she knew it was *her* truth.

"Because I care. It might sound stupid and, I don't know, maybe crazy, but you know what, we live in this insane world. People typically only think about themselves. I think that TV and pop culture has caused an entire generation to become numb to the violence and chaos of the world, and I'm sorry, but I refuse to become a zombie, to not feel when a woman dies, and especially when she's murdered. And yes, I do believe Lucy was murdered. And so what if she was obnoxious and had her issues, she was also a human being, and the thing is, Derek, we all have our bullshit. We all act like morons sometimes, but on the flip side I think most people are decent at their core."

She sighed and looked out the window, tears stinging her eyes. She hadn't realized that these feelings were who made her who she was until that very moment. For some strange reason she'd gone through life trying to convince herself, and even others, that she didn't really care that much—caring meant you usually wound up hurt—but the truth was, she *did* care.

Derek pulled the car off the road. Was he going to kick her out? Maybe her impassioned plea had convinced him that she was certifiably insane. Instead he grabbed her left shoulder with one hand and touched her cheek with his other, leaned in, and kissed her hard. It took her breath away. They kissed for several minutes and her world went from sitting in the little coupe on the side of a country road in the Barossa Valley to one of a warm, floating cloud in the middle of what had to be heaven. When Derek pulled away from her, it took her a few seconds to open her eyes. When she did, he was staring at her. "What?" she said, nearly breathless.

"And that is why I love you. But what I don't love is your poking around in this type of thing, because what I don't want is for you to get hurt. Promise me that you will drop this Lucy Swanson thing and let the gossip you heard back at Sarah Fritz's place stay there."

Hell, after a kiss like that, she was willing to concede anything. She nodded and whispered, "I promise." She said a silent prayer that she'd be able to keep that promise.

Chapter 10

Nikki and Derek completed the afternoon window-shopping in Tanunda, the town where they were staying. They'd changed their minds about going to Eden Valley. Derek wound up buying her a pair of Australian sapphire earrings, which she immediately put on. They made it back to the hotel right before sunset. Derek led her to the hotel bar. "What do you say we have a glass of champagne?"

"Sure. Are we celebrating?"

"Yes."

"Really? What?"

"That Simon has not been around all afternoon to bother us, and if we're lucky, he's found another room."

She laughed. They sat down at a window table. The room was quaint, with everything in white and wrought iron—again that old-world feel. Nikki finally started feeling like they were actually on a vacation, despite the nagging fact that Lucy Swanson had died so recently. Since making her promise in the car, neither one of them had mentioned it again. But it still bothered Nikki, who really wanted to know what in the world was going on back at the Hahndorfs' place.

Derek ordered a bottle of champagne and a traditional Australian appetizer—Oysters Kilpatrick.

After ordering, he got up to wash his hands. Nikki intended to ask him again about what he and Liam had been keeping so private about their business dealings.

Derek reappeared just as the waiter did, the latter with a bottle of Dom Perignon. "The best for you," Derek said.

"Thank you. That's really sweet."

"*You're* really sweet."

Wait a minute. When a guy starts in with the "really sweet" thing, doesn't that usually preface a "but" . . . ? And a "but" usually means that something isn't kosher. She eyed him. "Thanks."

Before he could reply, Kane Ferriss and Nathan Cooley walked into the bar. They spotted Nikki and Derek and approached their table.

Derek stood. "Hello, gentlemen."

"Derek," Kane said. "Sorry, looks like you're celebrating and we don't want to intrude, but we need to talk to you." They both looked at Nikki.

A pit in her stomach tightened into a knot. She had a feeling she was not going to get it untied anytime soon. How often did two powerful Hollywood types storm in on your little evening nip with the one you love and want to talk with you? Not often.

"I apologize again," Kane continued. "Today has been awful. That's an understatement, actually."

Nathan nodded sadly. "Miserable, but Kane and

I have hashed it out, and we've put too much time and money into this thing to just let it go. Sure, we could take the insurance money and split, but this movie needs to be made. We thought about seeing if we could get another big-name actress in here. Lucy had been a compromise really, because the leading actress calls for someone who is a little bit . . . older. But we couldn't get it done, timing wise, so we kind of settled for Lucy."

Kane nodded. "We started brainstorming about who we could get and then we remembered that you . . ." He pointed at Nikki and the knot grew tighter. "You are an actress. I was able to find some clips of your old show on the Internet and let me tell you, honey, how you didn't get swooped up and put on the big screen is beyond me. You're fucking brilliant, baby." Nikki cringed at his choice of words. "And we need you. We need you to play Lucy's part in what could be a huge hit."

"So? You'll do it, right?"

Oysters Kilpatrick with Champagne

Oysters Kilpatrick is a traditional Australian dish, and as with all oyster dishes, they pair wonderfully with a bottle of champagne or sparkling wine. Obviously, Derek had romance up his sleeve when he ordered food and drink considered by many to be aphrodisiacs, but his plans don't seem to be working out. Nikki was also probably on the same wavelength and not expecting Kane and Nathan to show up with their proposition. Will Nikki take the bait or chow down on the oysters and hightail it back up to the room with her hot guy?

24 fresh oysters, in their shells
rock salt
1 tbsp Worcestershire sauce
⅛ cup butter
4 slices bacon, rind and all fat removed, finely diced
sea salt, to flatten leaf parsley taste
fresh ground black pepper, to taste
2 tbsp leaf parsley, chopped
lemon wedges, to serve

Preheat the grill to the highest temperature.
Arrange the oysters on a bed of rock salt in a large, shallow, ovenproof dish.

Combine the Worcestershire sauce and butter in a small saucepan and heat the butter until it melts and the mixture begins to bubble around the edges of the saucepan. Remove from the heat.

Spoon a little of the Worcestershire sauce and butter mixture over each oyster, and top evenly with the diced bacon and season with sea salt and freshly ground black pepper, to taste.

Cook under a preheated grill for 3–4 minutes, or until the bacon is crisp.

Sprinkle with parsley, and serve with lemon wedges.

Serves 4–6.

Chapter 11

The next hour was like TiVo. Nikki went from fast-forward to rewind, pause, and then play again. After Kane and Nathan begged her to star in their movie, Derek invited them to sit down and have a drink and share the oysters with them. She was unable to find her voice for several moments, or what felt like an eternity, but Derek jumped right in.

"That sounds wonderful." He patted her knee. "Doesn't it, Nik?"

"It's a once-in-a-lifetime chance," Nathan said. "You know, timing and luck have a lot to do with success and this may be your time, Nikki. I know it's come out of horrible circumstances, but the show must go on. And we're willing to pay you nicely."

"Wait a minute, what about Lucy? I mean, did the police leave yet? Have they determined what really happened to her?" Nikki asked.

Both men stared at her. Kane said, "What do you mean what *really* happened to her? That snake of Andy's bit her and she died. And did you not hear the part about getting paid to star in a major motion picture, and with Shawn Keefer no less?"

"I just think there is more to it than that. And yes, I heard your offer." But come on, where were the ethics here? An actress had died and these guys were insisting that the show go on.

"Nikki," Derek said. "You promised."

"I'm sorry. I have an active imagination." She tried to smile, but it came out more like a grimace.

They all continued staring at her. Men were so stupid sometimes.

"It was a fluke. An accident," Nathan said. "Look, I know the timing sucks, but, Nikki, we have to have an answer. Will you do this movie with us?"

Okay, she was either in someone else's dream or nightmare—which one she could not be sure—but all the same, this proposition simply did not seem real. And, how about Derek getting so excited? What was up with that?

"Nik, I think this is something you might really want to consider," Derek said. "This was a dream you once had."

She was pretty sure her jaw dropped. She could find no words. Her brain and vocabulary didn't connect. "Dumbfounded" was the only word that came to mind to describe the feeling. She turned and faced Derek, finally regaining some composure. She placed her hands on his knees and leaned in close to him. "You know, this is a bit overwhelming and, um, probably not something I want to commit to in a matter of minutes, or even in an hour. Maybe we could discuss this *alone*?"

Kane stood up, Nathan following. The producer

said, "Sure, yeah, no problem. I can see that. But look, we have to have an answer either by sometime tonight or, at the latest, early in the morning. I'd prefer you called me tonight." He handed her his card. "Call the cell number there. I'm up late, so let me know ASAP. It'll cost me way too much to keep everything up and running without us going forward. If we have to can this thing, then I have to know as soon as possible."

"Fine. I'll get you an answer *ASAP*."

"Amazing," Derek said after they left.

"Um, yeah, amazing. What the hell was that about?"

"What do you mean?" Derek asked, shifting in his chair.

"First of all that entire situation was completely bizarre. Two Hollywood bigwigs practically beg me to star in their epic in which the former leading lady has recently passed away. Then you invite them for drinks so I can hear them out, and you suggest that I take their offer. Why? What the hell is up with you?"

He sighed. "When we met, when you first took the job at Malveaux, you had been trying to make it as an actress. Like I said, this was a dream for you."

"No, Derek, I'd stalled out. I left the dream behind."

He shook his head. "I know you don't think you had what it takes to be a great actress. But I disagree. I always have. What you don't know is that not long after we met, I got ahold of all of the episodes you'd done as Sydney Martini, and I have to tell you that I thought you were real good."

"Oh my God! You watched those? Why didn't you tell me? I am so embarrassed."

"That's why I didn't tell you. I knew you'd react like this, but you're wrong. You have no need to be embarrassed, because you really are good. And, I know there are other people who think so, too. I believe what happened with your acting is what happens to so many people out there chasing a dream. They give up just a little too soon. They don't stick it out."

She wasn't sure how to take that. "Wait a minute, I had to pay the bills. You know, I'm no spring chicken."

"You're what, thirty-two?"

She laughed. "You know how old I am." She was nearing her thirty-seventh birthday.

"Well, you look twenty-five."

"Sweet talker." For a minute she almost forgot they were arguing. "But I did, you know. I had to make ends meet, and the TV thing wasn't doing it for me. It was cable after all and I took the rock bottom fee, thinking it was my big break. What it turned out to be was my big demise, with no money to continue acting classes or to maintain the look and the whatever it takes to be all Hollywooded out."

"But you do have it, and you don't need classes or a look, because you're beautiful just the way you are."

Oh God, melting like butter, practically falling off the chair. Brain connect. "Thank you, but honestly, don't you think this is too weird? And, I don't know that even if this situation had fallen into my lap in a different way that I would have accepted it. My life is so different now. I mean, I manage a winery. Your winery. I have friends in Napa and I love what I do. I really love it. And, then there's . . ." She looked down at her hands and then back up at him. "There's us. Now, there's us."

"And you think because you star in this movie that it will change anything?"

"I, well . . ."

He took her hand. "I know that this is sudden and overwhelming and you're thinking tabloids and unwanted press. Am I right?"

"Kind of."

"I'm sure there will be some of that. But you can handle it. And, you know you're boring anyway. If the *National Enquirer* finds a story on you, surely someone like a Lindsay Lohan will beat you to the punch."

"Thanks. I think."

"No, I don't mean boring in a bad way. What I mean is, you're normal. Tabloids want exploitation and there is nothing to exploit about you. So, you take this role. Take the money, for God's sakes. Who knows, we may have a bunch of kids to put through college one day, and what if I start making crappy wine and the business turns to sour grapes? You'll need to support us." He laughed.

Kids. He just said *kids*. A bunch of kids. Yes, she did want kids. Sure. Soon. She would need kids soon because the biological clock was ticking, but she'd never heard him mention children before. This was a good thing. A little sudden, but good.

"Nikki? Are you listening?" She nodded. "Like Kane said, it's a once-in-a-lifetime thing. Maybe it'll be a hit like they're saying it will be, or maybe not. Maybe you'll find out that acting really is that thing you've been passionate about. That thing you gave up on, and then sometimes lie awake at night wondering about." She squinted. How did he know she did that? "Oh I know." He shook a finger at her as if reading her mind. "We all do it. We've all had hopes and dreams, goals we gave up on or couldn't make happen for whatever reason, and after everything is said and done, there are times we wonder, 'what if?' What if I'd done it this way or that way? Or tried that or this, taken this guy's advice or didn't listen to that guy? What if?"

Nikki called the waiter over and ordered a glass of Cabernet. Although the champagne was gone—most of it consumed by Kane and Nathan—she had the feeling that this conversation might go well with a glass of red. Derek followed suit and suggested they order dinner. They both ordered Australian rib-eye steaks.

"Your 'what if' song and dance sounds to me somewhat melancholy. Is there a 'what if' in your past?" Nikki asked.

He took both of her hands. "Almost."

"Almost?"

"Yeah, you. I thought about it and thought about it, and I've played out, what if you didn't choose me, or what if I hadn't taken a chance and called you while sitting on the tarmac? Or what if I'd been a chicken shit and not told Renee the truth and she was the one here with me now?"

Nikki didn't like the sound of that *at all*. Renee Rothschild was the daughter of a big-time San Francisco publisher who had published a book about the winery that Derek had coauthored. Nikki had worked on the book herself. Upon meeting Derek Malveaux, Renee had gotten all hot and bothered over his green eyes and chiseled features, not to mention those abs that Nikki was aching to run her fingers over. "What if" was right! Nikki knew if she hadn't heard that message from Derek before heading to the airport—if he hadn't made the call at that very moment—she would be in Spain. God, Andrés! She had to face it. Face him. Nikki didn't know how to answer Derek.

"I'll tell you what, I would be completely miserable because I know that I would have lost you, and Renee would be nothing but trouble. The only reason I showed any interest in her was because I thought I'd already lost you and I really didn't think that I was the best man for you."

"Why?"

"Come on, Nik. We both know that diving in, taking a chance—at least in relationships—hasn't been my thing. It scares the hell out of me. You, me—us—scares the hell out of me."

"Then why? Why take the chance, make the move?"

"It was that, or be miserable asking myself what if for the rest of my life. And, you and I both know that if you don't do this movie, you'll be doing the same thing. Maybe not now, or a year from now, but maybe ten, twenty years from now, you'll wonder, what if . . ."

The waiter set down their glasses of wine. She smiled and raised her glass. "Here's to 'what if.'"

Pan-Seared Australian Beef Rib-Eye Steak with Cabernet Sauce and Pear Risotto with Woop Woop Cabernet Sauvignon

Nothing like a good steak and a bottle of Cab to help make those "what if" decisions with a clear head. If you're not an Aussie and don't have access to their delicious beef, pick up some steaks at the local market and use the recipe all the same. It's delicious!

The Woop Woop Cab is full of intense flavors of spice, black cherries, and mulberries. It is a rich Cab that lingers on the palate for a long-lasting finish.

BEEF

4 Australian beef rib-eye steaks, trimmed
salt and freshly ground pepper, to taste
2 tbsp olive oil

PEAR RISOTTO

2 tbsp extra virgin olive oil
2 spring onions, chopped
1½ cups Arborio rice
1 large pear, peeled and diced into ½-inch cubes

1 cup white wine (try a rich Chardonnay)
4 cups hot chicken stock
white pepper to taste

CABERNET SAUCE

½ cup Cabernet Sauvignon (or Shiraz)
¼ cup beef broth

Season steaks to taste and let come to room temperature.

To prepare risotto, heat olive oil in a large saucepan over medium heat. Add onion and cook for 1 minute or until starting to soften, but not brown. Add rice and pear. Cook, stirring, for 2 minutes or until rice is well coated. Pour in wine, stirring until all liquid is absorbed. Reduce heat to medium-low, add chicken stock a ladle at a time, stirring constantly and allowing all liquid to be absorbed before adding the next ladleful. Continue until rice is creamy and al dente, about 20 minutes. Remove from heat and season with pepper. Cover and allow to sit for 2–3 minutes before serving.

While risotto is cooking, heat 2 tablespoons olive oil over high heat and cook beef for 1–2 minutes on each side. Reduce heat to medium and continue to cook beef for 3–4 minutes or to your liking. Transfer to a heated plate and cover with foil to keep warm.

For the sauce, pour wine and broth into pan and simmer over medium-high heat until mixture thickens, about 5 minutes.

To serve, spoon risotto into large bowls. Slice steaks, arrange over risotto, then pour wine reduction over top. Serve with more of the Cabernet and a large green salad.

Serves 4–6.

Chapter 12

The night didn't end with Nikki in Derek's arms, but yet again sleeping next to Simon, who was unable to procure another room. And this time, if anyone had been snoring, it wasn't her. Simon sang out like a buzz saw, while she tossed and turned and wondered about what it was she was about to do. Before turning in she had called Kane Ferriss and agreed to do the movie. He and Nathan Cooley expected her there at six thirty the next morning.

She finally did get some sleep but was awakened not long after by Simon, the scent of eau de vino on his breath and oozing out of his pores. Though a bit hungover, he insisted on escorting her to her first day on the set. Derek was asleep as they tiptoed past him. Nikki stopped at the door as Simon headed toward the elevator. "I'll be there in a minute," she told him. He nodded and she quietly walked back over to where Derek lay sleeping on the sofa bed. She leaned over and kissed his cheek.

He opened an eye, and a smile spread across his face. He pulled her down on him and twirled her around so that he was on top. She yelped in surprise. "I thought you were asleep."

He winked. "Fooled you. So, you're really doing it, huh?"

"I thought we were waiting for the right time and all that." Not that she probably couldn't get into it right here, right now, but she had promised to be at the set on time.

He planted a kiss on her. "No, silly. The movie."

She hesitated. "I think so, I mean I guess so. God, I don't know."

"Shut up and go and do it. I know you'll kick ass. Then next year, when we walk the red carpet, I can say yep, Nikki Sands is my woman."

She kissed him back. "Why are you so wonderful?"

He shrugged. "No clue. It must be your influence." He kissed her on the bridge of her nose and rolled off, just when she was getting awfully damn warm and comfortable. "Now go, you don't want to be late for the first day of shooting."

"Will you be by?"

"Yep. I'm meeting with Liam. We're going to finally tackle the contracts we've drawn up. His attorney will be there, and I've already faxed the contracts over to mine so we can have a conference call. We've basically handled Liam's problem."

"You still can't tell me what that is?"

"You know I can't. I have to keep my word to Liam."

"What happens when all the business is summed up, if I'm still doing this thing?"

"The movie? You will be. But I was thinking

that I could use a couple of weeks off. You work. I play. I may like you being a movie star. I get more time off, especially if we decide to cohabitate or even get married."

Instead of saying something charming and brilliant, Nikki did what she always did when she didn't know what to do—something stupid. She picked up a pillow and threw it at him. "Fat chance."

He pulled the pillow away from his face, looking awfully cute with his rumpled hair and sleepy eyes. "What does that mean?"

"Fat chance that I'll become a movie star." And with that she shut the door, and was walking on air. Okay, it was out there, on the line—cohabitate, as in *live together*, and even *marry*. Throw in the kid comment from the night before and talk about overwhelming. Oh God, there went that plummeting in her stomach again. Was it all too fast, and could she do what she knew her Aunt Cara would tell her to and go with it? And what about closure with Andrés? She needed to handle that. She hurried to the elevator, where Simon waited.

"Okay, peaches and cream, let's get a move on. This boy here needs a mimosa or a friggin' Bloody Mary, something off the hair of the dog that bit me, or whatever the saying goes, and you have a movie script to start reading. Chop-chop."

Nothing like Simon to pull you out of a moment,

or out of anything, really. She stood up straight, head held high, and took the elevator down to the lobby, praying that the confident look would not be detectable as phony.

When the door opened she was blasted by three people with cameras, all snapping her picture. "Nikki Sands, right?" one yelled. "You'll be taking Lucy Swanson's role in Nathan Cooley's movie. How do you feel about that? Isn't it harsh?"

She was so not ready for this. Get back in the elevator, go back to the room, and hide under the covers. But no, Simon covered for her. "Excuse me, Ms. Sands has no comment at the moment. Thank you."

"Who are you?" one of the cameramen asked.

"Her bodyguard, and watch out, sucker, I know Jiu-Jitsu. You know—Jiu-Jitsu? Brazilian wrestling? Not just wrestling, actually. I can kill a man with my bare hands," he snarled.

It took everything Nikki had not to burst out laughing. They got into a cab Simon had called, leaving the car for Derek. "Jiu-Jitsu?" she asked.

He laughed, too. "Oh, honey, have you ever watched it on TV? It is spectacular. Two sweaty men groveling on the floor."

"Enough already. I sure didn't expect that. How did they even find out I'd been offered this? And, they're right. It is harsh, only one day after Lucy was killed."

"Killed? You say that as in murdered."

Nikki noticed the cabdriver eyeing them in his mirror. She lowered her voice. "I think there was foul play."

"No! Come on. It was one of those bizarre things that happen. The snake got into the RV and into her bed, and there you have it. Sayonara." He slid a finger along the base of his throat.

"Simon, I'm serious. You don't think I'm doing this to become the next name on the front of the *Enquirer*, do you?" What she didn't want to add was the fact that acting in this movie would gain her access to people who had been around Lucy. She wasn't just going to work, she was going sleuthing. Being in that vineyard, on the set would give her the access she needed. But she didn't have to tell Simon, because he read her mind.

"Oh God, no, say it isn't so. That's it. You are cuckoo. Completely off your rocker. You wanna go play a Charlie's Angel, not Nicole Kidman. What the hell is wrong with you?"

"I can't help myself. Sure, I want to try the acting thing, but more than that I want to find out the truth about what happened to Lucy. Let's get real. The murder statistics aren't high in this area. If I had to put money on it, I'd say that Detective Von Doussa hasn't seen more than one or two in his day. He was shocked when I even suggested it."

"Well duh. Everyone is, sweetheart. You are the

133

only one who is screaming murder. Get over it. It was freaky. The snake snuck out, probably because Andy didn't latch the terrarium, and now lady luck is on your side. Make the best of it. Because, honey, I'm telling you now, when you walk down that red carpet, I'm going with you and I am so sporting an Armani tux. I always wanted one. Eat your heart out, Marco."

Nikki sank back, crossed her arms, and closed her eyes. She didn't give a rat's ass what everyone else thought. Sure, she'd learn her lines and she'd give the performance of a lifetime, but she was also going to prove that Lucy Swanson's death was not an accident.

Chapter 13

When Nikki and Simon rolled into the vineyard after security checked them through, the movie set was already bustling. Nikki made a mental note that buddying up to all the security guys would not be a bad idea. They were hulking men—not people you'd want to mess with. But Nikki had questions for them. There was always one guy up front when people went in and out of the vineyard; maybe he'd let in someone who wasn't supposed to be there during the party. Still, tracking all of them might not be so easy, but one of her first items in solving Lucy's murder would be to find out which guard was working the night of the party. Also, if that guard was on all night. Maybe he'd seen or heard something. Oh, and then there was the one security guy—the kid. The one that Andy had reprimanded for yelling for him when they were checking out the animals. What was his name? Will. That was it. That could be an in, a good way to go. She'd have to talk with Andy or Liam and see if she could get an introduction. She'd have to make up some excuse as to why she wanted to meet him, but she was sure she could come up with something.

Kane greeted her with a hot cup of coffee. "Good to see you didn't change your mind. I know this has been a lot to dump on you, but I can't tell you what this means to me, to all of us who believe in this film. I put a copy of the script in makeup, with Johnny. We'll film some scenes that won't include your character, Elizabeth Wells, in it. Then we'll do the first scene with you, the one that I've highlighted in your script. You're going to have to do a lot of quick memorizing, but since you've already been in the business, you should be able to adjust quickly. Also, there are a couple of books that had been written about Elizabeth, along with some old footage taken of her. Before she died she did some documentaries. I also met her and worked with her briefly on a documentary. When we get a chance we should sit down and discuss her in more detail."

"Elizabeth Wells?" Nikki asked. Where had she heard that name?

He lowered his voice. "It's pretty well known, but everyone is staying quiet about it because it makes Grace uncomfortable. Liam wrote this script in honor of Elizabeth. They had been lovers, and Grace knew her, too. This is before Liam and Grace were married. It would be convenient if you could speak to them about Elizabeth, but with Grace I don't see that happening. I get the vibe she's not entirely happy about this movie being made in the first place."

Oh yes, now she remembered, Sarah Fritz had talked about Elizabeth and Liam. So, it was true what Sarah had been going on about. No wonder Grace didn't exactly seemed pleased about the movie. And, what if Grace—oh wow—was willing to do anything to have this movie shut down? Could she go so far as to kill Lucy? If so, did that mean Nikki was in any trouble here?

"You'll get a chance to speak to Liam about Elizabeth. He's on the set frequently, but be delicate when you bring it up." He winked at her. "I'll get you the background stuff to study, but you better hit that script."

She tried to smile, but she hadn't read, much less memorized a script in years, and never for a feature, and now she had this dread pulling at her where Grace Hahndorf was concerned. A picture of Julie Andrews singing "Confidence" played out in her mind. "No problem. I can do it."

"That's the spirit," Kane said.

Not only had Nikki pegged it when she could tell Grace was not pleased about the movie, but now the words of Sarah Fritz haunted her. She could understand why Grace would not want Liam to have written the script. He'd loved Elizabeth. Yet, he married Grace, even though it was after Elizabeth's death. But they had Hannah together, which meant he must have loved her to have a child with her. But what if Grace had gotten pregnant early on in the relationship? Sure, they may have married because Grace wound up pregnant with Hannah, but Nikki found it hard to believe that they'd stayed married over twenty years because of the girl. Nikki would have to do the numbers, and find out how long ago Liam and Elizabeth had been involved, when she died, and when he and Grace wound up together. She figured Hannah to be in her early twenties, but she would need to know for certain to follow this particular thread.

From what she'd seen so far of the Hahndorfs, they appeared in to be in love, or at the very least affectionate with each other. Couples at odds typically gave off signals—body language, sarcasm, something—and Nikki figured she would have picked up on that. But she hadn't. Curious why this was happening now—if Liam knew his wife was unhappy about having this movie made, why do it? They didn't need the money. Maybe there would be some answers in the script.

"Kane, do you know where Shawn is?" Simon asked.

"He's finishing up in makeup right now."

"Well, Nik, I'll join you," Simon said. "Thanks, Kane."

Uh-oh. Simon was already getting way too comfortable, tossing everyone's names around as if they were all buddy-buddy. She'd have to nip this in the bud.

"We're thinking we'll be ready for you about nine o'clock. That gives you some time."

"Okay. Can I ask you something?" Nikki said.

"Sure."

"I've already had paparazzi hounding me at my hotel."

"Damn. Thought that might happen. We've been able to keep them out of here because of the security, but if any of the actors head out, I've been insisting they take one of the security guys with them. They're good at doubling up as bodyguards."

"It's a good idea, but the thing is, I certainly didn't expect them to find me so quickly. I only called and gave you my answer last night. I don't know, it was really unexpected."

"I'm sorry. All I can say is that as soon as word traveled that Lucy had died, we started getting calls. Then, when Nathan and I were tossing around this idea to have you star in it, there were probably people on the crew who might have overheard us. Who knows how the trashbloids get their info. There could have even been one inside the bar at your hotel yesterday. They're like flies on walls. But, don't worry about it. You know, why don't we get you a trailer out here? You can stay at the vineyard like everyone else. Like I said, no one has been able to bother anybody here. In fact, I think because it has been so closed off, a lot of paparazzi have gone back to L.A. With Lucy's death, though, it might stir the pot some. Honestly, they can get everything they need by just planting one or two of those maggots around. We'll get you set up out here and the problem will be taken care of."

She didn't know if she liked that idea. This was already getting complicated. "Maybe."

"Why don't you plan on it? It'll be easier on everyone. See you soon. Hey, the police are done with Lucy's trailer, so why don't you use it to change in? Someone from wardrobe will be over in a few minutes and then you can go and see Johnny."

Before Nikki could react to any of what Kane had said, he walked away. There were already issues with this project. The first was that she didn't want to be locked away from the outside world. Second, she didn't want to use Lucy's trailer for anything. It was so morbid. So the police were done with it? That was it then? She planned to talk with that Detective Von Doussa again.

"Come on, honey, let's go and see what wardrobe plans to put you in," Simon said.

"I don't want to go in that trailer."

"Don't be silly. The snake is gone and so is the dead actress."

"It seems wrong."

"Get over it."

"Simon," she growled.

He stomped his foot. "Lookie, this is no time to be a wuss, okay. Besides"—he lowered his voice—"maybe you'll find a clue in the RV that the police didn't."

"Funny." But he was right: maybe she would find something. She planned to look for Andy Burrow as soon as possible and see what the police had said about his snake and how they all thought it had gotten out . . . and what about the Kevlar suit he used around his reptiles? The one he was so sure had been moved? Nikki had plenty of questions to ask, and Simon was right about one thing: there wasn't a whole lot of time to waste. "Okay, let's go."

The crew eyed Nikki and Simon as they walked to the trailer. "I think they're talking about me," she said.

"Good."

"No, not good. That's not what I want."

Simon swung the door open, grabbed her arm, and pulled her in. "Of course they're going to talk about you. You're now the 'it' girl on this movie. Get over it. Play a diva."

She shook her head. "Not my style."

"Yeah, well, take some lessons from me."

She rolled her eyes and looked around the RV. It was weird being inside the space where a woman had taken her last breath barely two days before. She wondered how the cops could allow anyone in so soon. They must have deemed it all an accident. She sighed and glanced around. Nothing unusual. It was really a nice RV: plush leather sofa, kitchenette, dining table, queen-sized bed in the back, and a big bathroom. There was even a stacked washer and dryer.

"I don't know about her taste in music," Simon said, thumbing through a CD collection. "Okay, I get Gwen Stefani, totally, but I am so over the melancholy chick thing. She's got Alanis Morissette—God, how old—Sarah McLachlan, Tori Amos . . ."

"Hey, Tori Amos is one of my favorites."

"Sure, when you're on a downward spiral and you need to be pushed over the edge." Nikki shook her head. "Okay but now this is strange, she's got the Dead Kennedys and the Violent Femmes and the Ramones."

"Maybe she liked to listen to old-school punk and wind down with some man-bashing folk-type music."

"Weird," Simon said.

"I guess." It *was* kind of weird that a woman Lucy's age, which couldn't have been more than twenty-five, wouldn't be into some of the younger, hipper music that was out. But she certainly wasn't about to pass judgment on the deceased girl's music, especially since she was in agreement with most of it—minus the Dead Kennedys. That was a little too punk for her taste. She liked the Violent Femmes and Ramones back in the day, but probably wouldn't enjoy them the way she once had as a teenager. Her tastes had mellowed in music; come to think of it, in men as well. Thank God. Back in the day, Nikki had a bit of a wild child in her and she'd been unsuccessful in love, because picking the bad boy seemed to be a constant theme, until Andrés and Derek. Yeah, Andrés. Today, even if it meant at midnight, she'd sit down and write him a letter. But a *letter*? That was so impersonal . . . and didn't he deserve some sort of explanation? She knew she needed to call him. He deserved that.

"Nikki, yoo-hoo, I think someone is here for you?"

They heard a tap at the door. Simon swung it open and in stepped a petite woman with brunette hair cut in a pixie, carefully applied makeup, and an outfit that looked as if she could have stepped directly out of a J. Crew catalog. Long-sleeved, white button-up cardigan sweater and a pair of chinos. "Good morning. I'm Amy Applebaum. I'm in charge of wardrobe." She eyed Nikki up and down. "Okay, so it looks like we have to go up a couple of sizes with you." Nikki frowned and then remembered that Lucy had been a wisp, and reminded herself that there was nothing wrong with a womanly figure. "My assistant, Harv, should be right along with some outfits. Now your character Elizabeth is not exactly a fashionista. Unlucky for you, no designer duds to stash away." She laughed. Nikki was already not liking this woman. "You've read the script, I'm sure, so you know that Elizabeth was a conservationist and big-time animal kingdom chick. Completely over the top. Even started a zoo but then the croc thing happened and you know . . ." She tossed up her hands. "I don't know. I'm sure the zoo is still there. I'm not much into animals."

Now Nikki was *really* not liking the woman. Someone who didn't like animals? The script, yeah. She'd like to be getting to that, considering she was supposed to be filming a scene in a couple of hours.

"Oh good, here's Harv now. Chop-chop, darling. We have a lot to do here. Good thing we have some bigger sizes." She turned back to Nikki. "You never know on a movie set. Actresses do get replaced and you have to be prepared for all sizes. Alrighty then." Amy clapped her hands together and flashed a fake smile.

Her assistant, Harv, entered the motor home. Nikki's jaw almost dropped. An image of Marco flashed through her mind and she knew it did

Simon's as well as she watched him look at the man—same high cheekbones, dark hair and eyes, not to mention style. If Marco had a twin, this Harv guy was it. "Hello, darling. I pulled the outfits you asked for . . . in a size six." He lowered his voice as if that was horrendous. Nikki began to have serious second thoughts. "Ms. Sands, would you like to take a look?" Before she could reply, he stepped down and lifted a clothing rack into the trailer.

"You can call me Nikki," she said.

"Great. Well, Nikki, why don't you try these on, and let's see what works."

The three of them stood there staring at her. She realized after several seconds that they weren't going anywhere.

"What? Here?"

"Of course here," Amy replied.

"Can I have some privacy?"

Harv waved a hand at her. "Oh, honey, you've been in show business, you'll just have to get over the modesty thing."

Simon nodded in agreement. Who did he think he was? "Fine, but I'll step in here."

"Suit yourself," Amy said.

Nikki took the clothes, walked into the bedroom area, and pulled the curtained partition across. The clothes all fit a kind of outback theme—khaki or denim, T-shirts, that kind of thing. As she dressed she could hear Amy, Harv, and Simon talking.

"It's different being in here and not having

someone yell at you. I'm sorry about what happened to Lucy, but she was difficult," Amy said.

"Seriously difficult," Harv said. "May her soul rest in peace, though."

Nikki nearly tripped over the camouflage pants she was trying on. The way he said it sounded so insincere.

Nikki zipped up her pants and opened the curtain. "Everything fits."

"Good. You better get yourself off to makeup. Johnny will be waiting for you," Amy said.

"I heard you all talking about Lucy."

"Yeah." Amy crossed her arms. Long seconds passed without her saying anything else.

Oh, so it was going to be like that. Was Nikki already being considered an outsider? "I was wondering if the police were further investigating her death as a crime."

Amy shrugged. "Don't know. Must go. See you on the set. Glad that all fit. I was a little worried we'd have to get you a size eight." She motioned for Harv to follow her.

"Did you see that? Him?" Simon asked. "My heart be still."

"He looks like Marco."

Simon shook his head. "What? No he doesn't. No way."

"Simon, the guy is a twin to your boyfriend."

"*Ex*-boyfriend. Ex, remember? He walked out on me."

"Hmm. Right. You miss him, though, don't you?"

"We better get you into makeup," he replied.

"You know, I bet if you call him and talk to him, you can work this out."

"Snow White, I've moved on. Plenty of fish in the sea. Even around here."

"You haven't moved on."

"Whatever. Off to makeup. Grab your script. No time to stand around and gab. You have a ton of work to do."

"I don't think I need a reminder." She'd drop the subject of Marco for now, and bring it up another time. "What do you think about what they said about Lucy?"

"That's a no-brainer. It was apparent the woman was not easy for anyone to work with."

"I know, which could mean someone with a screw loose could want to kill her, and the way that Harv guy made the remark about her resting in peace, I don't know, I thought it sounded kind of like sarcasm."

"Let it go, Snow White. Let it go."

"I'd sure like to talk with that detective again," she muttered.

"No, Nikki dear. You are here to be a movie star. Just think Beverly Hills, swimming pools, and movie stars."

"Okay, Jethro, let's go." No use arguing with him. "Why did you come with me again this morning?"

"I'm your manager and bodyguard."

"Right."

Simon wrapped an arm around her. "And I know that you're happy about it."

Nikki nodded. Maybe, maybe not. Simon could be a detriment, but then again, she could turn his hanging around the set to her advantage. Granted he would need some convincing, possibly even some bribing. The crew didn't look like they were going to warm up to her anytime soon, but they might Simon. She smiled at him. "I know you'll be the best manager ever."

He rolled his eyes. "Okay, what do you want?"

"Nothing." *Yet.* But she had a plan for her friend. Yes, Simon was going to be put to good use.

Chapter 14

Nikki turned to Simon when they neared Johnny's trailer. "Instead of coming in with me, I have an idea. Maybe you can wander around, meet some of the crew . . . you know, pave the way for me. See if you can score me some brownie points."

Simon rubbed his chin as if he actually had facial hair. His skin was as bare and soft as a baby's. "That's probably not a bad idea. Build up your image as a good gal."

"Exactly."

He headed off with a smile on his face. Nikki entered the trailer and stretched out her hand to

147

the same young man who had been part of the post-barbecue trouble with Hannah and Lucy. "I'm Nikki."

"Johnny Byrne. Nice to meet you. Take a seat and we'll start with your makeup. It's pretty basic, because your character Elizabeth was a naturalist." He handed her the script that Kane had left there.

"Crazy stuff going on around here," Johnny continued. He motioned her into a chair in front of an array of mirrors and bright lights.

"Definitely."

Johnny looked to be in his midtwenties and she could see why Lucy and Hannah had taken off with him the other night. He was a good-looking guy in an Ashton Kutcher kind of way, with a boyish face and pretty brown eyes. Stereotypically he should have been gay, considering his job description. But from what Nikki could tell, Johnny was an all-American, red-blooded male.

"It must feel really weird to be one of the last people to see Lucy alive," she said.

He turned around to get his equipment out. Nikki read the back of his shirt: "Social Distortion." The other day it had been the Sex Pistols.

"For sure. One minute we're hanging, and the next . . . you know." He snapped. "She's like gone."

"You knew her pretty well, I take it? I mean, I

148

don't want to pry, but I did see you, Lucy, and Hannah take off the other night. And, I heard about what happened with Hannah's mom's car."

"Yeah. Mrs. Hahndorf was pretty pissed at us. She kind of wigged out. Thing is we were run off the road by some lunatic racing by who cut us off. But no one believed that."

"Can't really blame her since you were all drinking. She's a mom. They can smell a lie from miles away."

"It's not a lie."

Despite Johnny's claim, Nikki was skeptical and she wondered what Hannah might have lied about.

"At least none of you were hurt . . . until of course Lucy, later on."

He didn't reply.

He was starting to clam up and she couldn't let that happen. "You must have gone to some pretty cool places around here. I haven't had a chance to get out. Any good bars?" She knew how stupid that sounded.

"We went to one on Main Street. It was okay, I guess."

She knew she was pushing it, but what the hell. She wanted answers. "Main Street." That was funny, because each one of the little towns around here had a Main Street. "Did you guys meet any locals when you were out?"

"A few. You know, with Lucy being who she was and everything. But it's not like in the States where everyone is all obsessed with movie stars. Everyone was cool. One of the guys who works security here met up with us. Lucy told him to hook up with the group when he got off."

"Which guy? I haven't met everyone, yet."

"Will. He's a big, farmer-type kid. Local around here. I know he's a friend of Hannah's or at least they've known each other since they were kids. Nice guy. Lucy was working him, though, you know, doing one of her tease acts. Kind of felt sorry for him. I think Lucy was upsetting Hannah because Lucy was leading Will on."

"Did Hannah say anything to Will?"

Johnny nodded. "Actually I think she did, because when Lucy went off to the bathroom and Will started to get up and follow her, Hannah grabbed him and whispered something to him. He didn't look too happy, but he took off right after that."

This was all good and interesting stuff that Nikki knew she would have to digest and run through her brain. First she wanted some more information.

"You must've been pretty good friends with the girls." If Lucy was hitting on this Will guy, then maybe it was Hannah who Johnny had an interest in. Then again, Lucy didn't seem to have a problem hitting on anyone. She recalled her screaming at Shawn about him having a little *problem*, though Shawn had deflected that well enough. She could buy into Shawn not being seduced by Lucy. Still, Lucy had been quite a looker.

He shrugged. "I like to hang out."

"Oh come on, you went out with Lucy and Hannah two nights ago. The night that Lucy was killed."

Johnny set down the sponge he'd started using to apply foundation to her face. He looked at her reflection in the mirror. "That's the second time you brought it up. You know, I thought maybe since you were new on the set that you'd be different. But you're like everyone else around here. All you care about is the dirt."

"No. That's not it. I swear." Okay, that was partly true, but not for the reasons he thought. She didn't plan on going to any tabloid to sell them gossip. How to handle this one? Delicately. "Oh gosh. I'm sorry." Think quick. "It's just . . . well, no one is talking to me. I guess because I'm new here, and everyone seems to be talking about Lucy and what happened. I thought that maybe if I tried to join in, people would warm up to me. So maybe I was fishing, but it's not because I'm a snoop." *Not technically anyway.*

He picked the sponge and a jar of foundation back up and started applying it again. "Okay, you seem cool. I haven't been talking much to anyone about what happened. Like I said, everyone around here is all about gossip and rumors. I even heard one that I was sleeping with Lucy." He laughed.

"Jeez." Nikki had wondered it herself.

"That didn't happen."

"What about this Will? Did he make plans to hang out with Lucy the next day or even later that night before he left?"

"I doubt it. Lucy gets a thrill—got a thrill—from being a tease. I think Will could probably see it coming from a mile away. And, I'm pretty sure that was what the powwow between him and Hannah was about. Hannah gave the guy the skinny and he figured it wasn't worth being led on, only to have to wind up taking a cold shower."

"Probably, but still, it *was* Lucy Swanson. Don't you think that a local boy might have been interested in hanging with Lucy, even if all he could do was entertain the thought of being with her?"

"I don't know. I guess. I really don't want to talk about it anymore. It bugs me, you know? It's creepy and kind of disrespectful. Lucy is dead after all. I want to do my job and get back home, so I can put all that happened here behind me."

"You missing L.A.?" she asked. She knew what she was doing was risky, but Aunt Cara had taught her a lot about people's psychology, and she had to get Johnny to trust her. She had to get inside his head.

"Like I said, I want to get back home, but missing L.A.? I don't know that I can say I miss it."

Ah, the ambivalent type.

"What I mean is, there isn't much difference here other than the setting. That's as far as the job goes, you know. The job is always the same whether it's here, L.A., Japan, wherever. You still have the stars who think the world revolves around them, then you have the artsy-fartsy director . . . You know Nathan, right?"

She nodded.

"Right. Typical director, has a real temper. When things don't go the way he wants, there's hell to pay. If I were you, I'd get your lines down and stay focused, because that guy may act all mild mannered, but no way. He'll have your head on a chopping block."

Her plan was working. Here the guy was flapping as much as a *journalist* on TMZ, even though he'd been all high-and-mighty about not spreading rumors. In only a matter of seconds she'd discovered that Nathan was a hothead, which was good information on two fronts. The first being that she certainly didn't want to upset the guy, and she'd had no idea he had an anger management problem, though she wasn't surprised. The movie business was notorious for bad behavior, and not just by actors. The second reason was because it made her wonder if Nathan had a reason to get angry at Lucy the other night. But the key would be finding out who could handle poisonous snakes, other than Andy

Burrow. With Will being a local, with the possible motive of being teased by Lucy, he looked to be a decent suspect, too. And, being a security guard on the set, he would know exactly where to retrieve the brown snake.

"That doesn't sound good," Nikki said. "Any tips on dealing with Nathan?"

"Do your job. That's the best advice that I can give you. And do it well."

"Anyone else have issues that I should know about? The kind that might make it difficult for me here?"

"Kane, the producer, is cool, I suppose. His thing is to make the best movie he can, and he's always putting out fires. He's sort of the calming influence. The one thing you might want to know about him is that he totally kisses Shawn Keefer's butt. Those two are real tight. You know Kane made that guy a household name. Without him, Shawn would have probably just been another mediocre action star."

"Really?"

"Yeah. I think he's been in almost every movie that Kane has produced. It's kind of irritating that Kane does what he does with Shawn. He makes sure the guy has every comfort imaginable. But I can sort of get that. Shawn means money in Kane's pocket. And, I will admit Shawn has talent. But he also got lucky. A lot of people have talent in this business, but it also takes luck. Combine the two and you could be on your way to stardom."

"Makes sense. I already figured that Shawn won't exactly be a pleasure to work with."

"Yes and no. The guy is a total professional, you know. He knows what needs to get done, and he does it. He's always on time, always ready to go. Serious actor. Doesn't say much while in my chair, but that doesn't bug me. He's all about doing his thing. But for you and the other actors, he can dish out grief. He pulls the strings in a lot of ways around here and if he doesn't like the way things are going, then he can be pretty undermining." Johnny took a step back and looked at her face. "Okay, I'll add a touch of mascara, and then some lipstick. This is the scene where you first meet Shawn's character—the rough and tough but passionate hero, James." They both laughed. A few minutes later he took another step back. "Yep. Looks good. All I'm going to do now is pull your hair back into a sleek ponytail and you'll be ready to go."

She swiveled her chair toward him. "Thanks. Anyone else I should be wary of?"

"I don't really like Amy and Harv, the wardrobe couple. They're annoying and they stick together. The rest of us all kind of hang out, but not those two. They are on their own little island, and no one gets on with them. The grips, camera guys, they're all cool. They aren't staying here. So, they show up in the morning from their hotels, do their jobs, and head back. They have their own group. You won't hear much from any of them, but they all seem pretty cool."

"And the security? Good guys?"

"Couldn't even tell you. I can come and go as I please. They would have harassed Lucy the other night for sure if they knew she'd headed out of here. But not me or Hannah."

"So how did you guys get in and out? And what do you mean they would have harassed her?"

"That was easy. Will was working and Lucy told him to come hang when he got off work, which was in like an hour. What wasn't so easy was when Hannah had to call her dad to the rescue. Lucy took off and got a cab before anyone knew she was with us."

"Hannah's parents know that Lucy was with you two, don't they?"

"Oh yeah, they know."

Amy poked her head inside the trailer. "Nikki, you need to come with me. There's been a wardrobe change."

"See ya," Johnny said.

"Yep." He sure would, because she was not done pumping him for information. She wanted to find out every detail about Lucy's last hurrah. There could be a clue somewhere in what had gone on that night.

Chapter 15

"This is neat," Nikki said, walking into the wardrobe trailer full of racks of clothing. "Wardrobe-to-go." She chuckled at her own joke, which Amy did not seem to find amusing.

"Whatever. I got a call from Kane saying that he wants you in something that has some sex appeal to it. As if some zoo chick could have sex appeal. Let me see what I've got here . . ." She filed through the racks and tossed out a few things. Then she stopped. "Here we go." She handed Nikki a pair of olive-colored shorts that were definitely *too* short, and a tank top. Amy took the white tank and tore it on the side. "There, sexy and animal-like. Perfect. Put it on."

"It's freezing out there."

"Oh God, not you, too. One diva just bought the farm and here they bring me another."

"No. I'm not like that. But it is cold out there, especially for short shorts and a torn tank." Not even the cellulite on the back of her legs was going to keep her warm in the fiftysomething-degree weather. That was another concern—her drooping backside. She felt a woman her age should not be wearing short shorts. "How about a compromise?"

Amy stuck her hands on her hips and cocked her head. "Compromise, huh. Sure. Whatever. You're the star. Tell you what, I'm going to step out for a minute and have a smoke. See what you can find and we'll go from there."

"Okay." Nikki really did not want to seem difficult, but come on. She would find something. There had to be something in all this mess of clothes.

She filed through all sorts of outfits, both men and women's. One row had been specifically designated for Lucy. Her name was on the front of the rack. Everything was a size two. Did anyone really wear a two? She rifled through the clothes anyway. When something fell out of a jacket pocket, Nikki bent down to pick it up. It was a crumpled up piece of paper. Nikki gasped when she read what was written on it:

Lucy, watch out and keep your mouth shut. You never know what might come back to bite you.

The trailer door opened and Nikki shoved the note in her pocket. Amy stood there staring. "Why in hell are you looking at Lucy's wardrobe? There is no way you're getting into her skinny-ass clothes."

"She wore this?" Nikki pointed to the bulky jacket.

"The other day, when it was colder than it is today. That was actually hers. She put it over the shorts. That was one thing she was willing to do, wear what we told her. Unlike you. Yeah, she complained, but at least she wore what was suggested."

"Right. I found these." Nikki grabbed a pair of olive-colored pants, almost like the shorts, but being pants, it meant they'd cover her sagging rear and she'd be a lot warmer in them.

"Fine. But I'm not compromising on the tank. It's perfect. If I were you I'd get dressed and start memorizing the scene. They'll be looking for you soon enough."

"Right."

"And here." Amy pulled a wool sweater off a hanger and handed it to her. "This should keep you warm until you have to shoot. Plus there's plenty of coffee on hand."

"Thanks. I'll go inside Lucy's trailer and change." She was surprised that Amy was being decent to her all of a sudden.

"It's not Lucy's anymore. I don't care where you change."

Amy walked out and Nikki put the sweater on, then pulled the note out that she'd found in Lucy's jacket. She reread it. Lucy had probably laughed at it. Being a pain on the set was something she seemed determined to do. Still with what had happened, Nikki really wanted to know who had written that note.

Chapter 16

The moment came for Nikki to shoot her first scene. She'd had enough time to get a feel for the script, as things were running behind. Thankfully scripts were usually between 90 and 120 pages. She was a quick reader and found the story, set in the early eighties, fascinating. Elizabeth Wells, the naturist and conservationist, had grown up in wealth and privilege but didn't believe in materialism. She began working for a zoo as a teenager and her passion for animals grew from there. She set out to make people aware of endangered species and what they could do to save them.

She met James—who Nikki knew was really Liam—at a social event to raise money for animals. They were both young, and James was attending college. They fell in love, and their affair was tumultuous, because for Elizabeth it was always the animals that came first. She trained dingoes, kept baby koalas that had lost their mothers, and would take in any stray domestic animal that needed a home. Where Robert Redford had played the horse whisperer and Cesar Millan was the real-life dog whisperer, the role that Nikki would be playing was truly that of a woman who was a wild-animal whisperer. Reading over the script, she doubted she could do Elizabeth Wells any justice at all. The tragedy in all of it was that Elizabeth never had the opportunity to promote her causes in the way she'd planned. Her life had been horrifically taken from her by the very wildlife to which she'd dedicated herself.

The scene that Nikki would be performing took place after Elizabeth's initial meeting with James. He'd tracked her down at her farm in the bush. Nikki's nerves were in overdrive, and when they called her onto the set she said a quick prayer. *God, if you get me through this I promise to be a better person.* She knew it was selfish and maybe silly, but she believed in prayer, so she figured, why not give it a try? She was certain God already knew the human race could be a selfish group.

"You'll be tending to a dingo in his cage when Shawn's character James shows up," Nathan Cooley said. "You need to be irritated and feeling as if he has totally interrupted your day. You've gone over the scene, right?"

"Yes. Andy is close by, isn't he?"

"Over there. Go meet Buddha the dingo. You'll love him. Andy has him trained like a cocker spaniel."

She found Andy and Buddha inside a fenced area. The Hahndorfs had a small farm-type guesthouse that served as Elizabeth's house. "Hi," she said. "Nathan sent me over to meet Buddha."

"Yep. Hello there. You feeling good?" Andy asked. "Not afraid of animals, are you? Dunno

161

how they ever chose Lucy for this role. Girl was afraid of every animal on the set. But that won't be you?"

"No," Nikki replied, although looking at the wild dog with his dark, squinty eyes, she wasn't sure this was a good idea at all.

"Buddha, come," Andy called.

The wild dog did as instructed, wiggling the back end of his body. "He is lovely, isn't he? See here, the dingo can be tamed exactly as the wolf in North America. I've had him since he was a pup, along with his siblings. Their mother died and I found her den. We put on quite a show together back at the zoo. Go on, pet him, tell him how gorgeous he is."

Nikki reached her hand down and surprisingly found the dog to be like any other friendly dog she'd come across. It made her miss Ollie back home.

"Now, love, in this scene the dog will first be hesitant and then he does what you want him to do. I am going to show you the cues you'll need. He reads body language and understands the verbals that I will give you. Ready?" She nodded. "First, it will be your energy. Now, I have run through this scene with Buddha several times already. We have been practicing for weeks, even before arriving here. Thank God I finally have an actress who is willing to work with me and the animals. Between you and me there would have been no way this movie would have ever gotten made with Lucy. She could not take on my energy, which is what I'm going to ask you to do. Do you think you can?"

"I . . . think so."

"No, love. Wrong answer. Be bold. Take charge. You are now Elizabeth Wells, and as Elizabeth you are in control of the animals. Watch me."

Andy proceeded to run the scene through. With his cues and language, Buddha acted at first as if he were frightened of him by crouching down and slinking away from him, even growling. Andy squatted low. He glanced up at Nikki. "You have to remember that he is acting now. This is his job as much as it is yours." Then Andy propped himself onto all fours. He turned his head away from the dog and yawned. "You see what I am doing is letting him know that I don't care if he's being impossible. In fact, I am bored with it and want to be his friend. I am acting submissive." Andy took a few steps closer to the dingo, who backed away. He stopped and repeated his movements, even bringing his hand up behind his ear as if to scratch it. "This is in your scene, you realize."

"I do." Nikki had reread this scene a few times and was aware that she would basically be playing a canine through most of it. Then Andy sat back and put his head down. After a few moments Buddha came up and sniffed him, pawed his lap. Andy didn't move. Then Buddha lay down beside him and Andy gave the dog a rub. "You realize that if he were wild, these steps would take days."

"I do." She also knew that was a part of her line to Shawn's character James.

"Good. The thing you must remember is that you cannot have any fear. None. You are Elizabeth. You are me. Whatever it takes to keep you in a mode of *no fear*. You cannot get into your head, and allow yourself to think, that this dog is wild. He is not wild. He is a sweetheart and this entire scene is about acting, for both you and him. So follow what I have been saying, and you and my beauty here will do brilliantly."

"I'm in." Nikki took a few deep breaths and psyched herself. This was actually one of her favorite parts about acting—something that she really missed—getting into character. Getting herself into a place where she was no longer Nikki Sands.

"Good. I can't say it enough: I am thrilled you're on board. I don't think I could have worked another day with Lucy. I'm sorry she died the way she did, and I feel awful that it was Charlie who supposedly caused it, but she *was* impossible."

Nikki didn't know what to say. She liked everything about Andy—his demeanor, the way he was with both animals and people. But his diatribe about Lucy bothered her. Even more troubling was that Andy Burrow knew how to handle a snake, and it was presumably his snake that had killed Lucy. He was also probably adept at being stealthy. She couldn't shake the fact that, where Andy was concerned, two and two made four. The man had motive and know-how when it came to killing someone with the bite of a snake.

Chapter 17

Nikki did a few trial runs with Andy at her side, and then everything was set to go. She felt comfortable with Buddha, who was definitely better trained than her lazy Ridgeback at home. Actually, Ollie belonged to Derek. But he'd gone back and forth between her place and his, until hers had burned down. She wondered how it would all work when they returned.

She gave Buddha a doggie treat. Nathan and Kane came over and asked her if she was ready to shoot the scene. She was, with one exception—the Aussie accent she would have to pull off. She'd been practicing all morning, but still wasn't sure she had it right.

"Places everyone." Nikki took her place inside the farmhouse, where the scene would start with her walking out the front door, a cup of coffee in her hand. "Quiet on the set."

Nikki breathed in deeply. She could do this. She picked up the cup. "And action!" Nathan yelled.

Nikki walked out the front door of the farmhouse, took a sip of coffee, and looked around. A slight mist rolled through and she set the cup down on the railing to rub her arms. She still didn't get the tank top. Elizabeth would have been wearing a damn parka, but she was going with it. At least the coffee was real, and hot. She stretched and smiled. This was exactly what the script called for. She headed down to Buddha and said, "How are you today, old boy?" The dog growled. Nikki took a step back.

"Cut!" Nathan said. "Come on, what was that? Andy worked with you for what? At least an hour, and that on top of everything sets us back all day. You are supposed to have no fear. What the hell was that? No fear! For God's sake you are Elizabeth Wells! And the accent. Please Nikki, you are an actress. Think Nicole Kidman here, okay."

"Right. I'm sorry. It was instinct with Buddha." Right—think Elizabeth Wells, think Nicole Kidman. Before long she was going to have a regular party with all sorts of personalities carrying on in her head. She'd need some lithium to get through it.

"Get out of your fucking instinct and get into Elizabeth's. And work the accent."

Now she could see what Johnny was talking about. Nathan did have a temper, and over the next two hours Nikki got railed with it a dozen times before she ever moved to the inside of the cage with Buddha. Either her posture was wrong, the look was wrong, the way she talked to the dog was wrong. The accent was wrong. Hell, she even drank the coffee wrong at one point, which had grown cold. But finally—and oddly enough, because she was superstitious—it was on the thirteenth take that it all worked. The scene with Buddha worked beautifully, and she sounded as if she really had been born in the land Down Under. At that point she was pretty sure she was glowing.

She was inside the cage at the part where the dog finally lays his head in her lap and Shawn, as James, said: "That was amazing."

Immediately Buddha jumped up and ran back into his corner growling, which was what was supposed to happen, and Nikki, in character, came out of the cage and chewed him out. "Why are you here? I didn't hear you drive up! Do you know I have been working with that animal for weeks? Now look. You've probably set him back several more weeks." She grabbed him by the arm and yanked. "Get away from him."

Her ass chewing went on for a few minutes and as they reached the steps of the farmhouse, Shawn yelled, "Stop! Don't move. It's an adder." He scooped up the snake, which he tossed a hundred feet.

Nikki knew the snake wasn't real, but moviegoers wouldn't.

Nathan yelled, "Cut! Beautiful!"

Everyone seemed pleased and Shawn gave Nikki a pat on the back. They were able to do two more scenes and then they went on break. Nikki felt weary from the last several hours of work, but she knew break time would give her a chance find out more about Lucy Swanson and who might have wanted her in the ground, and that was what Nikki aimed to do.

Chapter 18

Simon ran up to her, a sandwich and a bottle of water in hand. "Oh my God, you were so good. So good, and Shawn—awesome. I couldn't believe it was you. I bought into the entire thing. This is it, baby, you are meant to be a star. Here I brought you some food. You need nourishment."

"You watched that agony?" Nikki asked and appreciatively took the food.

"Agony? That was *art*, Snow White. Art in motion."

"After hours and hours of shooting, and even then I don't know about art in motion. I can't believe you've been here this entire time."

"And where else would I be? I am your manager. Which by the way, we need to nail down the details on that."

She gave him one of her "you've got to be kidding me" looks.

"But we can do that later. For now, I want you to know you're brilliant."

"The director didn't think so."

"He was doing his job. He's teaching you your craft. Making you better at what you do. You'll appreciate it later. Be grateful."

Oh no, he was spouting the Sansibaba crap.

Thankfully, Kane approached them. "I'll let you two talk. If you need me, I'm going to have a bite myself," Simon said.

Nikki watched him hurry off and over to Shawn.

Kane laid a hand on her shoulder. "How are you?"

"Fine. Thanks." One thing she'd already learned over the course of the day: Nathan was a perfectionist, as Johnny had told her. She'd been ridiculed, screamed at, and at one point Nathan even called her stupid. He wasn't the same subdued man she'd met at the barbecue. He was out of control. "Honestly I don't know." She shrugged. "Nathan is tough to work with."

"You're doing a great job. I know he can get excited at times, but for someone who has been thrown into this, you have really come through for us. It can't be easy. You've talked to him outside of filming and you know that he has two personalities. He's a director, what did you expect?"

She laughed. "That's true. I want to do my best, but I don't think there is any way I can live up to Lucy Swanson. You guys really should have gotten someone else. Someone with more experience."

"I don't know about that. You've done awesome out here, and as far as Lucy, sure she was good. Great, in fact. I liked the girl. She had some emotional issues and was pretty high maintenance, but she didn't deserve what happened." He shook his head. "It's too bad. Now you'll probably see her dysfunctional parents all over the tabloids. They're total nut jobs. I met the dad once, and he's a real control freak. Used to manage Lucy until she got smart and realized that he was stealing her blind."

"Her own father?" Nikki was appalled, but an image of her mother ran through her mind. She didn't doubt that once her family knew she was coming into some money from the movie, sooner rather than later one of her siblings, or her mom, would be on the phone seeing what they could get out of her. Her family history was long and sordid and one she chose to forget. But in a way she had a feeling she could probably relate to Lucy Swanson in that department.

"Oh yeah, and her mom is a real prize, too," Kane went on. "Made Lucy feel like she owed her. She was one of those whacko stage moms when Lucy was young and I heard that she'd even been abusive to her. But who knows. It'll be interesting. I'm sure that Lucy had a will, considering she was worth some money."

"That's too bad they treated her like that," Nikki said. "You know, I've been wanting to ask you something about Lucy, because you seemed to have had a decent relationship with her."

"I don't know about that, but I was the one everyone turned to when she needed someone to calm her down."

"Did she have any enemies on the set? I mean, *real* enemies that you know of? I know that some people didn't care for her but still, was there any one person that stood out in your mind?"

He raised an eyebrow. "Wait a minute. You're not still on the train of thought that someone actually did away with Lucy?" He laughed. "Come on now. You gotta get off that. I did hear something about you being a regular sleuth up there in Napa. It must be true."

"Who told you that?"

"Your pal . . ." He cleared his throat. "I mean manager, Simon. And your bodyguard? He's clued us all in that he's well adept in Jiu-Jitsu."

She sighed. "Great. Okay, yes, I have been known to be a bit of a snoop, but did my *manager/bodyguard* also tell you that I've helped solve some of those cases?"

"He mentioned it. In fact, it got me thinking that maybe I should produce a TV series in Napa, kind of a hipper version of *Murder, She Wrote*." He held up his hands and formed a square with his palms and closed one eye. "I can see it now, we take the nighttime soap opera tack and throw in murder mystery with an amateur sleuth and I think we'd have one helluva show. Maybe after we wrap this, we should sit down and discuss it."

Nikki cringed. That was *way* too close to her real life. "Maybe . . . but back to this thing with Lucy."

"Nikki, this isn't Napa, and you *are* barking up the wrong tree here. It was a freak incident that caused Lucy's demise. And, if it wasn't, which I can't even fathom, then the only one I know who even has the knowledge about how to handle poisonous reptiles is Andy Burrow." He shrugged. "I know there was no love lost between Andy and Lucy, but Andy didn't murder her by setting that snake inside her RV. No way. The guy is a gem. He's not a killer. Things roll off of Andy's back. You need to put it to rest, learn your lines, let's get this movie done, and then we can talk about a Napa Valley murder mystery show."

"Yeah, okay." She hadn't learned anything that she hadn't already known about Lucy, other than her parents were jerks. She figured if anyone knew who Lucy didn't get along with big-time, it would have been Kane, but he wasn't remotely convinced that Lucy's death was murder. And, his thoughts about Andy letting things roll right off his back weren't exactly true. Andy was still carrying on about Lucy.

Kane interrupted her thoughts. "One more thing, Nikki, and I know we mentioned it this morning, but I am going to insist that with these early-morning calls, it would be best for you to stay here on the set. It'll go that much smoother and be easier for you. Plus you don't have to be concerned with the paparazzi."

"You know I really don't want to do that."

"But I think it's important you're here."

"What's important?" Derek approached.

Nikki was thrilled to see him and the butterflies swarmed in her stomach. She had that same physical reaction every time he came near.

"Derek. Nice to see you. I was telling Nikki that I think it's important she stay out here in one of the trailers. It'll be easier for filming, and that way she doesn't have to trek in and out of town every morning. She also won't have to deal with the paparazzi, who will continue to find her and hound her like they did this morning."

Derek looked at Nikki. She knew he would ask her about the morning incident. "It might not be such a bad idea. It would make it easier on you."

She could not believe what she was hearing. Okay, sure it was a pain in the ass to have Simon in the same hotel room, but the last thing she wanted was to be even farther away from Derek. Oh, but wait a minute—stupid. Why hadn't she thought of this a minute ago? Maybe Simon could have the hotel room and she and Derek could do a little camping. That could be fun. "I tell you what, I'll think about it."

"Good. Now we need you back on the set."

"But, I wanted to talk with Derek for a minute."

"Go ahead," Derek said. "I'll hang around."

"You sure?"

He nodded. "Of course."

She groaned inside. Here she hadn't seen him since she'd left in the wee hours, and all she wanted to do was wrap her arms around him.

He kissed her. "Now go, you don't want to get fired on your first day."

She turned and he smacked her on the bottom. She looked back at him and smiled. Mmm—yes, maybe getting him alone in an RV would be exactly what they both needed.

They were busy on the set for the next three hours before taking another break, and then they planned to film a scene with just Shawn Keefer in it. Nathan had told Nikki she could head out for the day. She wanted to avoid Kane, because she knew he'd ask her again about staying there. Until she spoke with Derek about her brilliant idea, she didn't want to commit to anything. Her fingers were crossed that he'd find the idea of staying with her in the RV as great as she had. She hoped he was still around. Already past six, she was starving for both food and him.

She found Simon and tried to ask him if he'd seen his brother but she could barely get a word in edgewise. He would not shut up about Shawn Keefer.

"He's marvelous," Simon said.

"He is good." Nikki had to agree. Shawn was everything they'd said he was—a consummate pro who nailed it every time.

"And the two of you together are fabulous. I so knew you could do this," Simon said. "I am so proud of you, Snow White. The chemistry between you two is fantastic. You'd never know he was gay."

"For the love of God, Simon. I've said it before, Shawn is not gay."

"Shhh. Oh sure that's what he wants everyone else to think, but, honey, I can spot them, and if I can get my hands on him, I'll make him see the error of his ways. If he doesn't know he's gay, then he should be told."

"Don't you dare! That's only a little fantasy you have going on in your mind and it isn't reality at all. You and Marco belong back together and that's what you should be focusing on."

"Whatever."

"Right. Whatever. By the way, have you seen Derek?"

"I think he's up visiting the Hahndorfs."

"Good. I'm going to head up there then."

"Ta-ta."

Although it was quite a hike up to the main house, she walked it anyway. She enjoyed running daily in Napa, and being out of her exercise routine bothered her. The walk would do her good. The air was cold and she pulled her sweater

175

around her. Though already dark, the road was illuminated from the lights on the set. The air smelled clean and she took a deep breath, enjoying the freshness of it and the serenity of the moment. Nearing the house, she could smell food and her stomach growled. She knocked at the door and was greeted pleasantly by Grace.

"G'day, Nikki. Nice to see you. Come in. We're getting ready for a bit of supper. Join us, won't you? Derek is here."

Nikki smiled and walked into the sitting area where Derek, Liam, Andy Burrow, and Detective Von Doussa were seated around the fireplace drinking wine. The four men stood as the women entered. Derek said, "I was about to come and see when you might be finished. The Hahndorfs have asked us to dinner. You are finished, aren't you?"

"Yes. Thank God. It was a long day. I've got to get back into the swing of this."

Grace handed her a glass of wine. "Try this. It's from a winery over in Langhorne Creek. I know, I know"—she waved her hands—"maybe it's blasphemy to drink another winery's product, but Liam and I have talked about expanding, such as Derek is doing with us. This winery makes fantastic Viogniers, which is a fairly new wine to Australia. Liam and I find them delightful. Don't we, darling?"

"Quite good." He held up his glass.

Nikki still did not think that these two had the

problem marriage Sarah Fritz had indicated. "Thank you." She took a sip and discovered the wine to be refreshing even though red wine typically would have been her choice on such a cold night. Her walk had warmed her some, and of course seeing Derek, she couldn't help being more than warmed by his presence.

Derek kissed her on the cheek.

"She did great today," Andy said. "Should have seen her handle Buddha. Gorgeous. Absolutely breathtaking. The dingo adores you, love."

"He's great. Thanks for helping me out with him."

"You ready for tomorrow? You've got the kangaroo that gets injured. She might be a bit tougher to handle. A sweetheart, but she also has a mind of her own. Make it early and we'll work together with her. She's been known to box a person or two. Why don't you come by before you head off into wardrobe and such. I know that's like six in the morning, but it would be a good thing to have an intro to my Sophie before we hit the set."

"Boxing? I don't know if I like the sound of that. But I think I can meet you early."

"Nothing to frighten yourself over, love. She'll do her job, just like Buddha. I'll teach you how to handle her and things will go splendidly. Always think positive. Your energy with the animals is huge. You have good vibes . . . not like Lucy, God rest her soul."

Von Doussa walked over to the bar area and poured himself another glass of wine. He was obviously comfortable with the Hahndorfs. "Like some more, Andy?" He held up the bottle. "Anyone?"

"Oh no. I've got to get an early start. Both Nikki and I do. Right? She and Sophie need to get to know one another. Too much wine and I won't be any good at all. But thank you."

Wait a minute. They were all sitting around chatting as if there hadn't been a dead girl on the back forty barely two days ago. What was the story? And what about the snake—Charlie? Nikki took a big gulp of wine, which wasn't exactly protocol but did wonders for courage at times. She knew she would irritate Derek, since she was about to go nosing, but she just could not help herself. "Did you find Charlie?" she asked.

Andy frowned. "No. I'm feeling horrible about it. Poor guy. Had him since he was a baby, you know. He's out there in that bush somewhere having to fend for himself. It's a crying shame."

Oh God, he was a snake not a poodle. "Were you able then to determine that it was Andy's snake that struck Lucy?" she asked Von Doussa.

"Not yet. We took the DNA as you know, yep, but . . . uh, without Charlie we kind of have a problem there." He sucked down half a glass of wine.

Looked as if Detective Von Doussa was a bit of a lush.

"It really could have been any snake," Grace remarked.

"We do have quite a few out here," Liam added.

"Yes, but what about Charlie? How did he get out? You said there was no way," Nikki said. "And what about your suit, Andy? The one you wear around the snakes?"

Von Doussa handled that one. "Andy and I have gone on and on about that and turns out that yep, maybe he was mistaken. Happens. I took a look at the pegs and I know that I couldn't have remembered which one I set my clothing on."

Nikki frowned. "Wait a minute. Andy, you were insistent about that. You said that you had routines and protocols and that you always had it on the same peg."

He chuckled. "The thing is, love, I am usually pretty darn routine. I have to be with what I do, but you know, I'm in a new place. The building housing the animals is new, and I do suppose that with the wine and being tired and all I could have put the suit on another peg."

Andy had been so certain, and it seemed odd to her how his story had changed.

"You have the suit and peg situation figured out, but you still don't know who let Charlie out of the terrarium?" she asked. Derek squeezed her knee, and she knew right then and there that she should shut up.

"That is still a bit of a mystery," Von Doussa said.

"Dinner is ready," Grace announced. Everyone stood and Nikki felt more than frustrated that no one was giving her any straight answers.

They all walked into the dining room. Grace called out for Hannah to come down.

They all sat. Hannah took her time making an appearance, then sat across from Andy. Nikki noticed the two of them eyeing each other, almost as if they had a secret between them. Let it go, she told herself.

The food smelled delicious. Grace had fixed a gingered pork roast and Liam opened a bottle of Grenache.

"To try and further answer your question about Charlie and how he got out," Andy said, "we don't know. We really don't. I am cautious, but snakes have been known to escape in the past, and Charlie is a curious sort."

"But you can't say then that someone did not take the snake out and put it in Lucy's trailer? You're assuming he escaped."

Hannah gasped. "Of course he escaped. Andy just told you, woman. Come on. That didn't happen, what you're thinking—that someone took him out to kill Lucy. Who would do that? How stupid—"

"Hannah, I forbid you to speak to our guest that way!" Grace said.

Liam glared at his daughter, who apologized and sat back in her seat.

"We do not think that is what happened," Detective Von Doussa said. "It's far-fetched, Miss Sands. It might make good Hollywood, but it didn't happen. As vigilant as Andy is with his animals, we believe it possible that he may not have gotten the lock on as securely as he thought. Brown snakes are wily and if Charlie could find an escape route, he would have."

Oh my gosh, who were these people kidding? They were all staring at her as if she were a lunatic. So they all really believed that the snake got out of the terrarium, found his way into Lucy's RV and into her bed no less, and bit her, and there it was. Sure. She had to pinch herself to make sure she was not in an episode of the old *Twilight Zone*. Nope. She was still in Barossa Valley at the dinner table of the vineyard owner who had written the script of a movie she was now starring in, because the former star actress had been killed by a snake that they all believed had gotten into her trailer on its own. Yikes. She glanced at Derek, who chewed on a mouthful of pork, and shook her head. Was he buying this shit, too?

The dinner wore on, with Andy Burrow the center of attention, making everyone laugh and fielding questions about his training methods. Even surly Hannah seemed amused. Nikki was not, though. She'd grown quiet listening to Andy carry on, thinking how gullible the group was. She didn't buy it at all. None of it. And as she watched

Andy work the room, she was reminded by something her aunt Cara once told her about sociopaths—they were typically charming people with a dark side they hid well. Nikki wondered if Andy Burrow wasn't simply hiding *his* dark side.

Gingered Pork Roast
with Two Hands Yesterday Grenache

Nikki was grateful for the scrumptious dinner and good wine, but she couldn't help thinking everyone around the table had had too much wine if they were buying into this. She did her best to keep mum, she really did, but it was too much to handle. It didn't stop her from enjoying the meal, though.

Of course she also enjoyed the wine. The Grenache is a soft red similiar to a Pinot Noir full of berry and floral flavors.

5 lbs center cut boneless pork loin
2 tbsp fresh crushed and minced ginger root
2 tbsp extra virgin olive oil
2 tbsp ground ginger
2 tbsp sea salt
honey

With a paring knife, form pockets on top of roast. Push fresh ginger into pockets.

In a bowl, mix together extra virgin olive oil, ground ginger, and salt. Place pork in shallow roasting pan and brush with olive oil mixture. Bake at 350° for 2¼ hours on a barbecue grill.

Brush entire roast with honey and continue

cooking for 15 more minutes or until internal temperature is 160°.

Let pork roast stand 15 minutes before slicing. Serves 4–6.

Chapter 19

"You were awfully quiet during dinner, at least after you didn't get the answers you were looking for," Derek said as they drove back to the hotel. Simon had told them he'd catch a ride with one of the crew. A group of them were going out for drinks. Nikki couldn't help be a bit envious that he'd made friends so fast, and so far most of the cast and crew seemed to be tiptoeing around her. If she only had an oven back at their hotel room she could bake her world famous brownies for an icebreaker.

"What does that mean?"

"You were hoping that someone at that dinner would buy into your theory that Lucy was murdered."

"Maybe I was, because I do think she was murdered."

"You promised me that you would not do this, that you would let it go. Please, you have to, and if the police are convinced that there was nothing devious involved, then trust them."

"The police aren't always right you know, and Detective Von Doussa seems more interested in drinking good wine than solving any crime."

"I think Von Doussa is on top of it. I think that the best thing you could do for yourself and for *us* is go with that."

Let it go. Right. She probably should. She didn't want to ruin things between herself and Derek.

"I'm sorry. You're probably right. I think I was tired and you know how I get. I know I'm inquisitive. I felt bad that no one was saying much about the fact that Lucy just died out there. It's almost as if she's been dismissed."

He took her hand. "You sure that's all it is?"

"Yes." She didn't want to get into her real thoughts with him, because she knew it would only lead to an argument.

"How did it go today?"

"Fine." Again, not another topic she wanted to delve into. So she changed it. "What about you? Business with Liam moving along?"

"We've actually got it all tied up. I'm thinking, since you'll be working on this movie for a bit longer, I might take a trip to western Australia— the Margaret River—and see if there isn't a winery there I'd like to negotiate with. They make fabulous wines in that area."

"Oh. When do you plan to do that?" She didn't like the sound of this at all.

"Tomorrow. That way I can check things out, you can focus on your movie, and then we can hopefully have some time to really enjoy ourselves."

She was being paranoid again. He wasn't trying to get away from her. No. In fact, he was trying to give her time and space to do the job she was now committed to, and also get more winery business done. *Grow up*, she told herself. If she was going to be in a mature relationship, she knew it was time to act like a mature adult. "I wish I could go with you." That sounded mature.

"I wish you could, too." He turned the corner and pulled into the hotel's parking lot.

"Wait a minute," she said before they parked and got out. "This morning there were some paparazzi hanging out."

"I meant to ask you about that. What happened?"

She gave him a brief overview.

"Jeez, Nik, I think Kane might not have a bad plan with you staying out there. At least while I take this side trip."

"Funny thing is, I was hoping that if I had to stay there, you would stay with me. I kind of thought that Simon could have the hotel room and that we would finally have a place to ourselves."

"That would be nice. I've already made my plans for tomorrow, but I'll be back in a couple of days. I like the way you're thinking, though."

"Really?" she said.

"Really. Believe it or not, I always wanted to take a camping trip in one of those monster RVs."

"Why don't you have one then?"

"It doesn't seem . . . prudent."

"And a jet is?" She laughed.

"Well, we don't have to wait in lines."

"True. You ready?"

"Why do you ask that with such trepidation?" Derek asked.

"Because I don't know who we'll find in that hotel lobby. Hopefully the paparazzi got their photos of me this morning, have written their crap about me being heartless for taking Lucy's place, and that will be it."

"I'm here with you, and I'm sure you're right. They're probably all too busy putting tributes together for Lucy Swanson like they did Anna Nicole Smith." He opened the door for her. They walked hand in hand into the lobby, hoping not to be greeted with flashbulbs. Fat chance.

A camera was shoved in Nikki's face as someone snapped photos, but even more disconcerting was a voice off to the side. A voice Nikki felt sure she recognized. "Hello, Nikki Sands. Who would have ever thought this is where we'd meet again?"

Nikki swallowed hard, closed her eyes, and knew that her real nightmare was about to begin.

Chapter 20

Derek whispered, "Who is that?"

"Marne Pickett."

A petite, blonde woman whose hair was coiffed into a bun and probably white under her dye job, shoved her manicured hand into Derek's. Her hands were the only dead giveaway that the woman was ancient. She'd been pulled, plucked, and injected so much that Nikki wondered how she ever blinked her evil brown eyes. "I'm a journalist. You must have heard of me."

"Marne, what a surprise," Nikki muttered.

"Really?" She arched her eyebrows. "Come now, Nikki. You had to have known that you starring in a film by Nathan Cooley and Kane Ferriss would have gotten me on a plane to the Down Under. I was already on the way after the events that led up to you receiving the role. I'd love for us to sit down and have an interview. *Spoonfed* is willing to pay you a nice fee for an exclusive."

"I'm sorry," Derek said. "I'm confused."

Nikki turned to him. "Ms. Pickett is a gossip columnist. Her *articles* are syndicated to all the major newspapers across the U.S., and she's also a reporter for the tabloid *Spoonfed.*"

"Ah. It was nice to meet you, Ms. Pickett. But Ms. Sands is tired." He pulled her toward the elevator, with Marne Pickett in tow.

"And you are whom exactly to Ms. Sands?"

"Marne, I'm not interested in an interview," Nikki said. "I don't have anything to say. I guarantee you won't find anything good on me. Not a thing."

"I seriously doubt that," Marne said and laughed. "Come now. Why don't we have a nightcap and discuss the goings-on with Hollywood here in the outback."

"I don't think so."

"Uh-huh, that's what I figured. You always did think you were above the rest. I would have thought you'd learned by now. Not many actresses get second chances. Especially at your age."

"You are such a—!"

The elevator doors opened and Derek dragged Nikki inside. He stared at her for a few seconds after they closed. "Well?"

"What?"

"Care to elaborate?" he asked.

"Can we get to our room first?"

He nodded. But the minute they walked in, the phone started ringing. Derek answered it then slammed it down. "Reporter."

"Marne?"

"Maybe."

It rang a second time. He picked it up, slammed it down again, and then took it off the hook. Before long someone was knocking at the door. Derek cracked it to see a bellhop standing there. "Yes?"

"Note for Ms. Sands." He handed it to Derek. Nikki read it:

You might as well give me the scoop, otherwise I'll find it in other ways. I can make life very unpleasant. Remember? Marne.

Boy, and how Nikki remembered. She handed the note back to Derek.

"I think you better tell me what's going on, but first I can see that this is going to be a problem. After what you told me about this morning, and now this." He pulled her suitcase from the closet.

"What are you doing?"

"I think Kane is right. If you're out there at the vineyard, you will be able to be on time and focus. Plus, the paparazzi can't touch you."

"I don't want to be there without you."

He crossed his arms. "I've already made plans for the next few days, so we'll be apart as it is." He blew out a breath. "I can't believe I'm saying this, but I'm beginning to wonder if it's all a sign."

"What do you mean?" she asked, not liking at all what she was hearing.

He sat down on the edge of the bed and reached for her hand. "Maybe you picked the wrong guy, Nikki. Maybe you should have gone to Spain with Andrés."

"What?" Oh no, no, no! He wasn't going to do this to her.

"Look at everything that's happened. Maybe this is God's way of letting you know you made the wrong choice. We haven't even had a moment alone together."

"Oh no. No. You're kidding me, right? You with the what ifs and this movie thing won't change a thing? Please. Why do you do this? *Why?* Every time things start to head in our direction, like we might actually succeed in a relationship together, you balk at the first sign of trouble."

"What are you talking about?" He dropped her hand. "I don't do that."

"Since we've met, we've done this roller-coaster ride—up and down, with the same old question: Will we get together, won't we get together? Drives me crazy. You know it and I know it."

"You were involved with another man—"

"For a while, yes, I was. Because no matter what kind of signal I was sending, you weren't exactly doing anything about it. But then you'd do something, some little thing, like make a joke that you knew only I would understand, or have me to dinner and we'd hang out and watch movies . . . but nothing. You never made a real move. I finally had a man go after me, and I liked Andrés. I did. He made me feel wanted. And, hell, who knows, maybe I could have fallen in love with him. He has it all. Charm, passion, brains, and looks. He was my friend, too, but dammit—he wasn't you. He isn't you, and *you* have this thing over me. I don't know what it is, but I also don't know if *I* have a *thing* over you. If you can, at the first sign of any trouble, just make stupid-assed comments like 'maybe you picked the wrong guy.' Maybe the question should be, are you happy you picked me?"

He hesitated. "Of course I am."

"Okay then. Derek, it's time to shit or get off the pot. Your words are words and your kisses, well, they are beyond anything I've ever experienced." She choked back the emotion catching in her throat. "But either you're in, even when we have a bumpy road—and you and I both know it hasn't ever been exactly smooth going—or you're out. I got on that plane to come here with you because I am *so* in. Then all this happened." She waved her arms in the air. "Who knew that it would? I didn't even know a movie was being made here, and then Lucy and all of it . . . well, it's craziness. Total craziness, and now we're caught up in it. But if I've learned anything from life at this point, it's that everything changes. It's all temporary and it will pass. We won't have jackass reporters hounding us, and I won't become the next big star, and we will get back to Napa Valley, and life will be what we've dreamt it will be."

He stared at her for a long time. "What if you're wrong?"

She started pulling her clothes from the closet and tossing them into her suitcase. "And what if I am? Does it matter? You were the one who said that nothing would change, that it wouldn't matter, and now you're flipping the switch on me. When you're in love with someone, does it really matter? You might want to think about that. Oh and practice what you preach." She didn't wait for his answer as she closed her suitcase and slammed the hotel room door behind her.

Tears welled in her eyes as she rode the elevator down. He wasn't coming after her. Dammit, maybe she *had* made a mistake. When the doors opened there stood Marne Pickett, her photographer next to her.

"Oh no, are you crying? Dear. Talk to Marne. Let me guess: Lover's quarrel? It does seem to be the name of the game in this business. I'm sure you'll find yourself a new man soon enough." The photographer raised his camera.

"Screw you," Nikki said and pushed it out of her face. Thank God a taxi stood out front. She jumped in and told the driver to just drive as tears rolled down her face.

Chapter 21

Marne Pickett, now there was a blast from the past—not a good blast either. Nikki closed her eyes and leaned back in the cab. "Miss? Uh, hullo? Where would you like me to take you?"

She sighed. The moon might be good for starters. She didn't have much choice. "The Hahndorf Winery, please."

"Good people, them Hahndorfs. Done a lot for the community. But that daughter of theirs . . . She's a troublemaker. Heard she wrecked her mum's car with that crazy actress. The one who died out there. Them brown snakes, gotta watch out for 'em. Kind of cold though for them to be sneaking about. Guess he was looking for a warm place to hide. He found one all right."

Enough with brown snakes and Lucy and wineries and movie shoots. Enough already! That's what she wanted to scream, but instead she nodded and did her best to tune him out.

Here was Derek running from her again. Enough was enough. She'd had it with men, and she still had to deal with, at the very least, a phone conversation—with Andrés. How was that going to go? *Oh hey, sorry I let you go to Spain without me, and I ran off with Derek who has done exactly what you predicted he would do—never commit, but hey let's be friends.* Sure.

And on top of it all, she knew that Marne Pickett would do everything in her power to make her life miserable. She'd done it once and she would surely do it again, and all over a simple misunderstanding. Nikki did blame Marne for helping her acting career go down the tubes. She'd met the woman at a publicity party for her show, and they'd chatted. It had been an amicable conversation and Nikki liked the woman, although she could pretty much see past the Hollywood glitz and plastic glamour, so she'd taken it all with a grain of salt, as her agent at the time suggested she do. But when Marne called for an interview that would be published in *Variety* and the *New York*

Post, Nikki's publicist jumped on it. The date and time were set. They were to have lunch at The Ivy, a Beverly Hills hot spot where those who want to be seen go to eat. Bad luck struck that morning when Nikki's car got a flat on the 10 freeway and she had forgotten to charge her cell phone. She did her best to change the tire as quickly as possible, which was not quick enough.

Marne waited a mere ten minutes and walked out of the restaurant, calling the publicist and telling her that she was going to ruin Nikki Sands for standing her up. Nikki couldn't believe it. She asked for Marne's number, and when she finally did get the gossip columnist on the phone, Marne accused her of weak lies and that she had the *real* scoop on Nikki Sands.

Marne Pickett had written about how instead of being grateful to have survived such a horrible childhood and embrace her career and Hollywood, Nikki'd done the worst and become a first-class prima donna. She even had the audacity to make appointments with people in the business, and then be offensively late or worse—not show up. Marne followed Nikki's short-lived career, making snide comments in her gossip columns about how Nikki was supposed to be the new "it" girl and how Marne predicted she couldn't even do a decent job on a soap opera. Nikki never really understood why the woman was so venomous toward her, but it was true that once someone like

Marne decided to go for the jugular, there was little to stop them. And now, here was dragon lady in Australia, back to haunt her. Could it get any worse?

Of course it could. After all, she'd been honest when she'd told Derek that their relationship had been one big roller-coaster ride—but then again, so had Nikki Sands's life.

Chapter 22

The guard at the Hahndorf's security kiosk, who turned out to be none other than Will, let the cab through. Nikki wanted to talk with him, but at the moment all she could manage was to find Kane Ferriss, get the keys to the trailer, and go to bed. She doubted she'd be able to sleep, with the jumble of thoughts, regrets, and memories racing through her mind, and she'd made a commitment to meet Andy before the roosters even crowed in the morning.

The cabdriver took her suitcase out of the trunk for her, then left. She rolled it over to Kane's motor home, which was dark, as was Nathan's. The whole set was pretty quiet. Great. Where was everyone?

Leaving the suitcase by the trailer, she walked back to the security kiosk. Will emerged when he saw her.

"G'd evening," he said in a thick Aussie accent.

"Hi." She was already planning her strategy with him. Granted, her main goal was to find a key to the trailer, but she figured she might as well kill two birds with one stone. And maybe it would get her mind off of Derek—doubtful. "How are you tonight?"

"Oh, you know, a bit cold out here. Winter will be on next month. You're the new actress here? Taking that other one's place?"

That was interesting that he didn't even mention Lucy by name. He'd had drinks with her the night she died. Was he simply trying to be professional or was there another reason? "Yes. Do you know where Kane Ferriss is, or maybe Nathan Cooley? I need a key to get into one of the motor homes."

"A group of them went out. Took one of the other security guys with them."

"Oh." Nikki wondered how late they'd be out. "You don't know when they might be back?"

"Nope. Don't keep a schedule." He laughed. "Let them in and let them out. That's about it."

"Thanks."

"Aren't you cold?" he asked.

"I'm fine." She only had on a light sweater over a long-sleeved T-shirt and a pair of jeans. She'd stormed out of the hotel so quickly that she only now realized she'd left her heavier jacket there.

"I wish I had a key for you. You can come stand in here with me. It's a bit warmer," he said, referring to the kiosk. "Or here, I can give you my jacket." He started to take it off.

"No, no. Keep it on. Please," she replied.

"I insist. Take it. I'll be fine."

"That's kind of you." He handed her the jacket. She didn't feel right putting it on, seeing that all he had was a long-sleeved button-down. It did warm her, though. "You're Will, right?

"Yes. How did you know?"

"I was there the other day when you got reamed out by Andy on the set."

"Oh. I kind of messed up there. Forgot my manners. My mum is always telling me that I have horrible manners and don't think of others."

"I don't think so. Gosh your mom should see you now. You just gave me your jacket. I'd say that's pretty gentlemanly."

From the dim light shining inside the kiosk it looked as if Will was blushing. "Thank you, ma'am."

"Now, don't call me ma'am. Call me Nikki, although again your manners are impeccable."

He smiled. "Wish you could tell my mum that. She gets after me quite a bit, always telling me when to be home, where I can go, what I can do. That sort of thing. She's a bit controlling, I suppose." He laughed. "But, she's my mum."

Nikki knew she was looking at him oddly, because the fact that he was a grown man living at home seemed strange; but then, maybe his mother

199

was ill, or they didn't have a lot of money. She shouldn't judge. She didn't know his story, but the story she did want to know was what happened the night Lucy died—the night Will had drinks with the gang.

"Have you gotten to know anyone on the set besides Andy?"

Nikki picked up some hesitation on his part before he answered. "A few people."

"Really? Who?"

He did a sideways glance as if what he was about to reveal was secret information. "I could lose my job if the word got out, though."

"Lose your job? Why? Because you're friendly with the actors or crew members?"

He nodded. "I'm not supposed to, you know, associate with the actors."

"Who said that?"

He shrugged. "I'm not supposed to do it. That's what I know."

Nikki wondered if that was a rule Kane had established or possibly even Liam, who'd supposedly gotten Will the job. "I'm not going to tell anyone. Heck, no one around here will really talk to me. I could use a friend. It's hard. Maybe if you know some of the people on the set, you could help me out."

Okay, so she was playing the damsel in distress with the "poor, pitiful me" act, and she was even working the whole doe-eyed, eyelash-blinking trick that so many men fell for. Granted Nikki found it appalling, but there was a murder to solve here.

"I know Johnny Byrne. You met Johnny yet? Good guy. Had some drinks with him. He does the makeup, you know."

"Right. That's all?"

He sighed heavily and frowned. "Oh, you seem like I can trust you, and you said you need some friends, I can be your friend."

"I would love for you to be my friend." Poor kid was one big oaf. She could totally see Lucy playing with him just because she could. But at the same time, big oafs can snap; had he? The thought made her wonder about her own safety. Was she out here playing with fire with her flirting to get answers? Still, she'd better go with it. Surely Kane, Nathan, and the rest would be along soon.

"That's nice of you. I know what you mean about friends. I don't have a lot either. My mum is real particular about who I can be friends with. I've been friends with Hannah since we was kids, but even with her, my mum sometimes has a problem."

Boy, his mother sounded like a piece of work. Nikki wasn't necessarily keen on the Guru Sansibaba that Marco idolized and Simon used to, but she'd read some of his literature and one of his seminars might do this kid some good—allow him to cut that umbilical cord his mother seemed to have choking him. "That's a shame. You know you could get some books on maybe how to distance yourself from your parents without it causing a rift. It's none of my business, but maybe you could talk with your mom about needing some space to live your own life."

"You think? Maybe I could talk to her."

Now what was she doing? Here she was supposed to be fishing for answers, instead she was doing family therapy. "You should, especially because it is your life and you deserve to hang out with whoever you want and do whatever you want. So, was Hannah the one who introduced you to Johnny?"

"Yep, and you can't tell no one, 'cause only Johnny and Hannah know, and they swore they wouldn't tell no one, 'cause I don't want to get fired."

"Tell no one what?"

"I met Lucy, too."

"No!" If he only knew that Johnny had already told her this. That kind of bothered Nikki in and of itself. If Johnny had made a promise to Will, who was so sure he'd be fired if anyone knew he'd been out with the three of them, then why would Johnny tell her—someone he'd just met—especially since he'd been on his high horse about not talking smack. Something wasn't kosher with that.

"Yep." He nodded.

"What did you think of her?"

He shrugged. "I . . . thought she was pretty."

"She was. Very pretty."

He nodded and Nikki thought she saw his eyes water. "And she was nice to me. We all had some drinks together the other night."

"You did?" This was going to be much easier than she'd anticipated.

"Yes, and she told me that she wanted to be my girlfriend."

"She did?" This one surprised Nikki. "What did you do?"

"I said that would be nice."

"Wow. Do you think she was being honest? Sometimes when people drink, they can say things they don't mean."

He nodded. "Hannah told me she was lying. That she was only teasing me, and it made me mad, so I left. Then the next day when I found out she was dead, I felt real bad about it."

"Oh no, Will. I can understand that, but you didn't know that she was going to die."

"I know, but I left without saying good-bye, because I felt hurt. I've had other girls do that to me, and I'm tired of it. I knew I shouldn't have believed her when she was saying all those nice things to me, but I did."

"Maybe she really did mean them, Will. You seem like a nice person."

"I try, but Hannah said she was lying, so I left and was never going to talk to Lucy again. I didn't. If I'd known, maybe things would have been different. Maybe I could have saved her from that snake."

"I don't think so. I doubt anyone could have saved her."

Nikki had a lot to think about here. She believed this guy. He was naïve and, to be honest, kind of dumb. He reminded her of a little boy, and she couldn't help but find herself ticked off at Lucy—even postmortem. She could understand Hannah's protectiveness toward Will, but she also wondered if there were more to it. If Hannah didn't like the way Lucy was behaving toward Will, had she done something about it? Especially after the car accident and then Lucy taking off and acting as if she hadn't been involved at all. Hannah's name came up again and again, though never in a good way.

Nikki wanted to ask Will a bit more about his friendship with Hannah, but before she could, Kane Ferriss and his entourage pulled up. "Hey, Nikki, so you decided to stay here after all?" the producer said.

"Yes."

"Great. Get in. We'll give you a ride."

"I can walk."

"No. Don't be silly."

She took off Will's coat and handed it to him. "Thanks for the jacket."

"Thanks for listening, *friend*."

The bodyguard climbed out of the front and let her in the car. "That all you need me for, sir?"

"For tonight," Kane replied.

"Good night then, mates."

They pulled away. "I love that mate shit," Kane said. "They all say it."

As they pulled away, Nikki saw Will and the other security guard talking. She would have to find another opportunity to talk to Will. She had a gut feeling that he was chock-full of good information that could possibly help her solve Lucy's murder.

Chapter 23

Nikki could not sleep. Thoughts of Derek and thoughts of Lucy dying in this motor home kept her eyes open and her heart beating faster than it really should have been, even though she'd chosen to sleep on the couch instead of the bed, where the snake had struck Lucy.

How had things gone so wrong with Derek? Had she been too hasty during their argument? Maybe if she'd talked with him a bit longer she could have reassured him that no matter what, everything was going to work out. But she'd been stunned by his words about it being a sign that maybe things weren't supposed to happen between them. Even worse, now she had the same thoughts. Now that she'd had some time to think about it, was he right? *Was* it a sign? First off, they'd come here together after quick decisions made by both of them. He'd been prepared to leave with another woman, and she'd been planning to go to Spain with Andrés. Upon reaching Australia, trouble started almost immediately, first in the form of Simon, then Lucy's death, now her acting in this movie and being hounded by paparazzi. Was this a karmic thing? What would it be like right now if she were in Spain with Andrés?

Andrés. It was past two o'clock in the morning and she needed to be up in less than four hours, but she could not get Andrés out of her head. She knew that she needed to make that phone call. She calculated the time: nearly seven at night in Barcelona. Before she could change her mind, she dug through her purse and found her cell.

She dialed the operator to get the country code for Spain and then punched it in along with Andrés's cell phone number. Maybe he wouldn't answer, and that too could be a sign—one that she had made the right choice and she would work all of this out with Derek. What was it with her and signs all of a sudden?

"Nikki? Is that you?" Andrés answered, and she heard other voices in the background.

"It's me." Her voice trembled.

"How are you?" he asked.

"I'm fine. Good, in fact." She couldn't tell him the truth. What would he think?

"I heard that you are in Australia. Making a movie?"

"Yes." She swallowed hard. "How did you hear that?"

"Isabel. She's beside herself that you didn't call to tell her. She read it on the Internet."

Oh great. Now her best friend was upset with her. She couldn't blame her. "The truth is, I didn't want to call her for the same reason I haven't called you. I was afraid that you both hate me."

"Nikki, Nikki. Come on. You know that we are not like that." The sound of his melodic accent made her close her eyes. She could picture him as if he were right in front of her. "I think it is wonderful and so does Isabel. Good for you. Your dreams are coming true."

"Thank you." Now she could also hear music in the background. "I did want to talk to you, even though I've been scared. I wanted to tell you that I'm sorry about the way I left you. I . . . well, you were on the plane and I got a call from Derek, and I'm . . . God, this is so hard."

"Nikki. Stop. It is okay. I understand. Yes, I was hurt, but I would have been more hurt if you came with me and your heart was with another man. All I ever wanted and still want for you is happiness. You deserve that."

The waterworks were starting again. No. *He* was

the one who deserved happiness. He was such a decent, good man. "I want that for you, too."

"I know that. I want it for myself, too. And, you know me, I am not one to ever give up on finding that. Although it is difficult for me, I know that I must move ahead because there is someone who is in my future. Do not worry about me."

She heard a woman call his name, and then laughter.

"I am sorry, Nikki. I have to go. My God, what time is it there? It must be the middle of the night."

She didn't reply.

Someone else called out Andrés's name. "I'm sorry. I'm at a dinner party and I need to help serve the tapas. I will be back in Napa in six or seven months. Maybe I will see you then. Derek is good?"

"Yes." She bit her lip. As far as she knew, he was good. He certainly wasn't with her.

"Wonderful." He said it as if he truly meant it.

It was true that all Andrés cared about was her happiness, and that made the gnawing feeling in her stomach even worse. Why couldn't he just hate her? That would make this a lot easier. Why did he have to be such a good guy?

"Take care. Good luck with your movie, and be careful."

"Good-bye," she said. She shut off her phone. It was over. It was really all over.

Chapter 24

Thank goodness Nikki had set an alarm. Without it there would have been no way she would have gotten up and over to the animal enclosures to meet Andy, because after hanging up with Andrés, she'd finally fallen into a deep, dreamless sleep. She checked her watch again. Who on earth gets up this early? It was a quarter of six and the sky was just getting light.

A quick shower, brush of the teeth and hair, and she was out the door and into the crisp morning air. She'd need some coffee. She stopped by the snack room and was surprised to see Amy and Harv up and at 'em, having their coffee and a smoke.

"Good morning," Amy said. She handed a box of something to Harv who slipped it into a leather pack.

"Good morning."

"Nice to see an actress who takes her call times seriously," Amy said.

"I try." She smiled, not wanting to get into a conversation with these two. "I actually am heading over to meet Andy and the kangaroo."

"Oh," they both said.

"Would you like us to set your wardrobe for the day in your RV?"

Why were they being so nice? Nikki felt like

she'd intruded when she'd come in. They'd looked surprised to see her. Were they being nice to her or was there more to it?

"No. I can come by the trailer and pick it up after I meet with Andy."

"It's really not a problem for us to do it for you," Amy replied.

"Really, it's fine. I'll be by." Nikki finished stirring in her creamer and headed to the animal enclosures. Now that was strange. These two had been total jerks to her yesterday, and now they were being so nice. Why was that? One thing she knew for sure was that she didn't know who had killed Lucy, and she knew those two hated Lucy. Furthermore, she didn't know if either one of them knew anything about snakes, and she did not want them inside the place where she slept. It wasn't worth the risk.

When she entered the area that housed all of Andy's animals, she stopped and listened. An almost eerie silence surrounded the place. Where was Andy? She hoped she hadn't dragged herself out of bed forty-five minutes earlier than she needed to.

What was that? Something broke the silence. It was faint, but . . . there. Nikki listened. It sounded like crying. Someone was crying. It was coming from behind the enclosure area. Nikki took a walk around to the other side. She stopped when she spotted who it was. "Hannah?"

The young woman looked up and brushed away her tears. Then she stood. "G'day. Sorry. I'm waiting for Andy. I wanted to help him get the animals their morning feed."

Nikki walked toward her. "Are you okay? What's wrong?"

"Nothing."

"People don't usually cry over nothing."

Andy Burrow appeared behind her. "Good morning. Sorry I'm late. Hullo, Hannah. Why don't you start on down the end with the snakes? Now be careful and don't forget the gloves. Okay? You had a chance to get any of the feed ready?"

"I was just starting. Yep. I'll get on it right now."

"Good. Thank you, and Nikki, are you ready to meet Sophie?"

"I suppose." She followed Andy to the kangaroo's enclosure, glancing back at Hannah. Something was bothering that girl, and Nikki really wanted to know what it was. "You know, Hannah seems a little upset this morning."

Andy paused. "Oh. I'm not too surprised. Probably had another row with her mum."

"They don't get along?"

"I'm not one to speak negatives, so I'm not going to say much here other than if Grace Hahndorf would allow her child to be who she is by nature, then Hannah would become exactly who she is supposed to become, and I guarantee both mother and daughter would be that much happier. Okay, get ready to meet Sophie."

They reached the marsupial's enclosure, and Nikki figured that was all she was going to get out of Andy. "Hullo, love," he said to the kangaroo, who Nikki swore had this look of suspicion on her face. "Come on in here with me, Nikki." She entered the area with trepidation. "Say hullo to Sophie."

Nikki kind of felt stupid saying hi to a kangaroo, but she was going to do everything Andy told her to do when it came to his wild kingdom. "Hello, Sophie."

The kangaroo eyed her. Nikki did not like the look.

"I think she likes you. Here, give her some of these nuggets." Andy handed her some kind of grain-type treats. He gave Sophie a handful first. She eagerly gobbled them up. "Okay, love. Your turn. Once she knows you have goodies she'll be a sweetheart for you."

Huh. Nikki wasn't so sure she believed that. Buddha the dingo hadn't had a look of "I'm going to kick your ass" in his eyes. Nikki approached slowly and reached out her hand. The kangaroo sniffed it with a soft, whiskery nose—reminding Nikki of a giant rabbit. After a second of sniffing, Sophie ate the goodies and then turned away.

"This is good. She likes you. Yep. Everything will be fine."

"How do you know?"

He chuckled. "See now, Sophie is sensitive, and I've learned that if she isn't going to treat someone right, then she'll misbehave from the get-go, even if you have a peace offering, like the goodies there."

"What would she have done if she didn't like me?"

"Tried to box you."

"Tried to box me?"

"Yep, and she can give a mean wallop, too."

"And what if she had done that?"

"I was here with you. I would have had it all under control. See, that's why I wanted you to come on over early, to meet the girl and make sure we had a match made in heaven. Guarantee she would have boxed the hell out of Lucy. But you're good. I'll bring some goodies with me to the set and no worries. Okay then."

"Okay then," Nikki replied.

As they headed out of the enclosure, Nikki again looked at Sophie and she wasn't convinced at all that the kangaroo wanted to be her friend—treats or not. She wanted to tell the animal that she'd refused to have a bite of what could have been its brother or sister the other night at the barbecue. She was on her side.

After leaving the enclosure, Nikki grabbed herself another cup of coffee before settling down into Johnny's chair for hair and makeup.

"Morning. What's up?" he said.

"Not a whole lot, just met my costar today—Sophie the kangaroo."

"Lucky you. I'm a cat person myself. Don't care much for dogs and definitely don't like anything wild."

"I love dogs, cats. Pretty much all animals. I'm not so big on snakes, though."

"Know what you mean. Never been one of those guys who liked reptiles or spiders."

"Right. So you wouldn't have put that snake in Lucy's bed." Holy moly, now why did she let that one slip out?

Johnny gave her a look that basically asked the same question. But he said, "Anyone hand you the latest in the local rag?"

"No. Why?"

"Maybe you should take a look." Johnny handed her the paper, already opened to a photo of herself trying to cover her face while leaving the hotel the night before.

"Oh my God. How did they get this so soon?"

"Not a lot of news to report?" He shrugged. "You seem to be *it*."

"That Marne Pickett," she growled and read the article beneath her photo:

It looks as though the latest diva to flash her assets on the Hollywood scene fancies herself as a regular Angela Lansbury sans the actual acting and finesse. Yes, Nikki Sands, whose television stint a few years ago as Detective Sydney Martini lasted as long as it takes for my nail polish to dry, has not only landed herself quite a deal with Ferriss Productions, filming an epic in the Australian outback with none other than the fabulous Shawn Keefer, but she's also busy snooping around into the death of Lucy Swanson, whose place she's taken. Sources say that Ms. Sands is asking all sorts of questions about Lucy's enemies on the set and who could have handled the deadly brown snake. Sources also say she's a bit mad. Let's be real, Nikki: no one planted a brown snake in Lucy Swanson's trailer. Count your blessings that you got a second chance in the acting world, and don't blow it this time. If I were Ms. Sands, I would be thanking my lucky stars I'd landed the role that should have gone to an actress with real talent. And there is also talk on the set of romance between Nikki and the man himself, Shawn Keefer. Her current lover, Derek Malveaux, owner of the well-known Malveaux Winery in Napa Valley, has sent her packing. Is it because she's a tad loony, or is there another man in her life? My advice to Nikki is don't go the way of Anne Heche—there are no Martians and there are no murderers on your set, darling. The world doesn't need another crazy starlet, so get real.

Nikki blew out a long breath. "Unbelievable."

"I thought you should know."

"Thanks. I think."

"Sorry."

"Where is this coming from? Where did she get all this, that I'm asking questions about Lucy's death and . . . oh my God, the stuff about me and Shawn."

"Here's the thing: you do ask a lot of questions, and personally I like you. But there are people around here who will spread gossip and rumors like wildfire, and even create their own stories. You've been on the set for what, two days now? Think about who you've talked to. I know you asked me a lot of questions yesterday about Lucy, and I know what you were getting at. But I didn't kill Lucy with a snake. I didn't kill her at all, and I didn't say anything to Marne Pickett. But you have to stop asking people questions. It makes them uneasy and it could create problems for you."

"It looks like it already has," she replied.

"I do have a confession to make, though, and . . . I've been afraid to say anything to anyone."

Nikki was all ears.

"When you were asking me about the other night with Hannah and Lucy, I sort of left some stuff out."

"You did?"

"Yeah. That night after we were run off the road

and crashed Mrs. Hahndorf's car, and Lucy took the cab back, well, when I got back with Hannah, I went to see Lucy. We drank some more, listened to some music, and things got a little heated as far as . . . well, you know, we were making out and stuff." He chuckled. "But then Grace banged on the door and came in all huffy, yelling at us, telling Lucy to stay away from Hannah. Liam showed up, too, and got Grace to leave. But it pretty much ended the mood between me and Lucy and I knew I'd better get some sleep, so I split. The cops questioned me a lot about her."

So, Detective Von Doussa was doing his job after all. He may have been covering his arse, as he put it, but maybe he did have an inkling that there was more to Lucy's death than an accidental snakebite. At least he was actually questioning people. "Why are you telling me all this?"

"Because I've been afraid this whole time that I am responsible for Lucy's death, even though I think the snake thing was a freak accident. I hate snakes." His body shook when he said this.

"What? Why?"

"The door to Lucy's trailer. I was drunk, you know, and I don't think I closed the door. I've felt responsible ever since, like I caused her death, like if I had made sure that door was shut, the snake couldn't have gotten in there."

Nikki had studied people enough through the years that she'd thought she'd become a decent judge of character. There was something in Johnny's voice, and also the way he was looking at her, that had her convinced he didn't kill Lucy, at least not intentionally.

"I didn't say anything to anyone because once I saw the cops were involved, and then you've been going around saying it was murder, I kind of got weirded out."

"I understand. But I don't think you caused Lucy's death. I really don't," Nikki said.

"I hope not. You still don't think it was an accident, though?"

Nikki might have been sure that Johnny didn't take Lucy out, and he did seem to be more friend than foe in this strange world, but all the same, she didn't know who to trust. She had no clue who was feeding Marne all the dirt, and she wasn't willing to take a chance on Johnny. She hadn't forgotten that he'd supposedly promised Will he wouldn't tell anyone that he'd been out with him and the girls. "You know, I've been rethinking all that, and no, I don't think Lucy was murdered. It was a fluke accident. That's all. I guess I let my brain get carried away." Nikki was lying through her teeth.

"That can happen in this business. We creative types love to make up all sorts of stories."

"Yes, we do." Although only a minute earlier Nikki's radar had told her Johnny was one of the good guys, however, with his last comment, she wondered if he wasn't just flying under the radar. He was a "creative type," too. Was he the one who'd just fed her one helluva story to get her to stop making waves?

Chapter 25

Nikki didn't have a whole lot of time to prepare for her scenes. She memorized her lines, made some notes, and asked Nathan a few questions, but so far she hadn't done a great job all morning and she knew everyone was growing frustrated with her.

"Cut!" Nathan yelled again. "It's all wrong. Nikki, come on now, you've read the lines, you're a professional, and by this time you should have had enough time to get to know this character."

Sure. Everyone gets to know their character in barely two days. Nikki smiled. Tonight she'd watch those documentaries and read what Kane had for her regarding her character, Elizabeth.

"I'm sorry, Nathan. I'm not sure what I missed."

"First of all, this scene is supposed to be filled with passion. Elizabeth is finally falling for James, and it goes against her nature because she has never been emotionally close to another human being. Her life is the animals. She finally allows herself to go to this man."

Nikki nodded. She knew Nathan was right. Here she was supposed to be acting out a scene where she is falling in love with Shawn's character, and all she could think about was Derek. It wasn't comfortable, and she knew she was in way over her head. She didn't have any feelings for Shawn, and that's why she had to remind herself that this was acting. She was only acting. She was supposed to be Elizabeth Wells, dammit.

Shawn took her hand and glanced at Nathan. "We're going to take five and do this scene again. I think Nikki just needs a cup of tea. Okay?"

Nathan scowled, but Kane said, "I think that's a good idea."

She walked off the set with Shawn, touched by his concern. They sat down at a catering table. "Look, I know this is your first go at a major picture, and it's been hard," Shawn said. "On top of it you have some added pressures. First, I'm sure this is the last thing in the world that you expected." She nodded. "Second, you're filling in for an actress who died only a few days ago and you're having to learn a part and become a character you're unfamiliar with. Not to mention, you are working with one of the greatest directors out there."

"Don't remind me."

"These guys would not have hired you if they didn't believe in you. I can see it, too. You've got what it takes to make this all work. What you need to do with this scene is pretend that James—me—is your man. It's Derek, right? I've seen the way you look at that guy. Before you go back out there, get yourself in a state of passion. Think of the most romantic moment the two of you have ever had together. See yourself in that moment, and feel it. Then take those feelings and bring them onto the set, and I guarantee you'll nail it."

"You think so?"

"I know so. Now why don't you take an extra ten? I'll let them know that you need a few more minutes and then let's get this thing done."

"Okay." Shawn started to walk back to the set. "Hey, Shawn?" He turned. "Thanks." He waved at her. Maybe he wasn't so bad after all. Sure, he could have selfish reasons for wanting to get the scene wrapped, but that was okay. He hadn't been mean to her.

Now, to take his advice and think about the most romantic moment she'd spent with Derek; it wasn't hard. There had been plenty. What was difficult was that she had no idea if there would be any more between them. If only she could talk to him. A twinge of guilt struck her, knowing that if things had gone as originally planned they'd likely be touring the outback right now. Who would have guessed it would turn out like this? Just thinking about him though made her warm all over. The other day, when she'd pumped Sarah Fritz for gossip, he'd been so upset with her. But when she'd explained her reasons for caring about Lucy and her demise and he'd pulled the car over to kiss her—now that had been downright *hot*. Ooh boy, right down to her tippy toes. Yes, that kiss and that moment would have qualified as "romantic," at least in her book. Okay, she could do the scene now.

And she did. Returning to the set, she took Shawn's advice and as soon as she closed her eyes and visualized Derek's arms around her, the moment was golden.

"And . . . cut! Bravo," Nathan said. "I don't know what Shawn told you, but that was brilliant. That's what I want to see more of, Nikki. Exactly what you just did."

"Thank you."

Shawn winked at her. Now this was the high that came with acting, or just doing any good job, for that matter. Her buzz was killed though when Nathan called her over. Something in his tone said that, even though she'd just given a great performance, he either wanted more, or there was something else on his mind.

"Yes?"

"Kane and I wanted to speak with you. We have some concerns."

"I watched the scene you were shooting. I knew we made the right choice with you, Nikki," Kane said.

"Okay," Nikki replied. "So what's the problem?"

"It's a bit troublesome that Marne Pickett has

decided to pick on you. We had no idea when you did your TV show that you had been such a diva." Kane chuckled.

"Oh my God, you two of all people should know how these things work. I was never a diva." She proceeded to tell them what had gone down back then.

Kane shrugged. "The woman is a bitch. I think we can do something to put a kibosh on her story-telling."

"You do?"

"Yes."

"Good," Nathan said. "The last thing we need is any more negative publicity surrounding this picture. Lucy's death has been enough."

"Thanks." Nikki was still confused by what they wanted with her, but she also felt relieved. If anyone could help stop Marne from spreading lies it was probably someone like Kane, who had influence. Then again, stopping tabloid writers from doing their thing wasn't easy for anyone to do. Nothing was sacred. Not even the president, or even Jesus. A few weeks ago she'd read a headline in one of the tabloids that aliens were on their way with Jesus himself on board. If people believed stories like Jesus hanging with little green men from Mars, they wouldn't have to work too hard to buy into the diva story about her. And, why did she care? Because it wasn't true.

Nikki looked at Nathan, who sweated profusely,

which was odd, being that it was only about fifty degrees. "Are you okay?"

"I've been feeling a bit under the weather today," he replied.

"Yeah man, you do look pale," Kane said. "You know, we've done quite a bit today. It's already after three. Why don't we let everyone knock off early and you go and get some rest. The last thing we need is for you to get sick."

"I really wanted to shoot one more scene. Damn. But I do feel shitty. I'm sorry guys, but maybe I should go and rest."

Kane slapped him on the back. "Do that. I'll let everyone know."

"Thanks," Nathan said as he left.

"Since we're stopping early, would you want to join me and some others for dinner?" Kane asked.

Nikki thought about it for a moment, but all she really wanted to do was try and get ahold of Derek. She also had to find Simon. She'd only caught a few glimpses of him all day. She wondered if Derek said anything to him when he got back to the hotel room last night. "Thanks, but I think I'll follow Nathan's lead and get some extra rest. I'm not used to these long days." Not to mention she hadn't gotten more than four hours' sleep the night before.

Kane nodded. "It can be rough. But you're doing a great job, and don't you worry about Marne. Nathan and I were just wishing you'd mentioned it when you'd joined on. Marne Pickett can be one pain in the ass, and if I'd known she had a bone to pick with you, then I'd have had a strategy in place to deal with her."

Nikki got back to the motor home and called in to her voicemail. There were no messages from Derek. He must have been busy. She could understand that. Maybe he'd spoken to Liam. She could head up to the Hahndorfs' house and ask. She did want to talk to Liam about Elizabeth and the script, and gauge Grace if possible. She needed to talk with Liam alone but wasn't sure how that would happen.

She still believed that Grace was against the movie being made. Since the character Nikki was now playing had been Liam's lover in real life, had Grace lost perspective and seen Lucy as the *real* other lover from days gone by? Compounded with the fact that Grace didn't think much of Lucy hanging around Hannah, could she have gotten it in her head to do away with the actress? Grace claimed to be squeamish around snakes, but had she been dishonest about that? Had she taken enough mental notes to be able to handle a poisonous reptile and plant it in Lucy's bed?

Nikki was tired, but restless at the same time. Since she had time on her hands and unanswered questions on the brain, she figured there was no better time than the present to visit the Hahndorfs.

Chapter 26

Hannah answered the door and showed Nikki in. "G'day," she muttered. "Mum and Dad are in the kitchen." She held a book in her hand.

"Thank you. Hannah?"

"Yes?"

"About this morning, is there anything I can help you with? I mean, are you okay?"

"I'm fine. I have some reading to do."

"Okay. I can show myself in."

Hannah went back into the den off the side of the entrance and sat back down on a sofa without saying another word.

When Nikki had first met Hannah, she had thought the young women was strange and sullen, but now she found her more sad and withdrawn. Something was going on here at the Hahndorfs' house, and from what Nikki surmised, it was not a happy scene.

"I don't think it was a good idea to help out, Liam. I know your heart is in the right place. Hiring Will could cause problems, and with everything else we don't need it. You have to stop taking care of others and start taking care of yourself," Grace was saying as Nikki walked into the kitchen.

"Hi. Sorry. Hannah let me in. I was coming up to see how you're doing and if Derek has checked in with you." She wondered why hiring Will could cause them any problems. Was it because Grace knew that he'd gone out with the girls and Johnny? Maybe he was truthful in telling Nikki that he could be fired if anyone knew. Maybe it was why Hannah had been so upset. If Will was not supposed to be with them, and Grace was the hammer she seemed to be on her daughter's life, that could be where the tension was coming from. Yet she still did not understand why it would be such a big deal for Will to have met the others for drinks at the pub.

"Hello, Nikki." Grace circled around the counter where she'd been dicing onions. "Nice to see you. How are things going down on the movie set?"

Nikki could not tell if the concern was real. "It's been . . . interesting. Kind of tough."

"Tough, how so?" Liam asked. "Have a seat."

"Nathan is a stickler and I've had some difficulty getting things just so. But we're off early today because Nathan wasn't feeling well. I was actually supposed to do a scene with a kangaroo."

Liam smiled. "Yes, I remember."

Nikki noticed Grace eyeing him, but decided she might not get another chance to ask Liam about the script, or Elizabeth. "I've read the scene a number of times and it gives a good sense of who Elizabeth is as far as her love for the animals and her generosity, but there is something I feel I'm not getting right," she said. "There is some part of Elizabeth that I'm not dialing into, and as an actress I want to do the best I can by someone who did so many wonderful things for conservation."

"How can I . . . we help you?" Liam asked.

Grace leaned back and crossed her arms.

"You wrote the script. You knew her. Can you give me some more insight into who she was as a person, how she acted around people?"

Liam looked at Grace and then back at Nikki. The tension spread out thick, almost making Nikki wish she hadn't asked about it, but at the same time wondering what the real deal was between these two.

"You'll have to excuse me," Grace said. "I should get back to fixing dinner. We are expecting company tonight."

Liam looked at her as if he was surprised by this revelation. Nikki felt Grace was lying about any company. She just didn't like the topic of conversation.

"You know, I can come back another time."

"Oh no. This is a fine time. I'm only trying to get everything pulled together." Grace's body language told Nikki that she was not welcome. "Would you like to stay for dinner?"

"Oh no, I'm tired." Grace's tone also told her the same thing. It was the first real waft of coldness Grace had sent her way since they'd met. And it sent a chill down her spine and gave her the strong feeling that there had been no love lost between Elizabeth Wells and Grace Hahndorf.

"So you haven't heard from Derek then?" Liam asked.

"No." He was changing the subject and Nikki knew that if he was going to reveal anything about Elizabeth, and why the movie was so important to him, then she'd have to get him alone.

"You will. I'm sure of that."

"Yes. I better let you get back to your dinner preparations. I'm tired."

"I'll walk you out." Liam stood and walked down the hall with Nikki.

She peered into the den to say good-bye to Hannah. The girl was gone, but the book she'd been reading sat on a coffee table, and Nikki caught a glimpse of it: *The Illustrated Guide to Poisonous Snakes.*

At the door, Nikki turned to Liam. "It would be really helpful to talk to you about my character, Elizabeth. I know you two were . . . friends, and I'd really like to gain more insight into her. You wrote the script. I think you could help me better understand her."

"Yes. Maybe that would be a good idea," he replied. "Tomorrow morning. Six o'clock. I know you have to be on the set. I'll bring you down a bit of breakfast and we'll talk."

Nikki shut the door behind her with a lot of questions whirling in her head about the Hahndorfs.

Chapter 27

Nikki needed to know the timing of Liam and Elizabeth's relationship and how Grace came into the picture. They would be delicate questions to ask Liam, but there was one person who might know the answers, even if they were likely going to be embellished. She decided to drive over to Sarah Fritz's winery. First she needed to find Simon. He could keep her company and throw down his Jiu-Jitsu act if anyone bothered her. She smiled at the thought of that. Hopefully, no Marne Pickett or paparazzi would be stalking her.

"Where have you been? I've been trying to talk to you all day." Simon ran up alongside Nikki as she walked to her trailer. "Then after they wrapped I thought 'oh, now she'll find me,' but no. What is going on?"

"In case you hadn't noticed, they had me jumping through hoops today. We shot quite a few scenes."

"I did notice, but I kept trying to get your attention. Didn't you see me?"

"Yes, and I'm sorry. It was one of those days. But listen, why don't we get out of here? Go for a drive? There's a winery down the road and maybe we can do some tasting. It's just now five, so they'll probably still be open."

"That does sound fun. Can we bring Shawn?"

"No. It's you and me time."

"Let's go then. You need a little powwow with your BFF." He smiled.

"Exactly."

They got into the rental car, with Nikki driving.

"Okeydokey, Snow White, I need to know what is going on with you and Derek."

"What did he tell you?"

"Nothing. He said that you had decided to take Kane's offer to stay at the vineyard, and that he was leaving this morning to do some business and that he'd be back in a couple of days."

"Is that what he said?" She sped up.

"I knew it. I knew there was more to it."

"What makes you say that?" Derek must've known this was where she would come. And if so, since he hadn't come after her, did that mean it was over between them?

"He was pissier than I've ever seen him. Snapping at me for this and that until I finally went to bed. He said that I could have the hotel room, but I can see you need an ear. I've decided to stay in the motor home with you."

"Joy." She didn't mean to be sarcastic with him. In reality she wouldn't mind the company, and she could bounce some of her theories about Lucy's death off of him. Okay, he didn't buy into her sleuthing, but in the past he and Marco had been a big help in solving a couple of capers with her. She knew she could bend his ear, and the gossip alone would interest him. Plus, she wanted to learn if he'd heard any good dish himself that might tie into Lucy.

"Now, tell me what happened between you and my brother."

She gave him the scoop while driving toward the Fritz Winery.

"Ah, I see."

"See what?" Nikki asked.

"He's afraid and you're afraid."

"I'm not afraid . . . Afraid of what?" She turned onto the dirt road that led up to the winery.

"You're both afraid to jump in and see where this relationship will take you."

Nikki held up a finger. "I'll buy that as far as your brother is concerned, but I am more than—or at least I *was* more than—gung ho to jump in and see where a relationship could go."

"If that were true, would you have walked out so hastily on him?"

"What? Come on, he was second-guessing the relationship just because we hadn't had a chance to really be alone together. He was acting as if it was an omen directing the future. And, I might add, he never came after me."

Simon laughed. "Would you have let him? You know you're stubborn, and once you've made up your mind when you're angry, I think that it's best to leave you alone and allow you to sulk, pout, and overanalyze."

"I do not overanalyze!"

"Sure you don't. Here is what I really think."

"Do tell, Dr. Phil."

"I think the two of you love each other so much you can't stand it and it scares the hell out of you both. Neither of you have probably ever felt so deeply in love with someone. Especially someone who started out as your friend. Okay, I know there was always an attraction between the two of you. But you've been friends for going on three years now. To take your relationship to the next level, no matter how much you love one another, is scary because there is the thought in the back of your mind: What if you lose him? Or he's thinking, what if he loses you? Your subconscious is doing double-time for both of you. Because you know that it's better to be friends and close to each other than take that next step and possibly ruin everything. Because we both know that relationships are never, ever easy."

Nikki didn't know how to respond at first. She took a minute to really think about what Simon had said as she pulled up to the winery and stopped the car. "Where did all that come from? The Guru Sansibaba?" she finally asked.

"No. Actually it came from me. But I want to tell you something and I already said it to my brother: Marco and I started out as friends. You know we met at the nudophobia meetings." That made Nikki smile. Recently they'd revealed that they'd met each other at anonymous meetings for people who were afraid to be naked and/or see anyone else naked. "We were good friends for over a year until we realized that there was something deeper that we could explore, and we took a risk. Right now, things may never work out with Marco." He shrugged. "I don't know what's going to happen. But I tell you, as much as I miss him—and it's a lot, and it hurts—I would not have traded what we had and what I learned by going forward in our relationship. Even today I am still learning because I allowed myself to fall in love and really love Marco. And, I think if you and Derek don't allow that for each other, then in the end you'll be worse off than if you didn't ever take a chance."

"You really are a good friend. And, you're not as selfish as people say you are."

"I know. What are you going to do about Derek?"

"I'm going to talk to him when I see him. I guess that's the only thing to do." She opened the car door. "Thank you."

"Anytime. This place looks quaint." He wrinkled his nose while surveying the area.

Nikki knew that when Simon said the word "quaint," he didn't think much of it. "Come on, let's go in."

They went inside Sarah Fritz's barn/winery. This evening there was no one hanging around, and Sarah looked to be putting everything away for the evening. "Oh hullo. G'day. How are you?" She looked up from washing a wineglass.

"Are you closed?" Nikki asked.

"Never really closed." She laughed. "Have a seat. What would you like to try?"

"What's your best wine?" Simon asked.

So Simon—only the best.

"I prefer my Sauvignon Blanc. I'm the wine-maker as well as the owner."

"I'll give that a try," he replied.

She poured one for herself and one for Simon. When he took a sip, Simon nearly choked and spit it out.

"Go down the wrong way?" Sarah asked. "Care for some?" she asked Nikki.

"No thanks. I'm driving."

"Can I have some water please?" Simon asked.

"Me, too," Nikki said, trying not to laugh. Simon must have felt the same about Sarah's wine as Derek had.

"You were in here the other day with that other gentleman. The one making a deal with Liam Hahndorf," Sarah said. "Wait a minute, you're now starring in that movie they're making there. I saw you in the paper this morning."

"Afraid so."

"That writer sure said some nasty things about you."

"Yes, there is no love lost between us."

Sarah leaned on her elbows and lowered her voice, even though no one else was there. "Do you really think that Lucy Swanson was murdered?"

"I don't know."

Simon put his hands on his hips and faced her. "What's going on?" Nikki sighed. Simon knew her a little too well. "You are on some kind of fishing expedition here, aren't you? You didn't bring me here for the wine."

"What's his problem?" Sarah asked. "And what's he talking about?"

"The other day when I was in here you said some things about Grace and Liam Hahndorf and Elizabeth Wells, and now that I'm playing her I thought you might be able to enlighten me a bit more." Simon kicked her in the shin. "Ouch." Nikki gave him the evil eye.

Sarah smiled. "You want to know about what happened back then?"

"Yes. Maybe you can help me understand who Elizabeth was and what went on at the end of her relationship with Liam," Nikki said.

"Have you spoken with Grace at all about Elizabeth?"

"No. It does seem to be a bit of a touchy subject."

"I am sure of that. Everyone knows the truth. Elizabeth and Liam were lovers. I imagine Grace is coming undone over this movie because it must stir up everything again for her. You want the story about what happened with the three of them?"

"Yes."

"Liam Hahndorf and Elizabeth Wells both loved animals. Elizabeth more than Liam, but he fell in love with her at first sight. They were inseparable. But Elizabeth and Grace were best friends, too, and Grace pined for Liam, like many women around here did back then. Myself included. He is a fine-looking man."

Nikki nodded. "Yes. So what happened?"

"Grace seduced him one night at a party. He'd had an argument with Elizabeth, who wanted to have another go with the great white shark. He didn't want to do it, and he definitely did not want her to do it. When they made her first documentary, she nearly got herself killed and Liam didn't want that."

Nikki stopped her. "If he loved Elizabeth so much, how is it that Grace was able to seduce him?"

"He's a man. Liquor him up and make the moves. We're women. We all know how to do it."

Nikki didn't like hearing this at all. She believed that a man or woman in love could handle being seduced by another.

"It also didn't hurt Grace's case any when she told Liam that the reason Elizabeth didn't want to marry him and never would was because she truly belonged to her cause. And, I believe that is true. I think Liam knew it also, and in a weak moment he succumbed to Grace. I told you she is controlling and manipulative. Once Elizabeth found out about the betrayal, that's when she took off on her own expedition, and the rest is history. It would appear that the night Grace and Liam tangled, she wound up pregnant with Hannah, and so there you have it. The man is weak, loses the love of his life, blames himself for it, and then does the honorable thing by marrying the pregnant cow."

"What about Hannah? She does not seem like a very happy young woman."

Simon sighed. "This is a bad soap opera. Oh, go ahead and pour me some more of that *wine*, if I have to listen to this."

"He always so gracious?" Sarah asked, pouring him a new glass.

"Always." Nikki turned to him, knowing what he was about to do. "Don't you dare kick me," she said, and then faced Sarah again. "Do you know anything about Hannah?"

"You know they've had some trouble with Hannah being a bit of a party girl, but my goodness, she is a grown woman. She and her mother have different ideas about her future. Hannah has always wanted to go into zoology. Ever since she was a girl. I've known her all her life basically, and she was always into the animals, which of course gets right under Grace's skin because that's who Elizabeth was. It's ironic that here Grace stole Liam from Elizabeth and they had this child together who wants to be exactly like Grace's nemesis. I think it's rather humorous. Hannah will get her way from the looks of it, though."

"What do you mean?" Nikki asked.

"I've seen Hannah and Andy Burrow hanging out together and if you ask me she has eyes for him and he looks to be returning the affection. That won't make her parents happy. They've known Andy for years, too. As a matter of fact, Hannah and Andy Burrow came to the winery last evening."

"Really? I was with them over dinner at the Hahndorfs' last night." Nikki glanced at Simon.

"They came in early, maybe five or so, and they were pretty cozy. Although at one point Hannah got upset and Andy comforted her."

"Andy is old enough to be her father," Simon interjected.

"Love doesn't know age. To Hannah, it's probably pretty romantic. Here is this Aussie hero type, one who is involved with animals like she wants to be, and he's doting on her." Sarah finished off her wine in one fell swoop.

"Did you get the sense that he meant it? You know, that he was really into Hannah?"

"My opinion, yup."

"Nikki, we should get back," Simon said. "I'm hungry and I want a glass of wine."

"What do you think that is?" Sarah pointed to his wineglass.

Simon frowned. "Nikki, come on."

"You better take your friend home. Looks like he turns into a pumpkin when it grows dark."

Nikki apologized and said good-bye. Back in the car she turned to Simon. "What was that all about? Why did you have to be so rude to her?"

"I don't like her. There's something wrong with her."

"You sound like your brother. I would have thought that you would have loved town gossip."

"No. What I would love is a good glass of vino and that tasted like horse piss."

"You drank it."

"I had to in order to swallow all her banter. She is a liar, Nikki. I can feel it."

"Now are you going to tell me you have a built-in lie detector, kind of like your gaydar?"

"No. I don't know what it is . . . maybe I'm like Derek in some way. I really don't like when people talk so negatively about someone who has been nothing but nice to me, and Grace has been. She came down to the set earlier and we talked. I like her."

"Wait a minute. She was down on the set today? I didn't see her."

"She was there for a little while."

"What did she want?" Nikki asked.

"I don't know. I guess to watch a bit. But we got

to talking and I was telling her about Marco, and she gave me some sage advice. She said that people will do anything for love, give up anything, go the distance. That's what love is. I thought it was beautiful, what she said."

Nikki didn't know how to respond. She had a lot going on in her mind. First off, everything that Sarah had told them about Grace and Liam and Elizabeth. Was it true, or was Simon right? Was the woman a liar? What she said made sense. It did. But what about Grace showing up on the set? Nikki hadn't seen her. She would have thought that Grace would want to stay as far away from the set as possible.

They made it back to the vineyard. Will was at the security kiosk. "Nice evening?" he asked.

"Oh hunky-dory," Simon replied.

Will looked at him strangely and Nikki said, "It was nice. Thank you." She drove on up to the RV. "You need to really behave yourself."

"I'm sorry. I'm a bit hungry, and it makes me grumpy if I don't eat. I think my sugar levels are dropping."

"Right. Why didn't you go into acting?"

"Funny. So what are we going to eat?" he asked.

Once inside the motor home, she hunted through the cabinets, which to her delight were stocked with food, bottled water, soda, and even wine. "Hey, check this out. Lucy must have demanded all of this." She pointed to the food. "I think I can whip us up something."

"Where is that wine?"

"On its way." She opened a bottle and poured him a glass.

"Now this is good," Simon said.

"I'm glad you're happy." She found tomato soup, macaroni and cheese, and fixings for a salad. "Comfort food coming soon."

"Goody."

They took out plates and bowls and ate their comfort food while splitting the rest of the wine. Talk turned to the set and the movie. "It's hard," Nikki replied when Simon asked how things were really going. "I don't know how I'm doing. I suppose okay, because we are getting through it, but under the conditions of first Lucy's bizarre death, and now Marne Pickett haunting me, it's kind of tough. How about you? What do you think of things around here?"

"Interesting. I've never been on a movie set before. It's kind of like its own little city here, with pretty much everything one needs all set up. And then you have the pecking order—which, by the way, I am not low man on the totem pole."

She laughed. "You're not, huh?"

"No way. They all buy into my Jiu-Jitsu act. I think I have them scared to death of me."

"Who is low man on the totem pole then?"

"Who knows, really. What I do know is that

Amy and Harv haven't scored points with many people around here."

"Tell me about it."

"I thought that Harv might be cool and we could hang out," Simon said. "But he's rude. And that Amy may know how to pick out clothes, but she's a real bitch. I tried to take her a cup of coffee because I heard her tell Harv she wanted one, and she said that she changed her mind, when I went to give it to her."

"Why do you think they're like that?"

"Who knows? Superiority complex."

"I know they didn't like Lucy much. Maybe they did her in."

Simon laughed. "Come on. Why?"

"Because she was horrible to them."

"So what? That's showbiz. Actresses are awful to people all the time. I doubt it bothers those two very much. You're not still on this kick about Lucy's death being a murder? Is that why we just took the trip down to that so-called winery?"

"Yes I am, and yes that's why." Nikki went into everything she'd discovered, from Hannah's book on poisonous snakes, to Liam's love for the real Elizabeth Wells and Grace's jealousy, to the fact that Johnny, Hannah, and Lucy partied with Will the security guard the night that Lucy died. Then of course there was Shawn's contentiousness with Lucy, along with Kane's. Nikki had started wondering if Kane might have killed Lucy just because she was setting the schedule back with her temper tantrums. A new actress could get the movie done on time and for less money. That could be, but if so, why wouldn't he have just fired her? Of course there was also Andy Burrow, who knew how to handle poisonous snakes, was certain that his suit had been moved, and then had changed his story.

"Okay, I'll play Nancy Drew with you. I think I'm just about tipsy enough." Simon retrieved a second bottle of wine. "There is a hole where Andy is concerned. Why would he tell the cops that his suit had been moved and set on a different peg and then change his story to say that he must have been mistaken?"

"Good question. Why exactly." Nikki took the refilled glass from him. "Thanks. Last one for me. I'm feeling it." She took a sip. "That is a really good question. Maybe it was to deflect attention away from himself as a killer."

"Huh?"

"Think about it. He tells this story about his suit before he even realizes that the cops have basically dismissed the entire thing as an accident. Maybe he was covering his butt before he even needed to. Once he realized that the cops were not handling this as a possible murder case, he sang a different tune." Nikki theorized.

"Maybe, but I think Andy is really on the up-and-up," Simon said.

Nikki shrugged. "I don't know. I've also wondered if security guard Will might have been dazzled—and seduced—by Lucy and then have turned on her. He may also know how to handle a snake. He grew up around here. They all seem to have antivenom or know how to treat a bite. What if Lucy did something to upset him after the fact? I already know she was teasing him at the bar and he left because Hannah told him Lucy was only putting him on. Actually, Hannah's another one I've had some serious suspicions about. There's something off about Hannah Hahndorf."

"What about her?"

"Hannah has been friends with Will since they were kids. They all had drinks together the night that Lucy died. Johnny said that they crashed Grace's car after being run off the road by someone else, which no one really believes. Hannah is also into zoology. She's buddy-buddy with Andy. I saw a book in the den where she'd been reading when I was there earlier—on poisonous snakes."

"Where are you going with this?"

"Okay, so if Hannah and Will are pals, and Hannah is friends with Andy, and Hannah wrecked her mom's car while partying with Lucy and Johnny, and Grace had a conniption. Then, Lucy treated her friend Will like he was a piece of you know what. And finally, Lucy had been demeaning toward Andy and his animals, both of which Hannah loves. What if Hannah did away with Lucy? She has the know-how and the motive. Andy Burrow could be thinking the same thing, or maybe he even knows for sure, since Hannah had been with him the night Lucy died, checking on the animals. Maybe that's why she was crying on his shoulder at Sarah Fritz's place. He could be covering for Hannah because he cares for her on more than a friend level, or simply because of his ties to her family. But what I *can* for sure tell you is that when Hannah found out Lucy was dead, her reaction was strange."

"Too much *Law & Order*, that's your problem," Simon said, slurring his words.

"No. I don't think so. I think I am on to something. I believe that Hannah Hahndorf may have killed Lucy Swanson. Now I have to prove it."

Chapter 28

The next morning before six, Liam showed up with food and coffee. Simon had agreed to Nikki's request for some space when she said that Liam was coming by and that she needed to speak with him. He'd gone for a walk to try and burn off the calories from the night before, although he wasn't happy about having to rise at such an early hour.

After they'd stayed up talking, with Simon telling her repeatedly that her theories were out in left field and she should really concentrate on her film, she'd done exactly that and picked up the articles about Elizabeth. She'd read about Elizabeth's contributions to the world of wildlife and what her ethics had been. It was interesting, but didn't give Nikki much insight as to who she was. She'd also watched one of the documentaries that Kane had given her, about sharks. Elizabeth, an attractive woman, had been kind to all animals. She also appeared shy, almost childlike, but she had a quiet strength about her. Nikki could see why Elizabeth would have appealed to so many people. She hadn't gotten all the way through the documentary because she'd grown tired and finally shut it off, vowing to watch all three that Kane had given her soon.

Liam knocked on the door after she'd showered, and she was relieved to see he'd shown up. She was nervous, too, but so far she'd found Liam Hahndorf open and generous. Although she knew it was a sensitive subject, she figured the best tactic to take would be to get right to the point. After she buttered a croissant he'd brought and took a sip of coffee, she sat down across from him.

"You have questions about Elizabeth?" he asked—again, that sadness in his eyes shone through.

"I do. You loved her."

"Yes. I did. Very much. Elizabeth Wells was a wonderful woman."

"I can tell by what I've read about her and by the

script you wrote. I want to portray her as best I can. Can you give me some insight?"

"I've seen some of the dailies, and I've been on the set a few times during shooting and to be truthful, your portrayal of Elizabeth is astounding."

"I didn't know that you had been on the set." She needed to start paying more attention. Both Liam and Grace had been around and she hadn't noticed.

"I have, a couple of times, but it has also been painful for me."

"You want this movie made, don't you?"

"Of course I do. It's important to me."

Nikki nodded. "I get the feeling it is not as important to Grace."

Liam didn't reply. He held his stomach for a moment. Nikki noticed the color drain from his face.

"Liam? Are you okay?"

"I'm feeling a bit ill. Sorry. Excuse me." He stood and went into the bathroom.

Nikki sat there, baffled. She was sure she heard him vomiting. Poor man. He came out a few minutes later, pale and sweating. "Sit down, please. Should I go and get Grace?"

"No. Please don't. It'll upset her. No, don't do that."

"Can I get you anything?"

"No. Sit down. I have to tell you something. It's

important that I tell you now. I didn't want anyone to know. But for you, for the part you are playing as Elizabeth, it is important that I explain everything. But first you must promise me, you can't tell anyone. Only a few people know, including Derek."

"What does Derek know? What are you talking about?"

Tears filled Liam's eyes. "He knows that I'm dying."

Chapter 29

Nikki was shaken by Liam's story. "Cancer?" She had to repeat herself. "You're sure."

He smiled. "I've known for about a year. It's my second bout with it, but this time it appears it's going to get me."

"Oh no. I'm so sorry, Liam."

He explained to her that seven years earlier he'd been diagnosed with stomach cancer, then it had gone into remission. It was back now, and had spread to his liver and his bones. "I wrote Elizabeth's story years ago. Remember how I'd told you that I'd been writing for a bit? Her story—your story now—is one of my first scripts, only meant for me. But learning that my demise was imminent, I dusted off the script and sent it to Kane, who had been involved with us on a documentary years back. I also sent it to Andy because of who he is, and because he also knew Elizabeth. She is one of the reasons Andy started his zoo. It was her passion for the animals that drew Andy in and, bless him, he has done wonders for the animal kingdom."

"This tribute to her is because of your illness?"

"Kane doesn't know and neither does Nathan. You and Derek know now, and of course Grace. We have not told Hannah."

"Does Hannah know about you and Elizabeth? I mean the past?"

"I am sure she's heard the rumors, but Hannah is a good girl and we have done what we could to shelter her. Her mother and I both told her that Elizabeth had only been a friend of ours, and that was it. I hope she is convinced, but I had to do this. You see, Nikki, when you're dying you start thinking about all the mistakes you've made, the people you've hurt, and you realize that if you had to do it all over again you would do everything in your power never to hurt anyone again. Never say a harsh word. Never tell a lie or connive. You'd avoid all of that, if you could do it over again. It's terribly tragic really that we don't come to these conclusions in our youth, when we are so apt to hurt others."

"So you think about these things and you want to make amends. My problem is, I have made too many mistakes and have too many amends to make." He laughed, but his laughter was edged with sadness. "It may sound crazy but I feel this need to make amends with Elizabeth even though she is gone, and I also need to make amends with my wife. I am still stuck between the two."

"I can see that." She wasn't sure she understood, but she could feel the man's pain.

"It's a long story. But basically I fell in love with Elizabeth. Grace fell in love with me. Both Elizabeth and I made mistakes. I made a bigger one, or at least I thought so at the time when I had an affair with Grace. It was a mistake because I blame myself for Elizabeth taking off on the trip by herself. The trip where she was killed. What isn't a mistake is my daughter and, I can tell you, I am convinced now that my marriage is not a mistake either. For a long time I thought it was. I married Grace because of the pregnancy. For years there has been turmoil between us. My plan was to leave when Hannah was old enough. Then I got sick the first time and Grace was my savior. For the first time in our lives we became friends. She was with me night and day, researching the best doctors, best treatment, all of it, and I fell in love with her. I did. I love her so very much and I know making this movie about Elizabeth is upsetting her, and the only way I know how to make it up to her is to make the deal that I did with Derek."

"What do you mean?" Nikki asked.

"We have money, yes. But I want to be assured that Grace and Hannah—and in the future

Hannah's children—will be taken care of. The deal with Derek and Malveaux Winery assures me of that. Grace is not a businessperson, and Hannah does not want this winery. She wants to go into zoology and she should, although we would rather she didn't because of the dangers. Her mother is against it, but I am trying to convince her to let Hannah follow the path she chooses. The friction between them is making the two of them miserable. With Derek overseeing the wines coming into the States, those sales will be the big profit maker and my family will never have a care in the world. It's all I know to do.

"Grace sees this movie as a competition between her and Elizabeth. It's not. Elizabeth is my past, and I want her to be honored for the woman she was. I am not honoring her because she was my lover. That is what my wife does not understand.

"I have so many regrets, but the biggest one is that I looked back so many times in my life at what I missed instead of looking at what I had. If only I could make Grace see that she is the love of my life now. Our marriage and our child were never a mistake."

Nikki smiled. "I think I know how you can help convince her you feel that way."

"You do?"

"Yes."

Chapter 30

At first Liam was hesitant about Nikki's suggestion, but after some convincing, he believed it could work. Nikki's problem was that in reality, either of the Hahndorf women could still be a killer. Hannah especially looked to be a good candidate, but at the same time, if Nikki discovered that to be true, it could cause great amounts of grief to an already dying man. Nikki did bring up the car accident and what Grace had said about Hannah lying to Liam. Liam's answer satisfied her. It wasn't the big deal Nikki thought it might have been. Hannah had originally told her parents that she'd been the one driving the car when the truth was that she had allowed Lucy to drive. Lucy had crashed the car, not Hannah.

Regardless of whether or not Hannah or Grace were murderers, Nikki was still going to do what she'd suggested, as long as Nathan and Kane went for it. It involved one little tweak in the script. If the schedule remained unchanged, then the scene she wanted to alter would be shot the following morning.

Nikki also pondered the remark that Sarah Fritz had made when she'd met her for the first time about Grace being the one behind the business. Liam had a completely different story. Nikki was starting to believe that Sarah Fritz's opinion of

Grace Hahndorf could be more of a personal nature than anything else. It was almost as if Grace had done something in the past to upset Sarah.

After Liam left, Nikki headed to the set. Shawn approached her. "Ready to roll?"

"I am."

"Good. I think it's all going splendid and you and me . . . well, I think we have great chemistry. What do you think?"

Nikki knew she was blushing. "Yeah, I do think we have good on-screen chemistry."

"Off screen, too." He smiled and walked away.

Shawn Keefer was flirting with her. Any woman in her right mind would be flattered by it, but it bugged her. The last thing she needed Marne thinking was that she saw Shawn on the side.

The first scene of the shoot was with Sophie the kangaroo since they hadn't gotten to it yesterday. Nathan appeared to be feeling much better and Nikki prayed she'd nail it because she didn't want to go through another day of reprimands.

Andy brought Sophie onto the set. It was a simple scene where all Nikki had to do was go in and feed her, exactly like she had done yesterday morning in the enclosure.

"Okay, love, everything should go as planned. Got the treats ready?" Andy asked.

"Yes."

"Good."

"Quiet on the set. And action!" yelled Nathan.

And action it was. Nikki walked up to Sophie as they'd practiced, held out her hand to feed the animal, who sniffed the hand, took the treats, and then without warning threw a jab at her. Nikki ducked, weaved, and ran with the kangaroo bouncing around the cage after her, jabbing at her all the while.

Andy opened up the cage. Nikki ran out and looked around at everyone who'd been watching and they were all in hysterics, including Simon. She looked back at Sophie inside the cage, who still had a look of "get your ass back in here so I can kick it" in her eyes. Nikki turned to Andy. "I thought you said she liked me!"

He shrugged. "She's a female, what can I say." He was chuckling, too. "Guess she changed her mind."

"I loved that!" Nathan said. "We're keeping it. It'll add a nice comedic touch to the movie."

"Glad everyone else found it so funny that a kangaroo wanted to kick my ass," Nikki said. But when she said it she couldn't help but start laughing herself.

Simon patted her on the back. "Nice going, Tyson."

"Thanks. I think."

After the bout with Sophie, the day passed quickly, with Shawn continuing to gently flirt. Nikki couldn't tell if he was really coming on to her or if this was how he always behaved on the set when he became comfortable with his leading lady.

After dark, Simon asked her what she wanted to do about dinner.

"I don't know. I wouldn't mind going into town, but that's not so easy with Marne Pickett hanging around. By the way, have you heard from Derek?"

"Nope. Heard from Marco?"

"No. I'd really like to check my e-mail. But I don't have a computer."

"Why don't you ask Nathan?" Simon suggested. "I know that he has a laptop in his monster home."

"Not a bad idea. Why don't you start thinking about what we might conjure up for dinner?"

"Oh I see, I'm the manservant now. Just because you can escape from a deranged kangaroo doesn't mean you can boss me around."

She laughed. "I beg to differ. Go make me some dinner."

She walked over to Nathan's RV and knocked. Nathan opened the door, a beer in his hand. Kane and Shawn were also inside. "Hey, guys?" she said. "What's going on?"

"Nikki. We were just having a beer, and thinking about heading into town for a bite to eat. You care to join us?" Nathan asked.

"I don't think so. That Marne Pickett might be lurking around."

"Oh, screw the bitch. We can handle her. Come on with us," Shawn said.

She was hungry and she knew Simon would be happy as a clam to go out to dinner with these guys. It might be too much for her, though. She still wasn't sure about Shawn's come-ons, and opening herself up to any more of them was probably not a great idea. "I'd really hate to run into Marne, and I was only coming by to see about checking my e-mail. It's been a while and my aunt usually writes." That's all they needed to know.

"Don't worry about Marne. We won't take no for an answer. Check your e-mail," Kane said. "We'll finish up in my trailer and be back in twenty minutes. You're coming with us. We all need a break. God, I sure can't wait until we get home."

"Are you kidding? I love this outback shit," Shawn said. "Nothing like camping."

"This isn't camping," Nathan said. "Camping is with a tent and a can of beans, and you freeze your ass off. Kane, you have to be spending a fortune to style us all out."

Kane gulped his beer. "Now you know why I want to get this thing wrapped up. Hey, is Andy going with us? Where is that guy?"

"I think he's hanging out with the Hahndorf girl again."

"Sounds naughty," Kane said.

They laughed. Nikki studied them. Guys were

just . . . guys, right? "Come on let's give her some space," Nathan said. "We'll be back and then we'll head out. Someone was saying there's this place in town that has great food. My laptop is by the bed back there. Can you believe we've got Wi-Fi even out here?"

"Thanks. I'll be quick. Oh, can Simon come?" She'd go, but not without her pal.

"Sure," Kane said. "Good idea. He can be the bodyguard. That way we don't have to call in one of those security dudes. He really does know Jiu-Jitsu, right?"

"He . . . knows about a lot of things."

"Good. See you two soon."

Nathan's computer was already on. She checked her e-mail. Nothing from Derek. And, sadly enough, nothing from Marco either. Aunt Cara had written wanting to know what was going on with her. She was in Greece exploring the ruins and would be traveling on to Italy later in the year. Ah, the life of a retiree. She was grateful that her aunt didn't read the tabloids and that she hadn't heard what Nikki was up to. She was sure she'd catch some grief from her. Aunt Cara had always wanted her to follow in her footsteps and go into law enforcement. She sort of had, in her own amateur way.

She prepared to shut down Nathan's computer and bite the bullet by going out to dinner with the guys, but then noticed Nathan's favorites. She knew it was wrong to look, but curiosity was not something that could be easily squashed. As she scanned the list of Nathan's faves, she suddenly wished that she hadn't. He had a folder for favorite actresses. No biggie, right? He was a director after all, so that made sense. What she found disturbing was all the files he had were on Lucy Swanson, like he was obsessed with her. So, maybe he just wanted to know all he could about her. After all, she'd been his star only a few days ago. But Nikki's gut said there was more. She searched the files and came up with one that held poem after poem about Nathan Cooley's love for and obsession with the young actress. She scanned as much as she could quickly because she knew they'd be back soon. What caught her eye was a line in the last poem he'd written—the day she died. It read: *If I can't have you in this life, I pray it will be in the next.*

A chill crawled down her spine. She reread the last line a few more times.

"Nikki? You coming?"

She immediately closed the file and spun around. Nathan Cooley stood in the doorway of the RV. "We're waiting."

"Sure. Right now." She forced a smile and couldn't help wondering if she was walking out the door with a killer.

Thank God she was seated in the back with Shawn and Simon. After reading what Nathan had written, she had no desire to sit next to him. Shawn was being attentive and told her again what a great job she was doing.

"Isn't she, though?" Simon asked. "The two of you are golden."

"Yes, I think we are," Shawn replied.

They pulled up in front of the restaurant. She reached for her door handle, but Shawn said, "No, no. I'll get it."

"Don't be silly," Nikki replied, but too late. Shawn ran around the car and opened the door for her, reaching for her hand. She took it, and then something happened that caught her completely off guard for more reasons than one. Shawn put an arm around her and said, "I really do want you to know that I think you're awesome."

Then he kissed her on the cheek, and as he did, a flash went off. Nikki, wide-eyed and in disbelief, turned to see Marne Pickett and her photographer in front of the restaurant. Shawn started ranting at the photographer and yelling at Marne to give them the film. The photographer fled; Marne laughed and sauntered away.

Chapter 31

"That was great," Nikki muttered as a waiter brought over an expensive bottle of Bordeaux. "I'm sure she'll run with that photo and make up all sorts of lies." She glanced over at Simon, who'd been told to stand at the front door of the restaurant in case Marne or any other paparazzi vultures showed up. He didn't look too pleased about it, and neither was she. She would have much preferred him at the table with her. She was tempted to tell them the only kind of protection Simon could possibly offer would be to bitch slap someone, so that his bodyguard image would be blown to bits and she would have a pal at her side, but she refrained.

Kane waved a hand at her. "Nikki, that's show business. That's what those maggots do. They cause all sorts of grief for actors. It's the price you pay. What you have to do is learn to ignore it."

"Ignore Marne Pickett? Please. And how do I do that?"

"He's right, love," Shawn said.

Love? Oh no, no, no. What was the deal here? First all the compliments, the comment about the chemistry between them, and now he was calling her "love." No one else seemed the least bit concerned that the paparazzi were following them around. "I'm involved with someone." Maybe not any longer, but these guys didn't need to know that, and if Marne Pickett twisted that photograph in her deranged mind, Nikki knew that she and Derek would have no chance in hell of ever working anything out.

"Derek Malveaux? Is he your guy? I thought you just worked for him," Nathan said.

Oh boy. Shawn had picked up on the fact they were seeing each other. He'd suggested she visualize Derek in her mind prior to doing the romantic scene yesterday. How had Nathan not noticed? "It's kind of a new thing. Yes, we do work together, but we are . . . dating."

"Cool. Where is he?" Kane asked. "Haven't seen him around for a couple of days? Did he head back to the States?"

She took a sip of wine and tried to keep her hand from shaking. She didn't know if she was trembling out of anger, fear, or from being put on the spot. "He's actually in western Australia checking out some business opportunities. We've started distributing international wines in the States and labeling them with the Malveaux name. I was supposed to go with him to check out some of the wineries, but the movie came up."

Kane nodded. "Good. I'm sure Derek will understand that whatever Marne Pickett chooses to write is a crock. What are you afraid of anyway? All they got was a picture of Shawn with his arm around you. It's not a big deal."

"No. He kissed me, too."

"Oh God, come on, on the cheek."

"Come on? You all know how a photo like that can be misconstrued. The next thing you know we'll be linked as lovers." She looked at Shawn, who smiled. "Doesn't that bother you?"

He shrugged. "I'm used to it. In one flick I did,

I was supposedly having an affair with Julia Roberts and her husband was leaving her, which was absurd. We all had a good laugh over it. Look, you're going to have to lighten up and roll with it. Like Kane said, these people are maggots and they make up all sorts of stuff. I can tell you one thing: publicity of us being lovers before the release of the movie isn't a bad thing. It gets people into the theater."

"It's a bad thing when you're in a relationship. That's why people break up all the time in Hollywood," Nikki replied.

"You've read one too many of those magazines," Kane said. "Now come on, it'll work out. Let's order."

Nikki wasn't sure that *any* of this was going to work out, but she could see that none of these guys were on the same wavelength as her, so she ordered her dinner and tried to get comfortable with them.

They made small talk about the movie industry before dinner came, and Nikki had herself two full glasses of wine. She was completely out of her element and knew she shouldn't be drinking, but it was helping her get through the meal, which was actually delicious. She'd noticed that Shawn was going through quite a bit of wine himself.

Halfway through the meal, with either enough liquid courage or stupidity flowing through her, she turned to Kane. "So what's your story? How did you get into this business?"

"It's not interesting. Shawn's story is better than mine."

Shawn shook his head. "Go on, tell her. Your story *is* interesting. What you probably don't know is that Kane started out as a filmmaker, producer, director, writer, even an actor. Man, you did it all. You are the man."

"I didn't know that you did all that," Nikki said.

"Yeah, documentaries were your thing, right?" Nathan asked.

Kane nodded. "I was into that for a while, but then I met Shawn and saw a star. That was my ex-wife's gig—the documentaries—so she stayed with it, and I went in another direction. Not a lot of money in documentaries. I wanted to produce big-time action films and mega movies. Shawn and I hooked up and we've done that."

Shawn nodded, but wasn't as enthusiastic about Kane's story. "That we have. Lots of movies together." He smacked Kane hard on his back. "I do whatever Kane needs. I am his superstar, aren't I? Love those movies."

"Don't you like making the big films?" Nikki asked.

"Oh I love it, *love*. Didn't I just say so?" He looked at Kane.

"It's getting late," Kane said. "What do you say we all head out?"

"I wouldn't mind another drink. I think Nikki and I should talk some more," Shawn said. "I get the feeling she could really understand me. Wouldn't that be a good thing, Kane?"

"Not tonight. I think we should get back. You ready Nathan?"

Nathan nodded and looked as bewildered as Nikki felt. They paid the bill and headed out. It was a quiet drive home and Nikki was relieved to get back into the RV with Simon, who was not pleased with her.

"Real nice. Thanks a lot, Snow White," Simon ranted once they got back inside.

She held out the doggie bag. "I got you food to go."

He snatched it from her. "Food to go. Woo-hoo. You're all tight and cozy with your movie-making friends, and what am I now, chopped liver? Having to stand at the door. Jeesh."

"'Jeesh' yourself. Get over it. You were the one who said you could go all Rambo on people. Kane assured me that Marne Pickett wouldn't be lurking, but she obviously was, and so you had to do your job. Remember, you were the guy who claimed to be my bodyguard." He started to say something. "Uh-uh, I would seriously think before I opened my mouth with one of your smart-ass comebacks. I want you to keep in mind that the reason you had to stand at the door tonight is because of choices *you* made. Not me."

He stared at her and then peered into the bag. "You should be somebody's mother," he mumbled. He took out the foam box from the bag and opened up his steak dinner.

Nikki left to put her pajamas on. When she returned, Simon had poured them both a glass of port. "Sorry," he said. "I guess I was a little jealous is all."

"It's okay. I'm sorry you couldn't have joined us. Trust me, I would have rather had you at the table. There were some strange dynamics going on between Kane and Shawn."

"What do you mean?" Simon asked.

"I don't know. It was almost like an undercurrent of dislike from Shawn toward Kane—something I had not picked up until tonight. Granted Shawn had quite a bit to drink, and so did I, so I appreciate the after dinner drink here, but I think I'll have a glass of water instead."

"Suit yourself, Snow White. I didn't get to party like a rock star."

She shook a finger at him. "Don't start that again."

"You know that a lot of times when people drink, real feelings come out. Maybe there is a problem between Shawn and Kane. I could try to talk to Shawn about it."

"Mind your own business."

"Look who's talking," Simon replied.

"I know, you're right. Hey I have to watch the

rest of those documentaries on Elizabeth. Care to join me?"

He shrugged. "Why not? I'm all about KPBS and National Geographic."

They settled back into the bed and first watched one on koalas, kangaroos, and other marsupials. Again, all Nikki learned from it was that Elizabeth was as decent as everyone suggested. The production credits went to the Ferrisses. Nothing new. She'd watched part of the shark documentary the night before, so she decided to pop in the other one. She looked over at Simon, who was starting to fade. "You should go to bed," she suggested.

"No, no. I'm good."

She didn't have the heart to make him leave. She started the movie, which to her horror was about reptiles. A young Andy Burrow was there, smiling and assisting Elizabeth, who handled all of the reptiles, from poisonous snakes to crocodiles to some kind of poisonous lizard. And then, something happened that made her pause the DVD, reverse it a few frames, then play it in slow motion.

Elizabeth had a snake in her hands—a brown snake—and then she handed it off to another woman. Nikki looked closely and replayed it again, then again. That woman . . . yes, she recognized her. She was younger and much thinner, but it was her, same scar on her face and same red hair—it was Sarah Fritz.

Chapter 32

The following morning there was a quick meeting with regard to the change to the script that Liam was suggesting. Nikki did not want Kane or Nathan to know that she was the one who had initiated it. The day before, she'd thought there was a good chance that one of the Hahndorf women had killed Lucy, and she hadn't ruled them out completely, but now there was a strong possibility that Nathan Cooley had actually been the killer, considering the poems and letters he'd written to Lucy. That reminded her of the crumpled up note she'd found in Lucy's jacket the other day. And what about Kane Ferriss and Shawn Keefer? And now, Sarah Fritz.

What she did know about Sarah was that she didn't have any affection toward Grace Hahndorf. She had no problem talking trash about Grace, and Nikki knew she'd been involved in that documentary with Elizabeth and Liam. The woman knew how to handle snakes. But what could be her motive for killing Lucy? That was one Nikki had not been able to figure out yet. She had to go back to the Fritz Winery again and speak with Sarah. There was no other way around it. She wondered if she could get Simon to tag along again.

First she would have to endure the day of shooting and then she would figure out how she could go and see Sarah.

Both the producer and director agreed with Liam's script change. They shot one scene prior to it. Nikki saw that Liam had brought Grace down to the set. She hoped the revised scene would work to convince Grace that her husband truly loved her and had not pushed for the movie to be made because he was still devoted to Elizabeth.

Elizabeth is sitting on the porch of the farmhouse, her head resting on her arms. James drives up, and she immediately stands and starts screaming at him to leave. She never wants to see him again. He comes toward her and she is still yelling at him. He begs her to listen. She takes a step back and squares her jaw. "What is it that you have to say?"

"I'm sorry, Elizabeth. We both know that it can't work between us. It never could. You don't love me, at least not the way I need to be loved. Your love is for your animals. For the wild. There isn't enough left for me, and I didn't mean for it to happen between me and Gail." He wipes the sweat from his brow.

James continues: "But it did *happen, and she loves me and I love her. I really do. It's best this way."*

"You're right. It is," Elizabeth says. "The animals are what is important and I can't ever be a

wife, James. Not ever. Go to her. Be with her, because that is where you belong."

James gets back into his car and Elizabeth stands on the porch with tears in her eyes.

"Cut! That was wonderful," Nathan said.

Nikki glanced at Liam and Grace. At first she couldn't read Grace's expression. Her face was pale and she stood there, not reacting for about a minute. Liam was watching her, too. No one else noticed because they hadn't realized what the two of them had done. Then Grace looked up at Liam and Nikki could see the tears. She put her arms around her husband and leaned into his chest. Liam stroked the top of her head. A minute later, Liam took his wife by the hand and they walked off the set. Nikki brushed her own tears away.

"Nikki, are you all right?" It was Shawn.

"Yes. Feeling kind of, I don't know . . ."

"Off? Too much wine from last night. I know I had too much."

"I think I'm having a hard time blending real life here into a movie." The scene she'd witnessed between Liam and Grace was exactly what she'd hoped for, but it also made her realize that what she was doing by making this movie had so many implications. These were people's lives, and all of it hit her at once, especially thinking about Liam dying. "You guys make movies. You *pretend*. And I don't know if I can keep doing this."

He put an arm around her. "Of course you can do it. I understand that the lines can get a little blurred, but you have to be a professional. You have to learn to go into character and out of character. When you're out, you do real life. This is only a job."

"Is that all it is?"

He nodded. "It is."

"Do you like what you do?"

"Sometimes I'm not sure, but I'm a professional, so I do it. I get it done. Now, what do you say we get back to work?"

"I would say that's being professional."

"Good."

The rest of the day wasn't as eventful as the morning, though they had to do a lot of reshooting because Nikki was not on her game.

Finally the day ended, and Nikki was back in the RV sans Simon, who had gone into town—oddly enough—in Harv's car. Harv had invited him. Simon was bored and Harv was hot, even though he was a jerk. And of course, in Simon's book Harv was gay. Nikki was sure he was at least right about that.

As tired as she was, both emotionally and physically, Nikki still wanted to talk to Sarah Fritz. She really wanted a buddy to go with, but she knew everyone was probably off having dinner or doing their own thing.

She did need to stop in at the wardrobe trailer

and see about a larger size pair of pants. Harv had given her a size too small for tomorrow's shoot, and even if she starved herself for a night and morning, it wasn't going to matter. Plus, although she hadn't seen hide nor hair of Marne Pickett around, she thought maybe it best to get a wig or hat or something, just in case. Without Simon to pull his bodyguard act, she might want to go as incognito as possible.

She hunted through her own wardrobe. There was a beanie—the one that her character Elizabeth wore. That would help. Throw on a pair of jeans and a big sweatshirt. No. She couldn't look like a bum. Maybe Amy's trailer, since she had to return the pants anyway. Yeah. If she could somehow get into wardrobe she might find something.

The sun had started to go down. She wrapped her coat around her. The nights were definitely getting colder. She knew that Napa Valley would be feeling plenty of heat these days as early summer set in there. Just thinking about her stomping grounds made her want to go home. As beautiful as it was in the Barossa, and as kind as the people were—most of them—she wanted to get back to the real world. *Her* real world.

She smelled a campfire and saw some of the crew pouring wine and warming themselves by the fire. She reached the wardrobe trailer and knocked. No answer. She pulled the handle, thankfully found the door unlocked, and went in.

She had her purse, which lucky for her was the size of a diaper bag. She put the pants back and got the new size.

Nikki knew that Amy kept the wigs and hats in a large trunk. She found it, lifted the top, and peered in. There was the perfect wig. Nothing outlandish, a simple black bob. With the beanie over it, she thought she could pull this off. She noticed Harv's leather bag next to the trunk.

Nikki knew it was wrong, but she'd been curious to see what he'd shoved into his bag the other morning when he and Amy were having coffee in the snack room. She opened it up and found a first-aid kit. Inside it, in addition to the usual stuff, were syringes and vials of antivenom. *Antivenom?* These two had their own antivenom case? Maybe it was for nothing more than being prepared after Lucy had been killed; still, it made Nikki wonder.

She put it all back in the trunk and shoved the wig into her purse. Then, she heard the door to the trailer open. Great. She hid behind one of the racks as Amy laughed and then shushed someone.

"Quiet. Come on, maybe we can play dress up."

Who was she with?

"You're a bad girl. I never would have guessed."

It was Kane's voice!

"Oh, you must have known by the e-mails. You didn't think I agreed to help you with your little charade for nothing, did you?" Amy asked.

Charade?

"Honey, it's not a charade. It's business, and it's going to work out perfectly for everyone. You included. You get that little extra we agreed on, and I think—for a little while anyway—you can have me."

Oh gross. Nikki had to get out of there. How was it she always wound up in these situations? It was like they fell right into her freaking lap, and as curious as she was about the charade they were talking about, and the money Amy was getting, she would have preferred to be far away from there. God, she didn't even think Kane knew Amy existed. When had all this come about? Now they were rendezvous-ing in the wardrobe trailer. Ick.

"I think you'll be happy about the information I passed on today. By the time we get home, Nikki and Shawn will be on the front page of every tabloid and they'll be all the rage."

Wait! What the . . .

"Good," he said.

"I told Marne about how Nikki didn't like the outfit we'd picked out for her and how Shawn was so nice to her and talked her into coming back on the set, and once she was out there the chemistry between them was hot," Amy said. "Red hot. Oh, and how about the Martian angle Marne put in?"

"Did you have anything to do with that?"

"Of course. I told her that Nikki was snooping

about Lucy, and then Marne thought up the perfect story."

"Do you think she found the note you put in Lucy's jacket?"

"Totally. She's a busybody, that one. It's good, because the more nutty we can make her look, the better the publicity. The public loves nut jobs."

"Publicity is everything. Right now, I have to turn the negatives into positives. Since Marne thinks Nikki is such a diva, that's what you keep giving her, and Shawn will be the lion tamer, making their love the source that tempers her rage. Kind of a Brangelina thing. Looks like it won't be too hard to get rid of the wine guy. He's not even around. I'll get Shawn to sweep Nikki off her feet. He can end it after the movie premieres, but for now I need to make this movie a hit. I can't let Lucy's death overshadow this production. I've also been thinking more about having Nikki do the TV series—the wine and mystery thing. I think I can hook her. With her live sleuthing it makes a great publicity campaign. I'm working on Shawn. He's being a bit belligerent about going along this time. He's started flirting, but it's not enough. He actually likes her, and that's causing him some type of moral dilemma. I need to sit him down and have a long talk with him."

"I'm sure he'll come around."

Nikki could not believe what she was hearing. Part of her wanted to step out from behind the clothing racks and pull an Angelina Jolie à la Mrs. Smith on them both, but she was riveted by what they were saying. Also, her sixth sense told her that keeping mum behind the clothes would serve her well in the long run. Marne Pickett was bad enough. But the betrayal by Kane Ferriss . . . !

"I can't say that I miss Lucy," Amy said. "Sure, it was a shame that she died, but Nikki is easier to work with."

Gee thanks, a kind word.

"I agree. She may turn out to be exactly what this movie needed. She'll bring us the kind of publicity that gets people talking, and once people start talking, they'll have to go and see the movie—especially if the stars are creating a stir in their private lives."

"Don't you kind of feel bad for Nikki, though?" Amy asked. "I'm sure she didn't know what she was getting into."

"Bad? Hell no. In the long run, she'll probably thank me. She's not the kind of person who will snap under this pressure. She's got a good head on her shoulders. I'm going to make her a star, like I did Shawn, and who knows, maybe those two will find a happy ending. God knows I've been trying to get Shawn to settle down for some time now. After the Fiona fiasco and all the cash she got out of us. I think Nikki will be different. But, I'm going to continue needing your help on this."

"You got it."

"Just keep feeding Marne the tidbits. I'll work on Shawn. I would say work on Nikki's pal Simon, but he's in love with Shawn and he's the wine guy's brother. We have to get him off the set because the sooner Nikki breaks her Napa Valley ties, the better off we'll all be."

"I'm already on it," Amy said. "Or at least Harv is. Simon doesn't only have eyes for Shawn. He likes my assistant, too, and Harv is a heart-breaker—love 'em and leave 'em. They are out and about tonight at my suggestion. Harv had been nasty to the poor guy, and I told him that it would be in our best interest to make nice. So he is."

"Should we seal the deal with a kiss?" Kane asked.

"Sure."

Nikki covered her ears.

"Maybe we should go someplace a little more comfortable," Kane said.

"You mean somewhere with a bed?" Amy asked.

"You said it."

Nikki waited until they left the trailer before letting out a breath. Then, she smiled. So Kane wanted a diva, huh? Fine. Because that was exactly what he was about to get.

Chapter 33

Nikki put on the wig, the beanie, and a big jacket. She took two beers out of the fridge in the wardrobe trailer, then snuck back to the car. A few minutes later she pulled up to the security station. Will looked at her oddly. She handed him the two beers.

"Hey, Will."

"Nikki? Is that you? What are you doing?"

"I am going crazy. I have to get out of here."

"You're supposed to be with your bodyguard."

"He's busy."

"Oh, I dunno then. I could get in some trouble. Kane would not be too happy."

"I know. But I only want to go for a drive. And I brought you some beers." She handed them to him.

He took a quick glance around. "Fine, but I'm off in an hour and if you aren't back, I don't know what to tell you."

"Thanks. You're a champ." She turned out onto the road, looking in her rearview mirror several times. The paparazzi must have given up for the time being. They were being handed a B.S. story regularly from an on-the-set source—Amy, the wardrobe queen. Ooh. That bitch.

She would get even later. Rest assured. For now she headed toward the Fritz Winery, which she hoped was still open. She thought about the other day, when she and Derek had driven to the winery. Thinking about him both upset her and made her smile. She missed him. Was he missing her? Would they—could they—work this out? She also thought about Simon calling Sarah Fritz a liar. Simon had never been known for having any kind of intuition that she was aware of. But he had not liked Sarah. Not at all.

Ten minutes later she pulled onto the Fritz property. The winery did look closed, but she saw a light on in the house, a few hundred feet up a dirt driveway. She took a chance and drove on up. Stopping the car, she took off the beanie and wig.

She thought twice before going to the door. What was she looking for, and what was she going to ask the woman? What did she want from Sarah Fritz? To find out more information about Elizabeth. And why hadn't Sarah mentioned that they'd worked together? Was she being ridiculous? The woman knew how to handle a poisonous snake, granted, but what reason would she have to want Lucy dead? There seemed to be no motive.

Nikki rapped on the door a few times. Sarah opened it. "G'day, Nikki. Nice of you to come by again. That's funny, because I was going to see about getting a message to you about inviting you for dinner. We had such a nice chat the other day.

Your friend was a bit off, but that's okay. I get kind of lonely when people don't come by too often. The winery has been slow these days."

Nikki figured she'd already had a drink or two.

"I'm sorry to hear that. Listen, I was wondering if we could talk."

"Of course. Come in. Would you like a glass of wine and something to eat?"

"No. I'm okay, thank you."

Sarah led the way down a hall and into a small, quaint family room. "I need to tidy up some. I apologize. My son has been working quite a bit and he comes and goes and leaves a mess."

"You have a son?"

"All grown up." She smiled. "But he still depends on me. He says that I'm controlling and won't let him move out, but that's not true. I wish he'd find a nice woman and settle down. Give me some grandchildren."

"Right." She smiled.

"I'm sorry. I don't mean to chatter on about my problems. You came here for a reason, I suspect?"

"Yes. Did you ever work with Elizabeth or Grace?"

"I did work with Elizabeth, after school. I was in one of the documentaries they did on her."

Nikki breathed a sigh of relief. "That was you then. I watched those last night and I thought I recognized you. What about Grace?"

"Grace? What about her?"

"I'm not sure I understand why you have such a personal beef with her."

Sarah sighed and ran her hand along her face. "See this scar?"

"Yes."

"Grace Hahndorf did this."

"What?"

"Yes. Driving too fast one day, hit my car, and the windshield broke and glass went flying. But do you think she went to jail for it? No. They're established here, the Hahndorfs. They have friends in the police department like that idiot Von Doussa. I hated her already for being the cause of losing the only friend that I ever had. I lost everything after Elizabeth died. Even my husband left me."

"Why would he leave over your friend's death?"

"I guess because I couldn't get over the sadness of losing her. Maybe it's why I hang on to my son so tightly. He says I do anyway. I'm not going to lose anyone else I love. And, that is exactly what is happening." Her eyes grew wide and Nikki didn't like the tone in her voice.

Sarah continued. "You like wine. Come on, take a walk with me. I have a great cellar in the back of the house."

"No. I think I should be going." Something was way off here.

"Sure. I see. You can ask me all sorts of questions and I take my time with you, even bring your rude friend over to insult my wine, but you can't indulge me?"

"I . . . have an early call in the morning. I do need to go." This had not been a good idea. She started toward the door.

"I wouldn't do that," Sarah said.

Nikki heard a click. She turned around to see Sarah pointing a gun at her. "I think you'll take that walk with me now."

As they headed down the hall, the gun in Nikki's back, she saw photos of a child from the time he was a baby until he was a grown man—Will. Will Henwood. *Her son.* She now knew that Sarah Fritz had killed Lucy Swanson, and why.

Chapter 34

They turned the corner into a small room. Sarah switched on the light. Nikki gasped. The room was filled with terrariums that held snakes—all kinds of snakes.

"These are my friends. Would you like to hold one?" Sarah asked and then started laughing.

"Sit down," she ordered and pointed to the single chair in the room.

Nikki didn't have a choice. "You're Will's mother."

"I am. I understand he's mentioned me to you."

"What do you mean? I had no idea he was your son."

"Yes, he does sort of leave out that his mother is Sarah Fritz, winery owner. What does he do? Goes against my wishes and takes a job over at the Hahndorfs. And I warned him, I warned him all about you people."

"I'm sorry, Sarah. I'm confused." Nikki knew that Aunt Cara would tell her to keep the woman talking as long as possible. See if she couldn't find a weapon.

Sarah knocked her to the ground with the side of the gun. "Confused! You're confused?"

She cackled and before Nikki could recover from the pain, she realized that Sarah was wrapping duct tape around her wrists and legs. Oh no. How was she getting out of this?

"No, *I'm* confused," Sarah said. "I don't know why anyone would ever tell a child they should separate from their mother. You're actually worse than that Lucy slut. She was easy to deal with. You are the kind of woman who goes around being nice and spouting your words of wisdom. All Lucy wanted was to seduce my boy, which I could not ever let happen."

Oh God. A nutcase. Mrs. Bates revisited.

"I take care of my boy. I do. I followed him to the pub that night to see that Lucy Swanson didn't get her hooks into him. But sure enough, she did. I could see it in his eyes. Lust. I ran her off the road and they crashed Grace's car. Will wasn't with them. But I know he would have been if she'd had any more time to work her charm. He would have wound up going with them. But he's a good boy. I taught him well, and he came home, instead of letting that whore get to him. I hiked to the Hahndorf place. I grew up here, remember? I know how to get around. It wasn't hard after that. I found where Andy kept the snakes, used his suit. I know the poor man thinks Hannah had something to do with it. I told you they were in here the other day and she was crying on his shoulder." She laughed. "But they aren't lovers. I like making up stories."

Simon had been dead-on—the woman was a major liar, and obviously insane.

"I have good ears. He begged her to tell him if she had anything to do with letting Charlie out. They were both so pitiful. Lucy was easy to kill. Passed-out little slut. You, on the other hand . . . God, why did you have to come here? I wouldn't have hurt you. I wanted to, because you think you're some kind of psychiatrist. But I wouldn't have. I could have gotten Will back under control. You're all the same. Women like you. Like Grace Hahndorf. You all think you are so much better than us. Than *me*. Than Will."

Oh yeah, this woman was totally loony tunes.

"My friend here. See this? *Look at me!*" Sarah screamed.

Nikki tried to focus. Sarah stood in front of one of the terrariums. "My pet. I call her Elizabeth. Do you know anything about death adders, Nikki?"

What Nikki *did* know was that anything with the word "death" in it was bad. Very bad. She watched as Sarah pulled on a set of gloves and took the snake out. This, she knew, would be the end. There was no way of getting out of this. Her life flashed through her mind as she heard Sarah open the terrarium and talk calmly to the reptile.

"I have a treat for you, Lizzie. A nice sweet treat."

Nikki shut her eyes. A door slammed and a man called out, "Mom, I'm home."

Oh sweet Jesus. She opened her eyes just in time to see the snake strike out and clamp down on Sarah's cheek.

The woman screamed; her gun flew through the air. The snake dropped to the floor. Sarah Fritz grabbed her face, still shrieking as the snake slithered toward Nikki.

Chapter 35

Nikki didn't know how long it was—a second, five seconds, longer . . . but what she did know was a shot rang out. Then, Will knelt at her side, his mother's gun in his hand. "My God! What is this? Mother? What have you done?" The dead snake was only two feet from Nikki. Will was either lucky or some kind of sharpshooter.

"Antivenom. Get it, Will!" she cried. "I've been

285

bitten. And we have to do something with her!"

Nikki looked from Will to Sarah Fritz. Was Will going to obey his mother? Would he hurt her to save his demented parent?

He went over to a box and removed a first-aid kit.

"Good boy. Now give Mommy what she needs and we can get rid of our problem."

He *was* going to listen to her. Nikki was doomed.

Will went to his mother's side, and plunged the syringe into Sarah's leg. Dread spread throughout Nikki's entire body like ice-cold water. She actually began to shake. What had she expected? Will had been controlled by his mother his whole life. Things wouldn't change now. Nikki was a goner. Tears stung her eyes as the reality of what was about to unfold grasped her. She couldn't fight back. Not with the two of them.

Will stood back from his mother while she rubbed her leg and then her face. She kept muttering, "Good boy, good boy. God it hurts. Hurts so bad."

Then Will grabbed the duct tape. What was he doing? Nikki was already all taped together. He couldn't possibly think she could escape.

He grabbed his mother's wrists. She screamed out, "What are you doing? Stop this! Will, stop this!" They struggled for a moment, but in her weakened state Will was able to wrap the tape around his mother's wrists. She continued to berate and scream at him. "Take this off now! Don't be stupid! You've been stupid all of your life! Will, I demand you stop!"

"Oh, Mum, please stop. Please stop this. You need help. You truly need help." He had tears in his eyes.

Nikki felt his pain. The man obviously loved his mother, but he could not continue to do her bidding when it meant harming others.

"Dammit, boy! Take this tape off."

"No, Mum." He wiped the tears streaming down his face, and then knelt down again by Nikki and undid the tape around her. "I'm sorry," he said.

Nikki hugged him, "So am I." She saw Sarah stand up from her chair, a look of hatred in her eyes, her wrists taped together. "Will!" Nikki yelled as Sarah brought her arms up and attempted to swing them down onto Will's head, but he turned and caught her just in time. Within seconds he had her seated back in the chair.

"Why, Mum? Why?"

"For you. I only wanted to protect you from getting hurt."

He shook his head, escorted Nikki out of the room, and locked the door behind him from the outside. Nikki realized that the hardest thing the young man would ever have to do was pick up the phone and call the police to tell them what his mother had done. But he did.

Chapter 36

The police showed up quickly and took Sarah Fritz away. Nikki again apologized to Will. He kept assuring her that he would be fine. Von Doussa was there to conduct the investigation and questioned Nikki on exactly what had happened.

She explained everything from the moment she decided to pay a visit to Sarah and about why she wanted to talk with her.

"You suspected Sarah had murdered Lucy Swanson?" Von Doussa asked.

"No. Not really. I had questions, and looking back now, I can see the answers, but the one element missing was I had no idea Will was her son. If I had clued into that and the things he'd told me about her controlling behavior as well as the things she'd said about Grace Hahndorf . . . Then seeing her in the documentary clip, it was right in front of my nose."

Von Doussa pushed his hat off his forehead. He looked disturbed. "Yep, well, it should have been in front of my nose. I'm the detective after all. That troubles me. I thought that Lucy's death was a strange accident. A coincidence of sorts, but you never thought that, did you?"

She shook her head. "Nope."

"Why?"

"I guess I have good intuition or something, or I'm plain curious. I don't honestly know."

"Good job. You did good work, Ms. Sands. I bet I could hire you on here. Come work Down Under with my police team. You know we have the MERIT system, and I have some pull."

She laughed. "Thanks, but I think I'm ready to head back to Napa Valley and manage the winery there." A thought crossed her mind—what if she didn't have a job back at Malveaux? She still had not heard a word from Derek, and she was beginning to believe that it was truly over between them.

"I'm going to wrap things up around here," Von Doussa said. "I may need to phone you if I have any more questions. I have the cell number you originally gave me in Lucy Swanson's file."

"Feel free to call. What do you think will happen to Sarah Fritz?"

"She'll probably go into a psychiatric ward for the rest of her life. From what you and her son have told me, she's completely mad. But don't worry about her or Will. He'll be fine. He's a good man."

"Yes, he is. He saved my life."

"Do you need a ride back to the Hahndorfs'? You've been through quite a trauma here."

"I'm okay. I really am. Thank you, though."

"Yep." He smiled and tilted his hat at her.

She was glad to get off of the Fritz property. She

still felt horrible for Will and hoped he would recover from the events of today. The horror of what could have happened to her back at the Fritzes' left her dazed as she headed back to the vineyard.

When she opened the door to the RV, Simon was sitting next to Shawn on the sofa. They were each sipping a glass of wine. Nikki wondered if she was missing something here.

Simon took one look at her and said, "Oh my God, Snow White! What in the world happened to you?"

"You wouldn't believe it if I told you."

"Try us," Shawn said.

"Yes. Do," Simon added. "Because you won't believe what we have to tell you either."

Nikki had no problem believing what they told her, especially after her evening, but what she couldn't believe was what the two of them had gone ahead and done.

She sighed and then looked at Shawn, who shrugged. "Oh my God. You didn't!"

"She is on her way here, right now."

"Now, as in *now*?" Nikki asked.

They both nodded.

"Oh well. I suppose we'll have more than one major headline for her then."

Nikki had just learned something that she knew Marne Pickett would love. Now she was going to get two stories for the price of one. Nikki had no idea what this was going to mean for the fate of the movie, but she had a strong feeling that by tomorrow afternoon, production would be shut down.

There was a knock at the door. Nikki opened it, and Marne Pickett walked in. Shawn had let security know to let her through. She looked at Nikki and said, "Oh dear, what happened to you?"

Nikki laughed. "You're going to love it, Marne. This is one time when I think you and I might actually be on the same page. But you have to make me a deal first."

Marne cocked an eyebrow. "What's that?"

"No more negative publicity about me." Nikki could let bygones be bygones and hopefully so could Marne.

Marne looked as if she was considering it. Shawn crossed his arms and said, "Make the deal with her Marne or you get nothing."

"Deal," Marne replied.

Nikki told her story first with gasps and "oh my Gods" from everyone in the trailer. Then it was Shawn's turn. Marne Pickett's face exploded in a shit-eating grin as she scribbled furiously. "Brilliant. Thank you," she said when Shawn was done. "You have no idea how many magazines we'll sell. But you're not worried about the backlash?"

"No. I'm more tired of pretending to be someone I'm not, and I wasn't about to do it to someone else I really like and have come to care for." He smiled at Nikki.

"Thank you," she replied.

The following morning Nikki went ahead with her initial plan of playing the diva.

She left the trailer and tracked down Amy and Harv. "I don't like what I'm wearing today," she snapped. "It's not working. You need to find me something else."

They looked at each other in disbelief. "What?" Amy asked.

"You heard me."

"But that is what you are supposed to wear—"

"I'm not wearing it! Are you deaf?"

"What is up your butt today?" Harv muttered.

"Last time I checked, I was the star of this movie, and you two are peons. You'll do what I say."

Amy shook her head. "No, Nikki, that's not the way it is. Kane is in charge here—"

"First, you'll call me Ms. Sands. Second, get Kane over here." Amy glowered at her. "Now!"

Amy and Harv turned on their heels and stormed off. Nikki almost started laughing; she was enjoying this acting job a little too much. A couple of minutes later Kane showed up at the wardrobe trailer.

"Is there a problem, Nikki?" he asked.

"Yes. There is. I don't want to wear this today. It's gross. I want something better."

"Okay. I think we can handle that."

"And I want an assistant. Also, I'd like my fridge stocked daily with 7UP. Not Sprite. Not Mountain Dew or anything else, but 7UP."

"I think we can get you 7UP." He crossed his arms.

"Good. And I want some of those Dyptyque candles, you know, the ones that J. Lo gets. I want those in cherry blossom, gardenia scent, and fig, oh, and brown sugar. Also, the trailer needs some brightening up. So, daily there needs to be Sterling Silver roses, and no substitutes. I don't like pink or red, only the silver. The sheet count on that bed, too—that is not one-thousand-thread-count Egyptian cotton, and I'd like those in white. *White*, not cream or off white."

Kane shook his head in disbelief. "Nikki? What the hell has gotten into you?"

"I'm a star." She shrugged. "You said so. Come on, we have a movie to make." She sauntered off, doing her best Mariah Carey impression. Kane threw his hands up in the air and followed her out.

Nikki played diva all day, and every time she caught a glimpse of Shawn, they shared a secret smile. Kane looked haggard and confused. Amy caught the brunt of her act; served the witch right. She didn't feel sorry for Nathan either; face it, the guy had a screw or two loose. But having a fetish was better than having blood on one's hands.

At the end of the day a package came for Nikki. She knew what it was. "Everyone," she announced. "I have something here I think you'll all want to see." She passed around copies of Marne Pickett's article, which was already being printed in the United States in three of the major tabloid magazines.

Snakes, shysters, and other sinister surprises on the set of producer Kane Ferriss's movie, set in the Australian outback, about the life and death of conservationist Elizabeth Wells, played by the talented Nikki Sands.

According to Nikki, Lucy Swanson was indeed murdered as she'd suspected all along. Police have confirmed that winery owner Sarah Fritz murdered Lucy Swanson out of a deranged fear that her son, a security guard on the set, was falling in love with Lucy. When Nikki confronted the killer, she was beaten and held captive. Surprisingly, the killer's son, Will, came to her rescue. Ms. Fritz is being held in a guarded psychiatric ward.

However, the horror doesn't end there. It would seem that Kane Ferriss and Shawn Keefer have been running a scam for years. I had the pleasure of speaking with Shawn, who decided to come clean. Shawn Keefer has admitted to being gay. For years he has been keeping up the ruse of a straight man at the behest of Kane. Kane had convinced Shawn that coming out of the closet would destroy his career. After some research, and word from an inside source, I found the money that Kane has made from Shawn's movies totals over $500 million. He's been known to say that Shawn is his cash cow. Shawn says he's been nothing but Kane's puppet, and he's tired of it.

Shawn knew he had to put an end to it when Kane approached him about wooing Nikki Sands. He told Shawn that if he could get Nikki to marry him within six months, Kane would sign him to three more movies with bonuses in excess of $30 million. Shawn told him he'd think about it, but when an unlikely source—Nikki Sands's bodyguard and Jiu-Jitsu master Simon Malveaux—saw the actor so depressed, he asked him what was wrong. I quote Shawn Keefer: "Simon has been a good friend. He listened. He convinced me that I am better than a lie. I am tired of living lies and having others live them for me. I am coming out and saying that I am gay and proud of it."

I applaud Shawn for coming out, and I applaud Nikki Sands for solving Lucy Swanson's bizarre death. I wish them both luck.—Marne Pickett

Nikki looked around; some were still reading the article. Andy Burrow glared at Kane in disgust. "You did this, mate? That's abominable. Shame on you. I don't do well with liars."

Liam and Grace had come down because Nikki had spoken to them earlier. She had told them everything that occurred; they took it surprisingly well. Hannah was with them and for once she was smiling.

"I always knew Sarah to be a little crazy but I never would have thought her capable of such a thing," Grace had said. "I'm sorry for what happened to you."

"I'm fine. I'm sorry for the two of you, because I have a feeling that this movie is not meant to happen. I'm sure production will be shut down."

Liam waved a hand in the air. "It's for the best. It is." He put his arm around Grace.

She kissed him. "I love you, Liam Hahndorf."

"And I you," Liam said.

Nikki had left feeling better about the two of them. She hated knowing that Liam was going to die, but she was pleased that he and his wife had put their differences aside and found the love between them.

Nikki still had a bit of a problem with the fact that, for years, Shawn had sold a lie to the public. But she wasn't one to hold a grudge against someone who decided to admit his wrongdoings and ask for forgiveness. Hell, who was she to judge?

Now done reading the article, Kane screamed at Shawn. "How could you do this?"

"I'm not like you. I don't need the money to keep me happy."

"Oh, not now, after I've made you a bundle. Now, you can go telling the world that you're gay, and it's my fault you've been in the closet all these years."

"I'm tired of being your tool. All you care about is money. I've suffered. Fiona suffered. And then you wanted Nikki to go through it when she has a chance to be happy with someone she really loves."

"Shut the fuck up, Shawn. Fiona didn't suffer and neither did you. I've gone the extra mile to keep the fact that you're a fag out of the papers, to make you a huge star. Without me you'd be nothing. You have no idea all that I've done for you with paying people to stay quiet."

"You did this for me? No, you didn't, Kane. You did it for *yourself*. I hope you never work in Hollywood again."

"You're fired! You are fired from this movie."

"No, actually I quit."

"Me, too," Nikki said. "I know what your plans were for me, too. I know you had your little plant Amy reporting lies to Marne, just so you could pump up this movie and then maybe a TV show you were pushing on me."

"You're ridiculous. You would've been a huge star because of me. Now what, you'd rather sell wines?"

"Actually, yes, I would." She started to walk past Amy, who looked shocked. Instead she stopped. "You're the nut job. Planting a note to make me look crazy; that was brilliant. In reality I wasn't crazy at all. Lucy was murdered. I have to ask you, though, what gives with the antivenom you and Harv had? Or was that staged, too, to keep me guessing?"

Amy looked down. "No. Harv thought he saw a snake after Lucy died and so we bought it for ourselves, just in case."

At least that had been innocent. Nikki actually felt sorry for Amy. One by one the other actors and the crew started to walk off.

"I want all of you back here!" Kane screamed, but no one listened.

Nikki, Simon, and Shawn walked to her trailer, where they took out a bottle of champagne and toasted one another.

Shawn gave her a hug. "You are the best. I love you."

"Excuse me, does anyone want to tell me what the hell is going on here?"

Nikki pulled away from Shawn to see Derek standing in the doorway.

"You should tell him," Shawn said, and walked out past Derek. "She's one helluva woman, pal. I'd hang on to her if I were you."

Chapter 37

"I think the man makes a good point," Derek said. "But first I think there is someone the two of you might want to say hello to."

Marco stepped inside the motor home. "*Bellisima*," he said and kissed her on each cheek.

Tears sprung to her eyes. "Marco."

"Marco?" Simon said. "How, what, I . . ."

Marco walked over to him. "I miss you."

"You do?" Simon asked. Marco nodded. "Oh God, I miss you, too."

"What do you say we go home? We let these two solve their problems and we go solve ours," Marco said.

"What time does the flight leave?"

"Soon," Derek said. "You better get a move on."

They all hugged good-bye and Marco and Simon were on their way.

Derek turned back to Nikki. "Guess we better do what Marco suggested and figure out our stuff, too. I've been hearing some things about you and Shawn Keefer and all sorts of interesting stories, and I think you might want to start talking."

Nikki told him the whole story. When she finished, he told her to stand up. "What?"

"Come with me."

"Wait. Don't you think we should talk about *us* before you start ordering me around?"

"No. Come with me and we'll talk."

"What are you doing? What is going on?"

"You have to trust me."

"Trust you! After this week? You left me high and dry. You never came after me when I walked out on you. And you didn't call," she said.

"You'll see why."

"No. I am not going anywhere with you. You have to tell me what happened between us and why you didn't come after me and—what in the world is going on?"

He kissed her on the lips again—long and slow and . . . oh so delicious. "Stop that. Just stop it now."

"Nope. You have to trust me now. I'll explain everything. Please. I promise it'll be worth it."

That kiss was nice. Worth it? Maybe. But what about commitment—and his seeming lack thereof?

"Give me another chance. Last one. I promise I will never hurt you again."

Oh no, were those going to be famous last words? Should she take a leap—yet again? Her heart said that yep, she definitely should, but that old brain of hers said *run away, girl.* Oh, the hell with the brain. What was the saying? It was better to have loved and lost than never to have loved at all? And he was promising her. She believed in promises, and she believed in him. "Okay, I guess I'll trust you."

"Do you need to let anyone here know that you'll be gone for a couple of days?"

"No. My movie-making days are over."

The next thing she knew she was seated in a limo. Derek poured her a glass of champagne. "To you," he said. "For this week. For discovering the truth about Lucy Swanson's murder, even when no one else believed you."

She held up a finger. "Except for your brother. It took some convincing, and I'm not so sure he ever believed me, but he did help me out a lot."

"Yes. He loves you."

"He's a good friend."

"He is." He kissed her cheek. "Nikki, I'm sorry. I know you've heard me say that before, and it probably sounds so lame, but dammit, you walked out on me in that hotel room before I ever had a chance to explain myself, and I got angry. I'm human, you know. I got angry over what you said about Andrés, about him being this and that and he sounded so perfect, and I started thinking . . ." He paused and took her free hand. "I started thinking that all the stupidity I was spouting was maybe true. I look back on that night and I see it now, and it was so stupid, so immature. I was testing you, seeing how far I could push you, or if you would walk. That's not a *man* thing to do. That's a stupid *boy* thing. I had all these stupid thoughts, like what if, what if she doesn't really love me? What if this whole thing has been a façade, and we both got caught up in something that wasn't real, but a fantasy—something we wanted to be real."

"Derek, it was never a fantasy for me. At one time . . . sure, I suppose. Isn't that how most relationships start out? You meet the man or woman of your dreams, you place expectations and even labels on them, and then you wind up together and your fantasy is perfect for a while. It's everything you expected and more and then wham, reality bites. You realize that neither of you is perfect or exactly what you expected. But the funny thing is, that's where true love lies. If you can make it past the *perfect*, past the Cinderella and Snow White stories, and into the reality of each other, you can make it. I believe that. What I was afraid happened between us that night was that you could never and would never see past the fantasy. I know we've already faced so much together before we've even begun, but isn't that a blessing in disguise? Doesn't it only mean that the best is yet to come?" She knew that she was being a Pollyanna, but it was where her heart directed her, and she couldn't deny it.

"Yes. I would count it as a blessing. Most definitely, more than that, I count *you* as a blessing. You know, you just took the words right out of my mouth and said them a whole lot better than I could have."

"Ah, but for men, isn't it all about the actions? As a woman, I would have to say that if your actions speak as loud as my words, then you're forgiven."

He clinked his glass to hers. "Mmm. Dom Perignon."

"Only the best."

Soon, the car stopped. They were at the airport and before long they were on the Malveaux jet. "I sent the boys back on Virgin Atlantic, but I did let them go first-class."

"You went and found Marco?"

"I figured it was the only way I was ever going to get you alone."

She laughed. Soon the jet screamed down the runway and they were quickly airborne. "You know, I don't think I'm ready to go home yet."

"Who said anything about home?"

After about an hour of more champagne and kisses, which left her tingly all over, the plane landed. A short drive out to a marina, they stepped onto a speedboat that took them out about thirty minutes to a luxurious yacht. "Oh my," she said.

He led her up some steps. There was a table set for two, crew members were dressed in tuxes, and the sun was beginning to set.

"Welcome to the coral reef."

"It's amazing. I don't know what to say, Derek. This is . . . Wow."

"I'm glad you think so." He kissed her. "This is only the beginning. Wait until you see what else I have in store for you."

She took his hand and stood up.

"What are you doing?" he asked.

"I'm done waiting."

"Okay, then." He got up from his chair, and led her to the master stateroom.

Three-Course Dinner with Wine Pairings

Finally Nikki and Derek get it all figured out. With Simon and Marco back together, these two can have that alone time they've been wanting. Their romantic dinner likely grew cold. It's doubtful it mattered to them. Not many of us get the chance to have dinner for two on a luxury yacht, but turn off the lights; if you have an aquarium, turn those lights on; get some ocean-scented candles and play some ocean waves off a CD; and create a little romance of your own.

For the perfect romantic dinner, here is what Nikki and Derek had (reheated, of course):

LOBSTER BISQUE WITH RIESLING

The 2006 Pewsey Vale Riesling Eden Valley South Australia is a medium-bodied wine combining citric fruit flavors of lime, lemon, and tangerine. It has a midpalate richness leading to a long finish. This is a wine to savor.

2 tbsp minced shallots
2 tbsp chopped green onions
3 garlic cloves, crushed
¼ cup white wine
2 tsp Worcestershire sauce

2 tsp Tabasco sauce
1 tsp dried thyme
6 tbsp dry sherry
1 tsp paprika
1 cup hot water
1 tsp lobster base (better than bouillon)
4 oz tomato paste
2 bay leaves
2 cups heavy whipping cream
4 tbsp butter
½ lb lobster meat, cut into small chunks

In a sauté pan, heat a little oil over medium-high heat and sauté shallots, onions, and garlic for one minute. Deglaze the pan with the white wine. Add the Worcestershire, Tabasco, and thyme and sauté for another minute. Deglaze the pan with the sherry. Add the paprika, hot water, and lobster base and combine well. Stir in tomato paste and add the bay leaves. Simmer for 10 minutes. Whisk in heavy cream and the butter and bring to a boil. Add the lobster and simmer until cooked through.

Serve with crusty garlic bread.

Serves 2–4.

Rosemary-Lemon Cornish Game Hens and Roasted Potatoes with 2005 De Bortoli "Deen Vat 10" Pinot Noir Yarra Valley Victoria Australia

The De Bortoli Pinot boasts light strawberry and raspberry flavors on the nose, along with a tad of fennel. It's a delicious, fresh, crisp wine with a focus on red berry fruit. It's a great value.

> 2 tsp crushed dried rosemary
> ½ tsp salt, divided
> ¼ tsp black pepper, divided
> 2 (1¼-pound) Cornish hens
> ½ lemon, halved
> Cooking spray
> 2 cups cubed Yukon gold or red potato
> 2 tsp olive oil

Preheat oven to 375°.
Combine rosemary, ¼ tsp salt, and ⅛ tsp pepper. Remove and discard giblets from hens. Rinse hens with cold water; pat dry. Remove skin; trim excess fat. Working with 1 hen at a time, place 1 lemon piece in cavity of hen; tie ends of legs together with twine. Lift wing tips up and over back; tuck under hen. Repeat procedure with remaining hen and lemon piece. Rub hens with

rosemary mixture. Place hens, breast sides up, on a broiler pan coated with cooking spray.

Toss potato with oil; sprinkle with ¼ tsp salt and ⅛ tsp pepper. Arrange potato around hens.

Insert a meat thermometer into meaty part of a thigh, making sure not to touch bone. Remove twine from legs. Bake at 375° for 1 hour or until thermometer registers 180°.

Serves 2.

CHOCOLATE SILK PIE WITH 2004 ZINFANDEL CHOOKSHED

The 2004 Zinfandel Chookshed is a juicy, succulent Zinfandel. With aromas of spring flowers, blueberry liqueur, pepper, and spice. It's expensive but worth the money.

CRUST

1 10-inch piecrust

FILLING

⅓ cup all-purpose flour
½ cup sugar
½ cup unsweetened cocoa
¼ tsp salt
1¾ cups 2% reduced-fat milk
4 oz semisweet chocolate, chopped

5 large egg whites
¼ tsp salt
1¼ cups sugar
⅔ cup water
grated chocolate (optional)

Prepare and bake piecrust in a 10-inch deep-dish pie plate. Cool completely on a wire rack.

To prepare filling, lightly spoon flour into a dry measuring cup; level with a knife. Combine flour, sugar, cocoa, and salt in a medium saucepan; stir with a whisk. Gradually stir in milk. Bring to a boil over medium heat, stirring constantly. Reduce heat; cook 2 minutes or until thick and bubbly, stirring constantly.

Remove from heat; add chopped chocolate, stirring until chocolate melts. Spoon chocolate mixture into a bowl; place bowl in a larger ice-filled bowl for 10 minutes or until chocolate mixture comes to room temperature, stirring occasionally. Remove bowl from ice.

To prepare meringue, place egg whites and salt in a large bowl; beat with a mixer at high speed until soft peaks form. Combine sugar and water in a saucepan; bring to a boil. Cook, without stirring, until candy thermometer registers 240°. Pour hot sugar syrup in a thin stream over egg whites, beating at high speed until stiff peaks form. Fold 2 cups of the meringue into chocolate mixture.

Spread chocolate mixture into prepared crust. Spread remaining meringue over chocolate mixture. Chill 8 hours; garnish with grated chocolate, if desired.

Serves 10.

Recipe Index

Center Point Publishing
600 Brooks Road ● PO Box 1
Thorndike ME 04986-0001 USA

(207) 568-3717

US & Canada:
1 800 929-9108
www.centerpointlargeprint.com